UPSWING

LADY LUCK: PART TWO

J.J. ANATOLIY

SYNOPSIS

The world's greatest antiheroes return in this wild ride packed with action, dark desire, and obsession.

Lady Luck never gives. She only lends...

And Emilia Fox isn't borrowing a damn thing.
The leader of Downswing just keeps taking her hits. Abducted by the world's most notorious assassin group - known only as Maman – she suffers both physical and psychological torture until she barely knows who she is, let alone how long she's been imprisoned. Emilia wants nothing more than to let her already questionable sanity just slip away. There is only one thing that is keeping her from giving in and giving up- her unfinished business with Korol, king of the Russian mafia that began nearly four years ago. Being a prisoner of Maman makes Emilia realize she possesses the key to winning the battle with Korol... but it may mean giving up the last piece of herself that makes her feel human.

And suddenly, it's not a question of if she will escape Maman's clutches and return to Downswing to end Korol's reign once and for all...

It's a matter of when.

But the devil's own luck is rotten to the core.

It's been two months since Emilia Fox was abducted and Viktor Orlov can't decide what's worse. The fact that his boss- his obsession- was abducted from right beneath his nose... or the fact that he must accept the help of their mortal enemy, Korol, to save her. As time goes on and Emilia still isn't found, the world is forced to wait with bated breath to see the wrath of Russia's most feared enforcer. Viktor didn't earn the nickname D'yavol- The Devil- for nothing. He will bring down the full wrath of the devil if his Emilia isn't found... and soon.

The devil will set the world aflame and bathe in the ashes without his queen by his side.

As secrets come to light, enemies become allies, and the world is turned upside down, the criminal underworld watches and waits. Can Emilia Fox rise from the ashes of her imprisonment to take her rightful place on her throne...

Or will she let the fire of insanity consume her?

Upswing

Lady Luck Part Two

J.J. Anatoliy

Copyright © 2018 J.J. Anatoliy

Cover Design: DoElle Designs

Formatting: Leslie Copeland

ISBN: 978-1-7321024-1-5

This book contains sexually explicit content which is only suitable for mature readers.

WARNING

This book contains sexually explicit content which is only
suitable for mature readers.
There are graphic scenes of violence inside this book that may
be a trigger to some.

Please read with caution.

AUTHOR'S NOTES

This is part two in the Lady Luck series. To get the most out of the storyline and the characters, it is *highly* recommended you first read Downswing: Lady Luck Part One.

There will be *hints* of male/male romance in this book. There will be an entire spin-off series that contains certain couples from the Lady Luck universe and yes, it will be male/male. This book is setting up the spin-off series along with continuing Emilia Fox's journey.

And as a reminder, the song that Emilia Fox sings throughout the book is *The Gambler,* written by Don Schlitz, made famous by Kenny Rogers. Her version is a tad bit... darker than the original. You can listen to a sample of it here.

ACKNOWLEDGMENTS

My beta readers, Bev, Melesa and Emily- Thank you ladies so much for taking this journey with me. Without your input and enthusiasm for Emilia and her crazy crew, this wouldn't be nearly as much fun. You guys are the real heroes.

Dee, my alpha reader. There are just too many things to thank you for, so I'm not even going to try and list them all. Without your wit, humor, and unconditional love, this story would never have been brought to life. So, on behalf of myself and all the voices inside my head shouting for their own stories... *thank you.*

Jess and Luke. Because even though we're growing older and you're expanding your families, I will never forget that there was a time when it was us against the world. I will never be able to convey how proud I am of both of you and how *lucky* I am to be your sister. Thank you for sharing your families with me and reminding me that I will never be truly alone. I love you both.

And finally, to my readers. Thank you for taking this wild ride with Emilia and Downswing. You didn't have to take a chance on this book, this series, but you did. And for that, you have my eternal gratitude. I hope you continue to have as much fun with Downswing as I do.

THE GAME SO FAR

Emilia Fox was taken from her home in Detroit and trans-
ported overseas to Russia by the king of the Russian mob-
known only as Korol throughout the criminal underworld. He
held the American girl for over a year, torturing and humiliating her during her forced stay in his country mansion. After
discovering that Korol was none other than Zakhar, the only
man she had grown to trust in Korol's employ, she escapes the
Russian mob king's clutches and even manages to take with her
the king's deadliest prisoners. It is revealed that Emilia Fox is
far more than she seems and is actually the great-grand-
daughter of one of the world's most famous serial killers. In her
younger years, Emilia's grandmother would take her and train
her in the art of self-defense and murder. The seemingly
normal American girl is no stranger to depravity, murder, and
ruthlessness. Korol's prisoners whom Emilia helped to escape
are all incredibly famous organized crime members themselves,
and as they listen to Emilia's story, they realize she will be the
perfect leader that they need. Together, they form a mercenary
group called Downswing, whose sole purpose is gaining

enough power and influence to face Korol head on and bring his kingdom to ruin. More than four years pass before they attempt to make their first move against the Russian mafia king. During that time, they forge alliances and make new friends in powerful places, hoping that will give them the edge they need to win the game for the crown. But before they make their move, Emilia Fox is stolen from Downswing's hideout in Russia by none other than *Maman*, the oldest, deadliest and most terrifying assassin group in the world. Now, Downswing must save their queen before time runs out and they lose their one shot at bringing Korol to his knees.

THE PLAYERS

Downswing:

Emilia Fox- The Queen of Downswing. The woman, the myth, the legend... the twice-crowned kidnap victim. She is the only person alive that can rend Korol's empire to rubble and ash. The reasons for this are still unknown, but she likes to say it's because of her mad skills at being a bad guy. No one agrees with her.

Viktor Orlov- nicknamed *D'yavol* (Devil) by all those who have been unlucky enough to end up on the wrong end of his fists. He was Korol's number one enforcer and held the reputation throughout the mafia underworld for being as ruthless and bloodthirsty as the devil himself. He was imprisoned and disowned by his former boss for daring to lust after Emilia Fox. He is now Emilia's righthand man and head of Security. He and Emilia have a few (or ninety-seven) unresolved issues.

Masamune Onodera- Disgraced fourth head of the Onodera group, the most violent Yakuza group in Japan. Has two underlings that rarely leave his side, Mari and Misaki Usami. All three seem to gain excitement from life-or-death situations.

Kiernan Fitzpatrick- No one knows his full background, but he is famous among the criminal underworld for once being the heir for several septs of the Irish mob in New York and Chicago. Considering he has no familial ties to any of them, there are many who are confused just how he became so powerful within the Irish mafia. When asked about this, he simply smiles and takes another drink of his whiskey.

Jazzy Prifti- The Albanian rebel who likes to make things go *boom*. Explosives extraordinaire and Downswing's main link to mercenaries across Europe.

Meiling Wu- Former high-ranking Triad member. Not-so-lovingly referred to as the Chinese Witch among the other members of Downswing. She won't admit it, but she is a fan of the nickname.

Roy Willows- The former CIA agent who retired from the agency after he was imprisoned by Korol and left for dead. He is now the sharp-shooting instructor and the Math tutor for the youngest members of Downswing, Kamili and Ludo. Emilia has called Roy her conscience and "the father she doesn't want to kill" on more than one occasion.

Fritz Schlusser- Terrifying German mercenary. Has approximately 1.7 million secrets. For some inexplicable reason, several of those secrets seem to revolve around Alexei Vasilek...

Ludo Flores- Former cartel royalty, bartered by his family to Korol to ensure they remain in power throughout Mexico and Bolivia. Ludo is now loyal only to Emilia. He also seems to have gained an extremely pale shadow who follows him in secret wherever he goes...

Kamili Okoye- Proud African queen. Her words. She was the young daughter of a sex trafficking kingpin and was taken captive by Korol after the mob boss ordered the murder of her father and stole his vast territory. Kamili is a sharp-shooting prodigy and typically responds to orders only from Roy or Emilia.

Cin Raymes- Real-life representation of the angry emoji. Kamili's words. He is also the last remaining son of the longest standing gang empire in Chicago. The gang empire that was taken over by Korol after Cin and Silas were kidnapped by said mafia king and thrown in his basement dungeon.

Silas Deveroux- Frenchman who *was* a high-ranking member of *Maman*, the ancient assassination organization that spans across the world. If one were to ask Grande Soeur, the head of *Maman*, Silas is still a high-ranking member, he's just having a years-long tantrum and will come home to her when the time is right. The Frenchman spends his days arguing with Cin... and his nights tumbling between Cin's sheets.

Cooper Reeves- Another new addition to the team. Completely nonconsensual on his part, or so he insists. He is abducted by Roy Willows during Emilia's capture by *Maman* to be used by Downswing for his vast hacking knowledge. Distant cousin to Cin, he was casted out from Cin's gang for being gay at an early age. He was saved by Cin, who used his own funds to house and feed the boy while he grew up. He is one of the most talented hackers in the world.

The Empire of Korol:

Zakhar Vasilek- Known throughout the criminal underworld as Korol, king of the Russian mafia. His organization spreads across continents. He is the most feared arms dealer in the world, along with being one of the biggest drug and sex traffickers. Has more money and power than any other mafia boss alive. Emilia Fox is his obsession and he will move heaven and earth to bring her back to his side and to his bed.

Alexei Vasilek- Korol's righthand man after Viktor was demoted and locked away, Alexei is now forced to work with Downswing by order of Korol to help rescue Emilia from *Maman*. Alexei seems to hate Fritz Schlusser with a burning hatred that runs so deep one could almost mistake it for lust. Or obsession. Or maybe loathing. One can never tell with these things.

Zane- ... (The author does not think she should describe him for fear he won't like it and will haunt her nightmares. The end.)

Anna Fuchs- The woman with all the answers. She is now Korol's second-in-command after Alexei's deception is revealed. The expressionless master of intel acquisition and security system build and analysis. The woman whose last name literally means, "fox-hunter". Emilia Fox doesn't appreciate the irony.

Lenora Mundez- Rumored to be the most talented sniper in the world. Former nun. Likes to say that she still helps others on their path to heaven. It just so happens she helps them with that journey a lot sooner than they might like.

Igor Schardt- Master of forceful persuasion. Chief logistics officer for Korol's sex trafficking ring. One of the most terrifying sadists alive and general dickhead (Kamili's words).

Ivan Karbelnikoff- The muscle. Big, dumb, and brutal, the man has close to inhuman strength and the brain capacity of a flea.

Niko Engström- Swiss man, former protégé of Viktor Orlov. Head of Security and Training for Korol's Russian base of operations.

Majid Khavari- Excellent chef. Likes long walks on the beach, mimosas with brunch, and fiery Chinese women who would rather have his head on a platter than his heart in her palm. Oh, and he is also the chief logistics officer for Korol's arms' dealings.

Sergei Kozlov- Head of prisoner relations, he is *not* one of Korol's personal bodyguards. He applied for the position years ago, only to be told his incompetence would forever keep him as nothing more than a mid-range lackey. He does have quite a history with Downswing. The only description Downswing gives to him is, 'prick running on borrowed time'.

EMILIA FOX'S BLOOD RELATIVES:

Catherine Smith- Grandmama. She is Emilia's paternal grandmother. Psychotic serial killer. Currently serving seventeen life sentences at the Women's Erie Valley Correctional Facility in Redford, Michigan.

Elijah Fox- Well...

Mona (Fox) Anderson- Mother to Elijah and Emilia. Has not had contact with either of her children from her first marriage since Emilia was kidnapped by Korol- though it is not by her choice. Though she has a sneaking suspicion, she does not realize the full extent Emilia and Elijah go through to protect her. And nobody knows the extent that her first husband goes through to make sure Mona is safe... especially from their own children.

Garridan Fox- Asshole, piece of shit, garbage dump of a human. Emilia's words. Also happens to be her biological father. No one in Emilia's vast circle of intel knows Garridan's true occupation and power among the criminal underworld. That secret is held by few people... one of them being Grandmama.

The Other Important Players:

Alex O'Connor- aka: The Hound. Emilia's childhood friend who was abused by her uncle for years until Emilia came along. Emilia killed Hound's uncle and her other abusers, freeing her from a life of terror and abuse. They were only teenagers at the time. Afterwards, Hound vanished and became a CIA agent under the tutelage of Roy Willows. She is now retired from the CIA and currently holds the title of Mistress in Leonid Sokolov's household. She also happens to be a certifiable sociopath.

Leonid Sokolov- The Pakhan (or boss) of Father of Assassins, the powerful assassin organization based in Russia. Father of Assassins is playing referee to the dangerous game that is going on between Korol and Downswing, per the request of Hound.

Leo helps Downswing when he can but refuses to form an official allegiance until Korol is brought to heel.

Ethyn Dubois- Assassin. Member of *Maman*, where he is known as Eighteen, he also works for Father of Assassins. Absolutely petrified of Silas... for good reason.

Grande Soeur- Leader of *Maman*, the assassin organization that has been around since the dawn of time. Grande Soeur is loved by few, hated by all, and feared by anyone who isn't a complete fucking dumbass. She is the one who orchestrated the second kidnapping of Emilia. Her reasons remain unclear to everyone except Jane Smith... and one other terrifying woman.

Jane Smith- The head of the Backyard of MI6, a secret organization within a secret organization. Jane helped Downswing escape Korol's clutches and now secretly assists Downswing with mercenary jobs across Europe and the UK. She made a pact with Emilia that she would keep Emilia's family safe so long as Emilia led the fight against Korol.

PROLOGUE

Somewhere closer than you think.

Ludo Alejandro García Flores realized that today was his sixteenth birthday.

Thwack! Hiss. Thwack!

"Again."

Thwack! Hiss, THWACK!

An agonized scream rent the air, echoing off the black stones of the cellar. The seconds ticked by like hours. The stale air of the dark room, combined with antiseptic and the tang of blood, sweat, and pain made the time slow to an even more agonizing crawl.

Ludo could do nothing but sit and watch, his breaths scissoring in and out of his chest like razorblades. He clenched his jaw, silently reminding himself to remain blank, reveal nothing. He refused to falter, refused to give even an inch. He needed his whirling thoughts to focus, remain strong. His commander would expect nothing less of him.

She wouldn't survive *anything less from him.*

The crack of the cane came swift, hard, and relentless.

And Ludo could do nothing as the screams and grunts continued to pierce the suffocating air.

Nothing.

"I think it is time for her shower." Four said after what seemed like an eternity but must have only been an hour, his cursed red eyes not leaving Ludo's trembling form. Ludo knew the albino assassin who had abducted them would continue to stare at him. The *pendejo* always did during these sessions. He was searching for weakness. And not just from Ludo. He was biding his time, waiting for Emilia to break down.

To break completely.

A few moments later, the two other assassins who Ludo swore he would see dead unhooked Ludo's commander, Emilia Fox, from the straps that had been holding her feet in place. She had been hanging upside down in the air, the soles of her feet belted with a cane. Ludo flinched slightly as her body slammed into the cold stone of the cellar. Emilia was trembling, her filthy body covered in bruises, scrapes, and filth.

After two months of being a prisoner of *Maman*, Ludo barely recognized his commander.

Her chestnut hair, which would normally look lush and inviting in the light, hung around her face, dirty and matted. Skin that was normally tanned and lightly freckled was white and sallow now, making her bruises stand out all the more. The mouth that had captured the hearts of many a man, those Cupid bow lips that were lush enough to make a man think of nothing else, were now chapped and bloody. Her cheeks were hollowed, her body the skinniest Ludo had ever seen it. And all of that paled in comparison to the real problem.

The eyes.

Those beautiful, stormy grey eyes which were often crinkled in the corners from laughter, were a shadow of their former selves. Ludo was beginning to see the edges of his commander's will beginning to crumble.

And it had started in her eyes.

Ludo had been forced to watch his commander's eyes over the past two months go from cold as ice, promising retribution and death... to dull, broken, *lifeless*. Her defiance still shown through when he was in the room, what little of it was left. She was trying to be strong for Ludo, which was a torture in itself. She had been through so much already and even Korol- king of the Russian mafia- hadn't managed to break her when he had held her prisoner four years ago.

But this... this was a different brand of torment. Torture, complete isolation, sleep deprivation, all at a non-stop pace. All with no explanation as to *why*. Ludo knew how much she wanted to give up, to just let go, and he couldn't allow her to do it.

That was why he never resisted being made to watch as she was tortured.

That was why he was still here.

She wouldn't give up if she was reminded why she was fighting. Why it was that she had to stay strong, hold onto the remnants of her broken sanity and stay alive. Ludo wouldn't allow his commander, his *princesa*, his friend, to give up without a fight. He knew that she had been struggling with something internally for a while, everyone in Downswing had known... but they had done *nothing* to help her. Ludo and the rest of Downswing had just assumed their strong commander would get a grip on her inner demons and emerge victorious, just as she always did.

But as Ludo watched his commander be strung up, arms tied to a hook in the ceiling and put on display for himself and the three operatives that he promised he would see dead, he realized that they had failed her. Downswing had failed her.

He had failed her.

His commander. His *princesa*.

Emilia's broken spirit had been coming.

And every last member of Downswing had turned a blind eye to it.

The knowledge shattered his heart. He couldn't prevent a single tear from sliding down his cheek as Thirty-Six, the biggest prick out of the three assassins assigned to torment Emilia, turned on the hose to full blast and sprayed the ice-cold water straight into Emilia's face. She sputtered, weakly yelling vile curses into the stream as Twenty-Two held her face still, forcing her to swallow, sputter, and gag. Her body thrashed wildly, and Ludo once again heard an audible *pop* as Emilia's shoulder was wrenched from its socket.

That was the second time in less than a week.

After an agonizing minute, when Emilia's struggles lessened and she began to sag against her bindings, Thirty-Six turned the spray to her torso. Emilia gave a loud gasp, screaming brokenly as the freezing water washed away the filth and grime from her latest torture session. Ludo noticed she was trying to hold herself up by her arms, and he flinched with the knowledge that her feet had to be in excruciating pain if she was forcing her dislocated shoulder to take the brunt of her weight.

God, his poor *princesa*.

Twenty-Two scrubbed her body with a washcloth he had produced from the tray at his side, his movements brisk and unfeeling. Emilia's struggling had ceased completely, though her body was shaking so hard the hook that was holding her bound wrists up shuddered and creaked rapidly. Ludo felt his own teeth chatter at the sound. Thirty-Six turned off the water after another few minutes. By that time, Emilia's eyes had closed, and her breath was coming in short, painful gasps that made Ludo's own chest ache. He gripped the chair he was sitting in, his knuckles whitening from the sheer force of his hold.

"Take her back to her cell. Solitary confinement for the next forty-eight hours. Turn on the lights, leave them on full blast. And pop her shoulder back in, Twenty-Two. I won't tell you again to hold her correctly." Four said in his deep, even voice. Those red eyes were still focused on Ludo, and Ludo found himself wanting to gouge them out and wear the red orbs around his neck as a trophy.

Ludo had been down to Emilia's cell only once, and he grimaced at the thought of her going back. The room was either washed in suffocating darkness- not a single ray of light allowed to shine through the cracks- or it was bathed in a light so blinding, it was impossible to escape the stark white reality of total imprisonment. Ludo knew that Emilia wasn't going to be allowed to sleep for the next forty-eight hours. That was what the blinding floodlights were for right outside the glass of her cell- to keep the incarcerated party awake and unable to escape the deafening silence of complete isolation.

Unable to escape the crushing reality of her imprisoned existence.

Though he hated Four, probably the most out of the trio that had been Emilia's constant tormentors, he couldn't help the shiver of excitement that raced along his spine at the effect the man had on the other two assassins. Twenty-Two paled at the words from his superior, swallowing audibly with a jerky nod. Thirty-Six's mouth pinched tighter, a flash of fear and dislike crossing his face before he could smother it. Ludo knew that even though Four's eyes remained on him, the assassin superior had seen that look on his subordinate's face. He had seen it, not for the first time, and as usual... said nothing.

This isn't right.

Ludo knew that there was something more at work here than just three assassins kidnapping Emilia Fox, the leader of Downswing. Four was playing a game, Ludo was sure of it, and he was using Ludo and Emilia in whatever scheme he was brewing. Ludo was almost positive it wasn't just Four playing this game- it was his boss, the mysterious leader of *Maman* herself, orchestrating the entire thing.

Something was going on with this infamous organization, something that was much more monumental than kidnapping an up-and-coming mercenary leader. Though Ludo had little to go on to support his suspicions, the calculating glances from Emilia confirmed that even though her spirit and body were slowly breaking down, she had the same suspicions he did. There were moments when he looked into her eyes that he could see his brilliant, ever-observant leader, just biding her time until she could strike. She had been watching Four and Thirty-Six closely when nobody was looking. Only Ludo, knowing his *princesa* like he did, knew she was gathering information, formulating plans in her crafty mind. His captain was one of the most brilliant, observant people he knew.

But there was no sign of his observant, calculating captain now.

Ludo felt sick with defeat as he watched the two fuckers Twenty-Two and Thirty-Six lower his beautiful Emilia to the cold stone of the cellar floor. He watched as Twenty-Two deftly popped her dislocated shoulder back into place and almost let his eyes close in despair when she didn't even flinch. When they moved away from her to replace the tools and washcloth back on the sterile table at their side, Emilia's eyes opened, capturing Ludo's tear-filled gaze.

He could only sit and tremble as he felt the weight of that dead, beaten gaze rest directly over his heart. Ludo forced the sadness down, staring right into the eyes of his Emilia with a fire so hot, he felt his chest tighten with the need to yell, to *scream*. He silently willed her to fight, damn it, *fight*. He *needed* her. Downswing needed her. Hound, her childhood friend, needed her. Korol needed her... to kill him. He silently, feverishly, madly willed her.

D'yavol needs you.

Emilia's eyes sparked, the cold defiance raging in her eyes for a fleeting, glorious moment. But the numb, broken look returned, and the pained glaze consumed that icy fire that Ludo was beginning to crave with all of his tortured soul. She licked her dry, chapped lips, and repeated the words that she had uttered every day for the past month, ever since her torture sessions had intensified and her imprisonment began to slowly break her from the outside-in.

The words themselves weren't what terrified him.

The fact that the words had replaced the song she had sung that had sent fear into the hearts of her enemies...The song that signaled her will to live, her will to fight, her will to *kill*.

That scared the ever-living fuck out of him.

"Go home, Ludo."

He clenched his jaw at the broken words, rage and panic crushing his windpipe, hollowing out his chest. A pale, gentle hand rested on his own white-knuckled fist still gripping the chair and he turned slowly to the bane of his existence, the person he wanted to see dead more than anyone in the world.

Four.

Four's red eyes held his, the unfeeling orbs revealing nothing. Ludo stared back, letting all of his pent-up wrath, misery, and determination show to the albino assassin. Four stared at him for a long moment, then finally let out a quiet breath, an emotion flickering so fast across his face, Ludo almost thought he imagined it. To Ludo's shock, Four leaned forward, his lips barely moving as he whispered, the low words intended for Ludo's ears alone.

"Obey, *minou*. Go home."

Ludo slowly uncurled the fist that was under Four's graceful hand, twisting so that his fingers tangled with the assassin's. Four held his gaze steadily, not flinching at the contact. He held the assassin's hand in his own, slowly but surely squeezing harder and harder with every passing breath.

And Four let him.

Ludo turned back to Emilia, whose eyes were still on him, the glazed, empty look seeming to stare straight through him. And Ludo knew what he had to do. He had to deal a blow that would shatter his poor Emilia. A jab straight in her heart that would shake her up, enrage her, bring her back from the abyss of broken insanity.

So, Ludo hit her where he knew it would hurt the most.

"It is my birthday today."

His quiet words seemed to echo in the silence. The only sound that he heard through the rushing in his ears was Four's swift inhalation beside him. Ludo stared into Emilia's confused, broken eyes for what seemed like an eternity.

Slowly, so very slowly, the dead sheen of her gaze lifted. Awareness crept into those grey orbs. Emilia's face, pinched from pain and hopelessness, slowly smoothed, line-by-line. Her breaths slowed to long, audible gasps of breath. The pain, hopelessness and defeat bled away. It started with her face and slithered down her entire body. Her muscles began to stiffen, tighten, shift. Ludo barely managed to suppress a sob of joy from escaping as he watched the shock that had erased the fog in her eyes be replaced with something far more valuable to him than all the gold, jewels, and money in the world.

Pure, unadulterated, icy *rage*.

"It's... your... birthday." Emilia breathed out, her voice but a croak, but the steel beneath it was unmistakable.

"Four." Thirty-Six took a step forward, his voice a lash of warning.

Ludo gripped the assassin's hand harder, the crushing force making his insides tremble with elation. Four's fingers tightened the slightest fraction against Ludo's.

But he remained silent.

"It's. Your. Birthday." Emilia's breaths came in pants now, and that icy burn consumed her. Her face contorted, her cracked lips pulling back in a snarl. Her muscles bunched up, her head sluggishly lifting from the floor.

It was like watching a snake. The slow, gradual unfurling of the deadly serpentine body. The slow hiss of breath while the snake danced, mesmerizing its prey. And all the while it was unlocking its lethal jaws, venom dripping, waiting for the moment to strike. The intense, icy burn of a predator's gaze, right before they snuffed the life from their prey forever.

And Emilia Fox struck.

Ludo's eyes widened as Emilia suddenly flung her body sideways, knocking into Thirty-Six's legs with such force, Ludo flinched. With a shout of pain, Thirty-Six went down, falling onto Emilia with a loud *oomph*. Ludo forced himself to stay still, but was rewarded with his patience when Emilia rolled, taking Thirty-Six with her so that she was straddling him.

She whipped her head back against Twenty-Two, who had rushed forward and was trying to haul her off the thrashing Thirty-Six. Her head connected with Twenty-Two's groin, forcing a strangled yelp out of the man. He dropped to the floor, clutching his balls, moaning pathetically.

Thirty-Six bucked up from the floor, trying to dislodge Emilia, but it was no use. Ludo watched with glee as Emilia reached forward and yanked the sterilized tray from the stand next to her. She raised it above her head, her eyes wild, and brought it crashing down into Thirty-Six's face.

And she screamed.

And screamed.

The furious, wrecked sound made Ludo tremble, the force of her wrath shaking him to his core. *This* was the prized queen of Downswing. The captain of one of the most feared mercenary groups in the world. The woman who had brought together criminals, mercenaries and assassins from all over the world and united them under one name, one cause. The cold, unfeeling killer let loose upon the criminal underworld. The princess of his heart.

And she was *terrifying*.

God, he fucking loved being scared of his *princesa*.

Emilia brought the tray down over, and over, and over again. She continued that same scream, the sound reverberating, making the room fairly tremble with the force of her swift fury. Ludo still gripped Four's hand in his own, and he turned to the assassin superior, a slow, glowing smile transforming his pretty face into a breathtaking picture of beauty.

"That is *mi capitán*. I will *never* leave her."

Four's expression remained its same calm, frightening mask. If Ludo hadn't been watching so closely, he would have missed the flicker of emotion, but this time he caught exactly what it was.

Pride.

For him. For Emilia.

God, he *hated* this albino bastard.

Ludo sneered at Four, turning back to Emilia still beating the now prone Thirty-Six. Twenty-Two recovered enough to tackle Emilia to the floor, her screaming dying down, her throat having gone hoarse from the sheer force of her fury. She struggled with the assassin, but he got the upper hand quickly and locked her wrists in the handcuffs he had pulled from his belt. Shock was clear on his face as he looked down at the panting, trembling mass of pure woman fury beneath him. His gaze trailed back to his partner, bleeding and struggling to stand. The rage on the sadistic Thirty-Six's face was plain to see, and the promised retribution in his gaze made Ludo sick to his stomach.

Twenty-Two tore his gaze from Thirty-Six and looked to Four, swallowed thickly at whatever he saw on his superior's face, then forced Emilia to her feet. She struggled against the bonds, her crazed eyes finding Ludo once again. She panted, her fury calming, her body slowly sagging with the weight of her injuries and exhaustion. But Ludo felt pride tremble through him at the healthy flush of color in her cheeks, the fury in her eyes, the spark that had returned.

This. This was his captain.

This was the queen of Downswing.

This was Emilia fucking Fox.

"Happy birthday, baby." The words tore from her throat, sounding wrecked and wretched. The words didn't matter. No, it was the cold, icy determination on her face, the promise in her eyes, the hard set of her jaw. That was what mattered.

Emilia Fox wasn't done yet.

Not by a fucking long shot.

ONE

Moscow, Russia

Viktor Orlov, known as *D'yavol* throughout the organized crime underworld, sat on the dirty ground, his posture so stiff that it physically hurt to look at him. He sat there, waiting, letting the people inside know that the devil had found them. Not even one muscle twitched as his black gaze bored into the house before him, the elusive mansion that housed the one thing he needed to find the treasure he had lost.

He sat motionless on the ground, staring up at the compound of Father of Assassins, the most feared assassin organization in Russia. He sat there, waiting for a sign, a hint, *anything* from the leader of the assassin group, Leonid Sokolov. The man who was harboring the only person that Viktor had found that knew anything about the kidnapping of Emilia Fox.

And he waited.

Alexei Vasilek, half-brother and righthand man to Korol, king of the Russian mafia, leaned back against the black SUV and heaved a long, tired sigh. He was still a 'guest' of Downswing and he couldn't be more exasperated about that fact. They were playing the most fruitless, frustrating game in the history of his career as a mafia underling.

The game of *Where in the World is Emilia Fox*.

And poor Downswing was losing.

The search for Emilia Fox, leader of Downswing, was *exhausting*. Her forlorn group was working in tandem with both the British and American Intelligence agencies, Interpol, Downswing's own numerous connections from around the world, and Alexei's boss, Korol, to find the girl. The searchers were scattered across continents, mob sects, and governments. The very eclectic members of Downswing had drudged up every single one of their contacts, and Alexei was shocked by how many people all over the world were willingly searching for a single girl. Hell, Korol alone had more connections around the world than any man alive and he was utilizing the full force of his power to locate the idiot Emilia.

And still, not one whisper of the girl had been found.

It was almost as if she had vanished into thin air.

Or she's buried six feet under, and this is all a huge waste of fucking time.

Alexei was technically a hostage to Downswing- Emilia Fox's mercenary group that had been founded specifically to take down Korol, his boss. But everyone knew his ass wasn't going anywhere until they found the stupid girl that had managed to get kidnapped, *again*. Korol had given him his orders, and that was to stay and help the floundering group find their mistress before they started receiving her body parts as 'gifts'.

Or worse.

As Alexei stared unblinking at the clear, end-of-summer sky above, he wondered why they hadn't yet received any *special packages.* They hadn't received *anything.* Not one word. No ransom, no threats, nothing.

And that was the concerning part.

They had inside information on the group that had kidnapped her and that was the single thread of hope that they were going on. Silas, a member of Downswing, was a former member of the group that had kidnapped Emilia. He insisted that the group, known only as *Maman*, had taken Emilia alive. If they killed someone- and fuck did they ever- they made sure *someone* knew about it. They had a signature known throughout both the criminal underworld and every Intelligence agency in the world.

A white lily. The flower of death.

Any member of any organized crime group, corporate or underground, would know *Maman*'s handiwork. The only time *Maman* didn't leave a body behind was if they were specifically told not to by their client or if they kidnapped the victim, imprisoning them inside their own compound.

And Emilia only had one enemy that would dare put a hit out on her.

Korol.

Alexei knew *damn* well his boss hadn't ordered the death of Emilia Fox. Only Korol had the pleasure of tormenting his Emilia, he had made that known when the capture of his former lover had been confirmed. The game they were playing was between the two of them, Korol had insisted, and somebody else had dared to usurp his queen from her throne. Somebody had stolen his property, right on the king's own turf. It was a clear sign of disrespect to touch something that very clearly belonged to the king of the Russian mob.

And when they found the ones responsible, Korol would make them suffer.

He would tear the world apart to find his Emilia Fox.

Every mafia group worth their salt knew the story of Korol and his runaway lover. The story had spread like wildfire among the many septs of the mafia. The story of Korol, the reigning mafia king and Emilia Fox, the usurper queen aiming to burn his criminal kingdom to ashes. Everyone knew the war that was brewing between them was theirs, and theirs alone. No one was to interfere until the world righted itself again and one of them emerged victorious. Korol had made that known as soon as Emilia Fox had escaped his clutches. The act of kidnapping Emilia from Russian soil was a challenge, pure and simple, to the powerful Russian mafia king. And Korol was not taking it well. He was becoming unhinged.

Alexei almost smiled at the thought.

"Is that a smile I see, *bärchen*?"

A shiver raced along Alexei's spine. He felt his lips start to curl back into a snarl, but bit back the emotion swiftly. The impossibly deep voice, along with its owner, had become the bane of Alexei's existence.

He turned, making sure his face remained expressionless, to his constant shadow- Fritz Schlusser. The towering German mercenary was one of the most famous mercenaries in the world. He had once been a prisoner of Korol's, captured by Alexei himself, almost four years ago. Emilia Fox had escaped with him and all of the founding members of Downswing four years ago. The motley crew consisted of dangerous killers from several different mob septs across the globe. They were all highly trained, highly skilled, and Alexei often found himself respecting the crazy bunch of assholes that Emilia had chosen to surround herself with.

The exception was the German.

His thoughts on the German were... different. Much to his despair, he entertained *very* specific thoughts when it came to Fritz Schlusser.

Thoughts like the pleasure he would feel at wrapping his long fingers around that thick throat of the German's and squeezing until his crystal blue eyes swam with agony, his chiseled face turning red from oxygen deprivation. He thought of how sweet Fritz's howls of pain would be in his ears as he whipped the hulking, blonde German with a thick, leather crop across his expansive back. He thought of how nice Fritz would look on his knees, head bowed, body broken by Alexei's hand. Those were the thoughts he focused on. Those were the thoughts that were most important when it came to Alexei keeping the calm, collected mask in place that he wore for the entire world.

Because beneath the calm, unfeeling, responsible man the world thought Alexei to be, buried beneath all of the lies he told himself, festering underneath the denial and self-hatred... was a man screaming to come out. A *weak* man. A man surrounded by impulse, rage, fire, and *need*. A man he had suppressed for as long as he could remember.

The true side of himself that he hated more than anything.

That man, his true self, imagined all of those same scenarios between the German and himself. Only, it wasn't the German on his knees. It wasn't the German who was being pelted by a thick, leather whip. It wasn't the German who looked, and *felt*, so good down on his knees. It wasn't the German aching to be filled, longing to roll around in the pain and humiliation like a dog in heat. It wasn't the German who longed to scream out, to beg. It wasn't the German that needed to submit. To be owned.

It was Alexei.

And Fritz Schlusser was the one wielding the whip.

Alexei pushed the thought down as swiftly as it had risen. He ignored the man inside begging for the pain, the humiliation, the mastery from the German. He stood now, calm, cold, collected. A man comfortable in his own skin, in his abilities.

He was Alexei Vasilek, the coldest, strongest, most ruthless man in Korol's ranks. He was power. He was control. He was strong. He was calm.

"Don't fucking call me that, you insolent piece of Eurotrash."

Okay, well, he had at least *said* the words calmly.

Fritz's eyebrow shot up, a small grin curling the corner of his lush mouth. Alexei was very proud of himself for not staring at those lips. He was extremely proud of himself for not imagining those lips smearing against his neck, feeling the German's breath on his flesh while Fritz tugged on his balls-

Fuck.

"You say this every time, *bärchen*, but you still have not asked me what it means." The low drawl made Alexei's knees quake, but he kept a firm hold on himself. Damn Viktor for putting the German in charge of watching Alexei. He hadn't had a restful sleep that wasn't bred from exhaustion in two months. The constant surveillance from the object of his innermost desires was getting to him. Gnawing at his control, eating at the walls he had so carefully constructed. He needed a moment's peace from the mountainous German so he could regroup. So he could breathe.

He needed a tactful retreat.

"I don't care what it means. Just like I don't care about anything that concerns you." Alexei said, his voice deadpan. He broke eye contact with Fritz and stepped forward.

A huge, searing hand clasped his upper arm, and Alexei felt the touch ignite him.

Everywhere.

"Now, *bärchen*, it is not good to lie. I thought I taught you better than that." The deep timbre of Fritz's amused voice skittered along Alexei's spine once again, and for all of the training and torture he had submitted his body to over the years, he couldn't suppress the shiver that escaped between the crack of his control. Clenching his jaw so tight his teeth felt like they could shatter, Alexei turned his head back a mere fraction, refusing to look the fucker in the eye.

"Let. Go. Now." Each word was a soft whip of sound. His lips barely moved. His entire body felt frozen but on fire at the same time. That single touch was managing to wreak havoc on his entire being.

"I do not think you want that at all, *bärchen*."

Fuck. The German had the deepest, richest voice. It reminded Alexei of liquid dark chocolate as it melted over him, blanketing all of his good sense, leaving behind nothing but a pool of need. All he could feel was the wall of heat at his back as the German stepped right up behind him. Alexei sucked in a sharp breath when he felt the German's chest brush his back. His nose was filled with the vanilla cedar scent that clung to the German no matter the time of day or night. He almost closed his eyes as he heard the rustle of his enemy's shirt as he leaned down, his breath hot on the shell of Alexei's ear.

"My *bärchen* wants what only I can give him."

Alexei had to bite his lip hard enough to draw blood just to keep himself from whimpering. He trembled, he shook, he needed-

He needed *to get a fucking grip*.

"The only thing I am of yours is your enemy. Do not make the mistake of touching me again." Alexei forced the words out and thank fuck they came out as unfeeling as his usual speech.

If he sounded a bit breathless, he sure as hell wasn't going to admit it.

Out loud.

He shrugged from the German's grip, stalking up to Viktor with his signature long-legged stride. He was *not* running away.

He was simply regrouping.

And there is one more lie to add to the rotting pile of deception at my feet.

He shoved down the need that had reared its ugly head from Fritz's touch and moved with a singular purpose. Alexei stopped right beside Viktor, crossing his arms over his chest and raising a brow at the large monstrosity of Father of Assassins' compound that reminded him of three separate houses jammed together by brick, wood, and mud. He licked his raw lip, tasting blood and inwardly cursing himself for the show of weakness.

"*D'yavol-*"

"Al."

That caught Alexei's attention. He turned to look down at Viktor with a raised brow, only to find the large man staring up at the house, cold fury in those creepy black eyes of his. That wasn't unusual, Viktor was usually furious over something or other. He'd earned the nickname *D'yavol* a thousand times over- the man could be truly terrifying when he chose to be. The unusual part came from the nickname he had called Alexei. That nickname seemed from a thousand lifetimes ago- when Viktor had been V, Alexei had been Al, and they had been brothers.

And not just in combat.

Alexei turned back to the huge compound, shoved those memories down, and forced himself to feel nothing. The past was the past, and nothing could ever change what had happened. Viktor had betrayed Alexei, his organization, his family. All for a woman. And now, Alexei's boss, Korol, was going mad from the loss of that same woman.

Sometimes Alexei hated Emilia Fox.

And sometimes he thanked whatever god was listening for sending her to them.

"Are you getting sentimental on me, *bratik?*" Alexei drawled, shoving his hands into his pockets, calling Viktor the Russian word for 'brother' on purpose. *D'yavol* hated it when he called them brothers. Yet another sin to add to the list that Alexei had built in his mind for his former brother-in-arms.

"We are no longer brothers. But you were once my friend." Viktor said quietly, his icy gaze still on the compound. "You were the one person I would let watch my back. You were the only man who would walk into hell with me and come out smiling."

Alexei nodded, frowning. He knew this. They had been inseparable before, both terrifying in their capacity to kill, maim, or torture any person who got in the way of Korol and his empire. Viktor had trusted Alexei with his life, and Alexei would have gladly given his own to keep his brother safe.

Plus, Viktor attracted fights. And fighting was the only time Alexei allowed himself to be free and let all of his pain, rage, and inner demons run the show.

He had liked having Viktor around just for that reason alone.

"Are you ready to go to hell with me once again?"

The low words froze Alexei in place. He looked down at Viktor, who hadn't moved a single inch. He slowly raised his gaze up to the tattered, mismatched house. He had seen the glint of a few sniper rifles through the shuttered windows. He had seen the men hiding in the trees surrounding the house, and he knew damn well there were dozens of men- some of the most highly trained killers in Russia- behind the doors of the big compound. Ready and waiting for Downswing to make a move against the impenetrable house. This was the compound of Father of Assassins, for fuck's sake, nobody had made a move on the compound and lived to tell the tale in the history of the organization.

Alexei smiled.

"Who better to go to hell with than the devil himself?"

Viktor

Sixty-two days, four hours, thirty-six minutes.

That was how long it had been since Emilia had been ripped from my side.

It was sixty-two days, four hours, and thirty-six minutes too long.

I was done waiting.

Standing up, I turned to the tall, slim man who had once been my greatest ally. It seemed an eternity since I had fought with Alexei by my side, but I was short on options.

All of our endless searching had come up empty. There wasn't a single piece of evidence left behind by the bastards who had stolen Emilia from me. Our first move in finding Emilia had been attempting to track Ludo, since the Mexican boy had been abducted right along with her, though none of us had any clue as to why. The tracking device that I had inserted into Ludo's arm had been deactivated minutes after our security team had sprung into action. The signal had gone dead on the outskirts of Moscow. We had tried to drum up information on every ship, truck, and plane leaving the country.

Nothing.

We had eyes and ears all over Europe, Great Britain, the US, Russia- as did Korol who was using his considerable influence to assist in finding Emilia. I had contacted Jane Smith, a leader of MI6 who had been our private sponsor from the very beginning, and even her people had come up empty. And her spies were everywhere. *Maman* wasn't the most famous assassin organization because they were sloppy, but everyone slipped up eventually. I had been counting on it. I had tried to be patient and just... wait. Wait and hope.

Nothing. Two months of searching by mafia septs, Intelligence agencies, and mercenary groups from around the world and still not a fucking sign of my Emilia. I was at my wit's end, clinging to the last piece of evidence I had. My last resort.

Ethyn Dubois.

The former member of *Maman* who had told the group exactly where to find Emilia. The current member of Father of Assassins who had ratted out my captain to his former organization.

And Father of Assassins had him on lockdown.

He was somewhere inside the mismatched walls of the compound before me. I had found the secret compound of Father of Assassins, and I wasn't leaving today without answers. Or without bloodshed. Hound had called me shortly after the discovery of Emilia's kidnapping two months ago, and in her hysteria had told me what the Frenchman had done. The call had been cut off, and that had been it. We had tried, over and over again, to initiate contact with Father of Assassins, to demand they answer our questions, to produce the man that had played a part in our Emilia's abduction.

Our calls fell on deaf ears and absent bodies.

I had scoured the city for any member of Father of Assassins, and again, nothing. I had tried to corner anyone who I thought might know where Hound was hiding and again... *nichego*. Nothing. Not a word. I had hoped that I wouldn't need the group that had gone radio-silent on me, but to my dismay, no other lead had led to anything more than more frustration. More helplessness. More burning *rage*.

So now I had to go with my Hail-Mary plan that had been in the making for two long months.

The plan to get to Ethyn Dubois and make him talk.

By any means necessary.

I nodded to Alexei. Turning back, I tried not to flinch with surprise to find Fritz standing directly behind Alexei, his eyes burning a brand into the back of the Russian's head. I blinked at the fierce light in his eyes. Before he managed to school his features, I could have sworn the look I saw was pure possession. And if anyone could recognize that look, it was me.

I wore it every time I thought of Emilia.

"Fritz. We're moving in. Now." I said, banishing the look from my mind. I didn't know- nor did I care- what was going on between the two men. All I cared about was the fact that I was finally about to launch an attack against Father of Assassins and would probably die for my trouble.

Not that I give two fucks about that, either.

I wasn't going to sit on my ass for another minute while Emilia, my Emilia, was still missing. That was the only thought consuming me. I didn't care if we were ready or not, today was the day we were moving in on Father of Assassins, something nobody had done and lived to tell the tale. But I wasn't the most patient of men on a good day. After two months of not seeing my Emilia, not knowing where she was, *how* she was, who was hurting her...

It was enough to drive me to the edge of my bottomless rage.

And nobody would survive the aftermath if I stepped off the crumbling edge.

I will light the world on fire and laugh as the ashes rain down.

Fritz nodded in acknowledgement of my outlandish

demand, which surprised me, and raised a hand to the communication device in his ear.

"It's time."

Raising a brow, I watched with a twinge of amusement as three of Downswing's biggest assholes hopped out from the SUV. The handsome former Yakuza member, Masamune Onodera, walked forward, hands in his pockets, a bored look on his face. He looked as if he could be anywhere else and be more entertained than he was at that moment.

He couldn't fool me, the fucker lived for impossible odds and bloodshed.

He was probably hard beneath his dress pants.

My gaze traveled to Kiernan, the Irishman, who was whistling and twirling a bat in his hand. He grinned at me, waving the bat over his head like a madman. Snorting, I turned finally to Meiling, the tiny former Triad member, her long black hair with the red tips blowing in the wind. She stopped in front of me, looking at the red tips of her nails and raised her amused gaze to mine.

"So, you finally stop being a pussy bitch now, *D'yavol?*" She drawled, her white teeth flashing in a predatory grin.

"Can I hit Ethyn with Una when we get him? I promise I won't scrabble his brains too bad, *a mhac*." Kiernan said, grinning and twirling his bat, whom he had named Una. His reasoning, he had told me one drunken night, was that the name in Irish meant 'one'. As in, it only took one hit to bring his enemies to their knees.

I noticed with another twinge of amusement that the bat - Una- had old bloodstains on her.

"This is suicide, you know this." Masamune drawled, heaving a bored sigh. I almost smiled at the excited gleam in the Japanese man's eyes.

"Where are Misaki and Mari?" I asked, turning back to the

large compound. I wasn't a fucking idiot; I had noticed the glint of the sniper rifles pointed at us from the shutters of the house. I knew about the men surrounding the property, hiding in the trees, and I knew we'd probably make it no further than the front door before being brought down in a hail of gunfire.

I just didn't give a shit anymore.

Finding Emilia was my only concern. If it meant killing everyone in sight, I would do it with a smile on my face. And everyone standing with me knew it.

"In position. Rifles are ready. They have a lock on the men in the woods. They could take out twenty before needing to reload and reposition. Or before getting themselves killed." Masamune shrugged. He had sent for the two sisters from Japan after his release from Korol's prison more than four years ago. The duo had been indispensable to Downswing and their booming mercenary business. I liked them a great deal, they were warriors through and through.

I liked them enough to potentially sacrifice their lives to find Emilia.

They should feel honored.

"Good. And everyone else?" I glanced to Kiernan for confirmation.

His response was a wink and a grin that could have been at home on a madman's face.

Guess it was right where it needed to be then.

"Good." I said before withdrawing the pistols from the holsters wound around my back. Turning back to the behemoth of a house, I pushed my shoulders back, clenching the pistols in a death grip at my sides.

"Suppose we should finally say hello." I said softly, bloodlust and fury brewing right below the surface.

It was time.

I heard Alexei chuckle darkly at my side before he withdrew his own pistols. He turned to me, a glimmer of morbid glee flashing in his eyes. He whispered his next words, his voice almost soft and loving as he turned back to the compound of Father of Assassins.

"And woe be it to the man who brings forth the fury of the devil."

TWO

"Boss, they have drawn their weapons. Awaiting orders."

Leonid Sokolov, Pakhan of Father of Assassins, puffed on his cigar, the smoke curling around his well-kept beard like the hand of a lover. He sat in his formal dining room, in his favorite chair, staring at the man who had brought the devil of Downswing to his doorstep.

"It seems they have finally found us." Leonid said in a conversational tone, tilting his head at the blonde man who was currently bleeding on his very expensive rug.

Ethyn Dubois, former member of *Maman* and current member of Father of Assassins, sat in an uncomfortable wooden chair used for torturing enemies of the group. His eyes were nearly swollen shut from his recent session with the madwoman who ran Leonid's household. His lip was bleeding and his naked chest was riddled with bruises and cuts, both old and new. He sat in nothing but a pair of his tight, brightly colored boxer briefs, and his legs were riddled with similar bruises as the ones on his chest.

"Took them long enough." The man sighed, though the

confident words were somewhat dimmed by the weak rasp that was Ethyn's voice. He hadn't been allowed to speak, eat, or sleep in days. Leonid still had to smile at the man's cheekiness, one of his favorite things about the assassin.

"Yes. Yes, it did." Leonid stood, and every man and woman in the room stood to attention. He walked leisurely to Ethyn's chair, standing right behind the man and patting the wood of the chair fondly. "And now what am I to do, eh? I cannot enjoy my favorite vodka if I so much as hurt a hair on any member of Downswing's heads. Especially Viktor Orlov." Leonid sighed, looking down with pity at the Frenchman.

"I suppose I should just give you up. I may lose a bit of leverage, but in the end, nobody gets hurt. Well, besides you. They'll probably beat you within an inch of your life. And then have their very own Frenchman *really* torture you." Leonid said softly, watching closely for Ethyn's reaction.

Ah, and there it was. The slight flinch, the miniscule flash of terror.

The very emotions Leonid had tried, and failed, to bring forth in the man during the entirety of his two-month imprisonment and daily torture. Something about Silas Deveroux, the young French member of Downswing, terrified Ethyn Dubois. Ethyn, who hadn't flinched during any of Alex's creative torture methods, who had merely raised a brow at Leonid's threats and beatings.

Leonid didn't know whether to be intrigued or insulted.

After a tense moment, Leonid raised a brow in surprise at the soft, mocking laughter that suddenly burst forth from Ethyn.

"I'm already a dead man. It shouldn't matter that Silas Deveroux is the one to finally wield the final blow."

A tremor went through Ethyn's body, the mocking smile at

his lips melting, leaving behind nothing but the blank, broken look of a condemned man.

"Fuck." Ethyn breathed out, closing his eyes in despair.

Leonid decided he was intrigued.

And insulted.

But mostly intrigued.

"Downswing is bursting with interesting members, is it not?" Leonid said softly. Ethyn didn't respond, merely sat with his eyes closed, hanging his head in defeat. Leonid felt a vibration in his dress pants, and he reached down to pull out his cell. Seeing the text on the screen, Leonid gave a small, secret smile.

He let a minute pass, his guards and the security team still holding their rifles and pistols in position, ready to fire at a moment's notice. Ethyn didn't move, still sitting motionless, his head hung down and his breaths coming in uneven pants.

Leonid finally heaved a sigh, clapping Ethyn firmly on the shoulder.

"Lighten up, Ethyn. Death hasn't come for you just yet."

Every person in the room turned slowly to Leonid, including Ethyn, mouths agape and eyes wide with disbelief.

"What?" Ethyn croaked after a long moment of shocked silence.

Leonid gave a deep, belly laugh. He took out his cell, pressed a number, and held the phone to his ear.

"*Zvezda moya*, I received confirmation. We are ready whenever you are."

Ending the call before the answering scream could pierce his eardrums, Leonid turned to smile down at Ethyn. He took out the knife from his belt, and Ethyn didn't even flinch as he brought the blade down in a swift, efficient arc.

The rope binding Ethyn's wrists fell away, leaving behind raw skin and blood dripping down his bony fingers. Ethyn could do nothing but stare up at the leader of Father of Assassins, larger than life, smiling widely down at him.

And then came the sound that Ethyn knew better than his own reflection in the mirror.

The scream of Alex O'Connor, otherwise known as The Hound.

The madwoman who ran the household of Leonid Sokolov. The childhood best friend of Emilia Fox, who had been searching night and day for the leader of Downswing. The former CIA agent who had stolen the heart of Leonid, one of the most feared men in Russia. The woman who had tortured Ethyn nearly every day, beating him to unconsciousness.

The crazy, psychotic bitch of a woman who was about to save Ethyn Dubois' ass.

VIKTOR

It was so quiet.

The entire world seemed to have hushed, waiting with bated breath for our final walk of glory. I walked forward slowly- Alexei to my right, Meiling to my left with Masamune, Kiernan, and Fritz at our backs. As we walked forward, I could almost feel the tightening of the trigger fingers surrounding us. We trudged on, silent save the incessant whistling from Kiernan as he twirled Una through the air with deadly precision. Meiling hiked up her dress as we walked- earning a catcall from Kiernan- and flashed the holsters strapped to her inner thighs. She swiftly pulled her pistols, flicking off the safety as we made our way to the large door.

My hands tightened with anticipation at the fantasy playing through my mind of finally feeling Ethyn Dubois' throat under my fingers. Beating him over and over again until his blood ran in rivers at my feet. Hearing his anguished pleas for mercy, knowing I would beat him for all eternity if I could.

And then throwing his ass to Silas.

"The flank draws as much fire as they can. We get Meiling inside to clear the room, Alexei will follow as protection, I go for the prize. And for fuck's sake, someone make it out alive with that prick and hand him over to Silas. On my count." I said and received nothing but a chorus of grunts.

"Three. Two. O-"

"What the fuck do you think you're doing, Ugly?!"

We all stopped in our tracks at the sound of the familiar shriek coming through the front door. I didn't bother to raise my weapon.

"Get back from the door, Hound." I yelled, a snarl of distaste curling my lips.

I hate this bitch.

"No. Put your guns down or Lo-Lo won't let me come out to play. You're being even more stupid than usual, Ugly Gorilla."

I really, really *fucking hate this bitch.*

Clenching my jaw, I thought it over for a moment, but still gave the nod to my team to follow her instructions. I wasn't stupid. I would rather work with Father of Assassins to find Emilia than die in a hail of gunfire. Not because I cared about living, but because the only thing I cared about was seeing Emilia returned to me. This was the first time that anyone from Father of Assassins had bothered to speak with us and I was going to make the most of it. Any intel at this point would be welcome, considering I was going mad from my relentless rage and helplessness.

Hound wouldn't dare hurt any of us, anyway. It would piss Emilia off too much.

My Emilia.

Rage, my constant friend, swarmed through my veins but I forced it down immediately. I had to remind myself repeatedly as the door creaked open that plugging Hound full of bullets wouldn't be the smartest idea. Not only would it piss off Leonid Sokolov, one of the scariest bastards in existence, but Emilia would never forgive me.

Slowly, a tall, lithe woman stepped out from behind the thick door. Her long, strawberry blonde locks blew in the breeze, and she stepped down and into the light of the faint rays of the sinking sun.

My first thought? She looked like shit.

Dark circles hollowed out her usually vibrant green gaze. She was pale and even thinner than the last time I had seen her. She looked like she would break if a strong gust of wind caught her. I couldn't help but marvel at the change in the loud, brash madwoman that was Alex O'Connor. This hollow shell was nothing like the vibrant, crazed woman we had all come to know because of Emilia. The sight should have made at least a tiny sliver of satisfaction snake through me, but my heart constricted instead.

Hound gave me a sad, tired smile.

"*D'yavol.* You look like shit."

I grunted.

"Was just thinking the same about you, mad dog." I said softly, raising a brow. She huffed out a hollow laugh at that, folding her arms and looking up at me with a vacant, lost look.

"We have news." Hound said quietly.

"Yeah? How long you have this news, crazy lady? *Two months?*" Meiling said, her eyes narrowed in dislike. Hound bit her lip, looking down.

"No," Hound said, lip quivering. She took a deep breath, raising her gaze after a few moments. I frowned in confusion at the unexpected look of sympathy and rage that transformed her gaunt face into savage beauty.

She sighed. "You'd better come inside, Ugly. This news is a little sensitive and... I just really don't think you're going to like it. I'd rather the snipers in the trees not shoot you when you go ballistic."

My blood froze in my veins.

"Hound. Is she-" I couldn't finish.

Fuck, no. It couldn't be true. My Emilia. She couldn't be-

Hound's eyes widened, her mouth dropping open. She let out a gasp, her eyes welling with tears.

"No! God, no! Don't even SAY that!" Hound cried, covering her mouth. She let out a little sob, but visibly shook herself. She lifted angry eyes back to mine.

"Don't you *ever* say that to me. *Ever*. She's alive. We're bringing her home *alive*." She said, the words sounding so commanding and final, I believed her.

Not that I would have accepted anything less, anyway.

"Fine. Tell your men to stand down." I said finally, nodding. She lifted her fist into the air and gave a high salute. With her signal, I could have sworn I heard the click of safety mechanisms being snapped back into place on numerous sniper rifles.

"There. Happy? Now follow me, you've wasted enough time being stupid." Hound said, rolling her eyes. I ground my teeth, reminding myself for the one-hundred and sixty-seventh time that I couldn't kill the infuriating woman.

"What are you doing with *this* asshole, anyway?" Hound sneered over her shoulder, hiking a thumb to Alexei. The man in question gave her the finger, not even glancing at her. Hound smiled the tiniest bit before she schooled her features.

"I think you know why he is here." I said, stifling the words I truly wanted to say.

I think you know a hell of a lot more than I do. And that pisses me off enough to kill every single person in sight.

"True. But do you?" Hound's answer was so quiet, I almost didn't catch the sad words. Frowning, I glanced over to Alexei who merely shrugged. I let it go for now, not knowing or caring what the hell she was talking about.

We stepped up to the double doors of the front entrance, where Hound stopped. She turned, looking at all of us solemnly.

"We're going to the dining room. When we get there, remember that we have information you don't, and any move you make will decide how much information Leonid will give you. And trust me, you're going to want to hear this. *All* of it." With those cryptic words, she thrust open the doors to Father of Assassins, and we stepped inside.

The click of several guns sounded, and I came face-to-barrel with all of them. At least twenty men and women stood inside the large entryway, pointing their numerous guns at me. I raised a brow, bored, looking drolly to Hound.

"Stand down." She barked, and the assassins complied instantly. They all lowered the guns, though the tension running through the room was still coiled, ready to snap. I followed the crazy woman down the hall, coming up to the double doors of the formal dining room. She looked back at me, giving me one last look of warning before pushing the doors inward.

There, sitting at a long, wooden dining table sat the Pakhan of Father of Assassins, Leonid Sokolov. Large body folded into a leather chair, he sat holding a lit cigar, a glass of vodka at his elbow. Ten more assassins surrounded him, guns at their sides, their watchful eyes narrowed on me and my group. I glanced to the other man at the table, who was bleeding onto the rug, his handsome face mottled with bruises. He was naked save a pair of brightly colored briefs and his mismatched eyes were focused solely on me. His long blonde hair hung in a tangled mess around his face, and his lip was split, blood dotting his chin.

My eyes snagged on the tattoo at his exposed hip.

The lily. Flower of death.

The tattoo of *Maman*.

My hands instantly clenched into fists, and a growl tore its way out of my throat.

"Leonid-" I growled, but the larger-than-life king of assassins interrupted me.

"*D'yavol.* So nice to see you again, comrade. Please, have a seat. We have much to discuss, yes?"

THREE

Viktor

My eyes never leaving the tattered form of Ethyn Dubois, my lips still curled back into a snarl, I moved slowly to the spot to Leonid's right. I sank slowly into the wooden chair, watching out of the corner of my eye as the rest of my crew did the same. Alexei sat next to me, and Leonid turned his attention to my former brother-in-arms.

"Alexei. It has been a long time. Fate has a way of pushing us together in the most interesting of ways, eh?" Leonid's deep voice boomed, amusement in every syllable. I growled again, impatience and bloodlust making me extremely short.

"Shut up, Ugly." Hound huffed, plopping down into the chair next to Ethyn. The pale blonde man, currently bleeding all over the place, still managed to infuse sass into the massive side-eye he gave the crazy woman.

"Ah, Viktor. Where to start? I am glad you finally managed to find my compound, though it took a little longer than I would have thought from the revered *D'yavol.* I am sorry for my silence these last few months-" Leonid began, but Masamune cut him off.

"We do not want your apologies." Masamune said quietly, his tone suggesting he was moments away from going for the Pakhan's throat. "We want answers. Now."

There was a reason Masamune was sometimes my favorite.

"Aye, like why do ye suppose a man who claimed to be a neutral party in our war against Korol suddenly cut off all communication with us when our lady disappeared? *And* harbored the one man who knew anythin' about it." Kiernan spoke now, rubbing Una's bloodstained wood lovingly against his palms.

And sometimes Kiernan stole Masamune's place as my number one.

"And why you, crazy lady, why you let him do that? You supposed to be Emilia's friend. Why you turn your back on her, huh?" Meiling said, her voice a hiss of disgust.

So, really, they're all my favorite.

Hound's eyes widened a moment before she leapt to her feet, her body vibrating with rage.

"I would never turn my back on Foxy! *Never.* How dare you say that shit to me when we've been-"

"Alex."

Leonid's voice boomed in warning. Hound snapped her jaw closed, the madness of her gaze seeming almost frantic. She finally huffed, slumping into her chair once again, crossing her arms over her chest like a pouting child.

"Yes, Sokolov, what *have* you been up to these past few months? Korol has also tried to reach you and found you to be... unavailable." Alexei said, tilting his head at the Pakhan. I still gazed straight ahead at the man I had dreamed about torturing for two long months, the one man who was rumored to be behind the kidnapping of my Emilia.

The Frenchman who wasn't leaving my sight.

"I imagine the same as everyone here. Looking for Emilia Fox." Leonid answered evenly, snuffing out his cigar and leaning back in his chair. He pursed his lips, rubbing a hand over his beard.

"Not much in this country goes on without me knowing. I would not be the leader I am today if I let things happen that are beyond my control. Especially in my own territory. You know this to be true, Alexei, for your boss handles his business with the same diligence and control." Leonid said. Alexei nodded in affirmation.

"So, when Emilia Fox was abducted from her safehouse, a place only Downswing, Father of Assassins, and MI6 knew her to reside in, I felt that something... was off. And yes, Ethyn came to me immediately with his tale of having called a member of *Maman* and telling them all about Emilia Fox."

At the blatant confession, I felt my face go blank.

Rage filled my every breath. Pain was right behind it, knowing my fears had been confirmed. Disbelief that Leonid would keep this man from me. And the need for revenge, so thick and heavy, it beat the same stucco rhythm as my heartbeat. My emotions swirled all together, but I kept them bound tightly inside. My face was blank, but I knew my eyes said exactly what my thoughts were at that moment.

Leonid Sokolov had just sealed the fate of the man in front of me.

Ethyn Dubois was a dead man.

"Now, now, *D'yavol*. That is enough of your scary face." Leonid scoffed, standing to his full towering height. He looked down at me, face bland, posture tense. It looked as if he was searching for something in my expression, but my patience was wearing thin. Leonid suddenly looked down, his shoulders drooping slightly. He shifted from foot to foot, and I, along with the rest of my crew, stared in amazement at the larger-than-life man looking... reluctant? No, contrite?

Leonid looked up, and I arched a brow.

No. Leonid looked at me with *pity*.

"You see, *D'yavol*, I did not contact you for two reasons. One, you were gunning for my operative Ethyn, here. No thanks to my lovely companion Alex, who went off half-cocked and decided to call you without knowing the whole story." Leonid slid a glare at the redhead, but she rolled her eyes, as if this was an argument they had hashed out many times.

"Second," Leonid continued. "Because I was waiting for confirmation of something I had suspected from the moment I saw the pictures that *Maman* sent out right before Emilia Fox's abduction. And today, I received that confirmation."

Leonid stopped, and again, he looked at me with pity in his eyes. I snarled at him, my impatience a living, breathing monster inside of me.

"Spit it out! What you waiting for, big scary man?" Meiling burst out, throwing her hands into the air.

"Well... it's just..." Leonid trailed off. He closed his eyes and heaved a long, disgruntled sigh. "You're not going to like it."

"Tell me. Now." I ground out.

Leonid looked at me and all pity, reluctance and sadness bled from his face. A blank mask settled in its place, and he squared his shoulders as he finally told me what I needed to know.

"I received confirmation that Ethyn was *not* the one who gave Emilia Fox to *Maman*."

The silence following Leonid's statement was deafening.

After a long moment of staring at him incredulously, I crossed my arms slowly across my chest.

"Oh?" I whispered silkily. "And is that why you've kept him from me for these past two months?"

"Yes." Leonid said simply.

"Bullshite." Kiernan spat.

"Yeah, scary man, you telling us lies now." Meiling chimed in, scoffing.

"I needed time." Leonid said. "Yes, Ethyn played a part in the kidnapping of Emilia Fox. But not in the way you think."

My gaze slid to the silent man, who was still bleeding on the expensive rug beneath our feet. He was pale, shivering every so often, but that was the only outward sign that the man was uncomfortable in the least. He sat back, lounging, his busted lips twisted in a mocking sneer. I almost leapt out of my chair and pummeled his face.

"Hound told us-" I began, but Leonid cut me off.

"She did not know then what we know now." Leonid cut in. He began to pace slowly behind Ethyn Dubois' chair, his hands clasping behind his back.

"You see, D'yavol, I have had my suspicions from the beginning that the events of the last few years were not simply advantageous happenstance. For instance, why would some of the world's most ruthless, terrifying killers and organized crime members be all in the same place, at the same time, facing a common enemy... who by all rights should have just killed them on sight?" Leonid paused, looking at me.

I frowned.

"You have to be more specific. Ugly is a little slow." Hound said, giving another of her epic eyerolls. Ethyn huffed out a raspy laugh beside her. Alex's response was to jump up, wind her arm back, and deliver a swift punch to his face. Ethyn grunted, turning his face back to me and spitting blood out onto the table.

"Alex, be a good girl." Leonid admonished softly; his tone besotted.

My entire crew rolled our eyes. Myself included.

"As I was saying," Leonid continued. "I am speaking of years ago, when you met each other for the first time. Why in the world would all the members of Downswing be together, under Korol's roof, held captive but *alive*, all at the same time?"

I looked over at my crew and noticed the same confused look that I was certain was stamped across my face. Except two people. Frowning, I noticed that Alexei had gone stiff beside me and Fritz was staring down at my former brother-in-arms with a look I couldn't identify. The only thing that was *very* apparent was that neither one was pleased with the question.

What the fuck?

"And I found the answer to my question. Along with information that has eluded you for these two long months."

Leonid paused in his pacing, facing me, standing directly behind Ethyn.

"Would you like me to elaborate? Or would you like the honor... Alexei?"

My head snapped around. I stared at Alexei, who had gone still as stone beside me. His face was the same impassive mask he usually wore, and if I didn't know him so well, I would have said Alexei didn't know what Leonid was talking about.

But, I did know him.

I had known Alexei all our lives. I knew him better than anyone.

"Al?" I inquired softly. Some would mistake my tone for affection, but Alexei knew better.

It was a threat.

"I... do not know what you speak of." Alexei finally said.

I stared at the man who had been my only light in the darkness of my life with Korol. This man who had been at my side for as long as I could remember, this man I had known better than myself. And I realized something that made my rage nearly explode once again.

He's lying.

"Ah, it seems you have been a very naughty boy, *Alexei Vasilek*." Leonid said quietly.

"Wait. What? *Vasilek?*" Meiling screeched, leaning forward onto the table and whipping her head to stare at Alexei.

"That means-" Kiernan stuttered.

"Yes. Alexei is the half-brother of Zakhar Vasilek, otherwise known as Korol, king of the Russian mafia."

Deafening silence met his pronouncement. Alexei's already-pinched mouth tightened, and he glared at the large Pakhan who was airing his dirty laundry without a care in the world.

"Woah." Kiernan breathed, falling back against his chair.

"Now that you say that, yeah, yeah, I see it. In the eyes. They both have those creepy eyes." Meiling said loudly.

Masamune nodded.

And Fritz said nothing.

His only response was to continue that fathomless stare that drilled right into the back of Alexei's head.

Silence reigned, long and tense. A muscle in Alexei's jaw ticked in time with the clock in the room. Finally, after a minute of the loaded silence, Alexei finally spoke.

"*Pizdets.*"

Fuck.

"Yes, you bad boy, you have been caught." Leonid said smugly.

"How did you find out?" Alexei whispered. My frown deepened, confusion reigning supreme.

What the hell is going on?

"Well, to be honest... I have been suspicious for a while. But it was when I remembered your capture of Fritz Schlusser that I began to reconsider my understanding of the events in question. The story was beyond all comprehension. Young Alexei, Korol's lapdog, managed to bring in big, bad Fritz Schlusser all by himself." Leonid said, rubbing his beard. "I remember thinking to myself at the time- Now, how in the hell did little Alexei Vasilek manage to capture Europe's most wanted mercenary? The man who had escaped MI6, the CIA, *and* Interpol? The German man who I, myself, had considered killing because he was such competition? And the answer to that came to me when I remembered how Downswing escaped from Korol's compound three years ago-"

"Almost four years now, Lo-Lo." Alex interrupted, tilting her head and smiling a vacant grin.

"Yes, thank you *myshka*. Almost four years ago. The answer to my question is simple, comrades. The answer is... you didn't capture him, Alexei. He came with you. Willingly."

Shock.

Shock and disbelief radiated through me like a lightning bolt. I felt it fry my brain cells, zap all strength from my body, and stop my heart.

"No, that's crazy, he-"

"As crazy as Alexei Vasilek capturing Fritz Schlusser?" Leonid asked quietly, his stare boring into me.

No. It was impossible. I remembered that night. Alexei had called me out of the blue after being absent for four weeks. Zakhar had sent him on a mission to Germany to speak with a few German businessmen who were buying into Zakhar's drug trade that ran through Germany and Austria. Alexei's mission had been to bring home contracts from our mafia allies, that was all. It had surprised the fuck out of me to get a call, saying he was bringing in someone worth his weight in gold if brought back alive.

But I didn't question him. He was Alexei, my brother-in-arms, the man I trusted above all others. I had hopped on a plane and gone to retrieve Alexei and his prize. When I had arrived, he had shocked the shit out of me by having a trussed up, unconscious Fritz Schlusser at his feet.

I had known who Fritz was. Hell, anyone in the organized crime world knew the German mercenary. I had been so impressed with Alexei, I remembered celebrating on the plane ride home. My Alexei, bringing in a member of the mercenary royalty. The man who never missed a mark. The unkillable German boogeyman. The man who was considered one of the world's greatest escape artists. No prison, government, or mafia sept had been able to hold Fritz-

My thoughts came to a grinding halt.

No prison had been able to hold Fritz.

No prison...

Holy shit.

"*Chto za huy.*" I breathed.

"Wow. Took you long enough, Ugly." Hound drawled, giggling maniacally.

I turned slowly back to Alexei; my breath trapped in my lungs.

"Why?" I breathed. Alexei stared straight ahead, the tick in his jaw increasing.

Leonid went on, not even giving me time to absorb the information.

"And there it is. The *why*. That is what I have been unable to figure out. And Alexei's lucky streak seemed to have continued after he brought in Fritz Schlusser. He went out on mission after mission and magically found – and captured – some of the organized crime world's best and brightest." Leonid paced, his hands behind his back as he spoke in his booming voice.

"Jazzy Prifti, the Albanian rebel who just so happens to be one of the world's leading experts in explosives. Kiernan Fitzpatrick, the Irish conman that was the heir- apparent to *three* different mafia groups in New York. He is related by blood to none of them, my sources tell me, he is just *that* good at talking people into doing exactly what he wants them to do."

I turned a raised brow to the Irishmen who *blushed* in response.

Fuck, what else didn't we know about our people-

"Meiling Wu. The Triad woman who killed the leader of the Wo Sun Yee clan in Hong Kong and took his head as a souvenir. She took it right to the next Wo Sun Yee clan meeting, walked into the boardroom, and threw the former leader's head onto the table. She walked out without a scratch on her and the nickname that is still whispered by Triad groups today. *Yāo*. Demon."

My jaw hurt from dropping open so much.

I turned wide eyes to Meiling. The *demon* pursed her lips, tapping her index finger against her plush mouth.

"He insult my dress." She said finally, shrugging.

Jesus Christ.

"Yes. He deserved it." Leonid agreed, though he gave the Chinese woman a long side-eye. He cleared his throat and continued. "Ludo Flores. The young prince of Mexico's largest drug cartel empire. Kamili Okoye, the daughter of the former human trafficking kingpin, Ibrahim Okoye. And then we have the package deal, Cin Raymes... and Silas Deveroux."

Leonid stopped, and looked down at Ethyn. The man was no longer wearing that eat-shit smirk that he usually sported. A flash of something that resembled fear came over his face, but he quickly looked down, his hair hiding his face before I could be certain.

"Well. Let's just say that those two are... *special*. I still do not know the full story where they are concerned. What I do know is that when Silas Deveroux worked for *Maman*, he was known only as 'Two'. All of *Maman*'s assassins are assigned numbers based on their proficiency and worth as a killer. And he was ranked second in the entire organization. And that? *That* is truly terrifying."

"Oh, oh, I have information from the CIA, too. Had a contact look into some things for me and she found some dirt on your boys. Cin and Silas burnt down half of Chicago right before being captured by Korol. Rumor is they went after the two biggest gangs in Chicago and killed their leaders. These leaders were CIA-sanctioned and everything. But Cin and Silas slipped right through the agencies' fingers and killed them. Heard it was a bloodbath. Now, that is pretty freakin' cool. And scary." Hound chimed in happily.

At this point, I could do nothing but stare. Yes, I had known some of the information provided. Of course I did, we had spent three – almost *four* - years together as a tightknit group. But it was becoming abundantly clear that Emilia and I had let the founding members of Downswing keep far too many secrets from us.

"And finally, we have Masamune Onodera. This one was a little tricky for you, eh Alexei? The renegade Yakuza member, the famous fourth head of the Onodera *gumi*. The man who some say has made a deal with the devil himself to never die. The unkillable Japanese warrior."

"Not to mention he's the boss of those two scary witches he brought with him after he escaped Korol. The Usami sisters? Those two are *crazy*." Hound nodded, her vacant eyes seeming to dance around the room.

"Korol had to be the one to offer peace with the Onodera clan in exchange for Masamune. But that wasn't what Korol wanted when he was discussing war with the Japanese, was he? He didn't want peace, he wanted complete annihilation. It took a little bird to whisper in his ear, tell him that peace was more profitable. That having a man like Masamune Onodera would be nothing but beneficial to his organization. And that taking the Yakuza prince as a hostage was by far the most profitable decision."

Leonid's eyes fairly sparkled with a fierce light; his expression thunderous as he laid the accusations on the table for all to see.

"It took the words of the head of his personal bodyguard team, his most trusted advisor. Alexei Vasilek. His own flesh and blood. *You* were the one to convince him to house all of Downswing's psychos under one roof."

"How rude!" Kiernan sputtered, frowning.

"Let it go. He's right." Meiling said.

Masamune nodded.

Leonid glared at the interruption but continued.

"*You* were the one to convince Korol to keep them alive. *You* told Korol that they had their use, that he could use them to further his own agenda. And all the while, you had an agenda of your own."

"Bad, bad boy." Hound murmured.

"And that is when I figured it out. You never *captured* Fritz Schlusser. He came with you after you offered him a job that was pure suicide. A job so impossible, I still cannot fathom why he would ever agree to help you. A job he helped you with by telling you the names of the craziest fuckers on the planet. He told you how to capture them. Barter for them. Do anything you had to do to get them all under one roof, united under one cause. You offered Fritz Schlusser the job of the century."

I glanced again to Alexei, whose jaw seemed on the verge of snapping, he was clenching it so tight. My eyes snapped to Fritz, whose face was now an impassive mask. He merely lifted a brow. Leonid bowed his head to the big German, then his eyes slid right back to Alexei.

His next words were whispered, but they echoed around the room, all the same.

"You hired Fritz to kill Korol. You hired him to kill your own brother. And to do that, you used Fritz to help you forge the perfect weapon. A group of the world's craziest, most lethal killers. The group now known throughout the criminal underworld... as *Downswing*."

FOUR

Viktor

The room was full.

Full to the brink from the whispered words that had just condemned Alexei to a life on the run if his secrets came to light. And they would, eventually. Now that we knew, it was only a matter of time before Korol found out. The room was full of disbelieving stares and silent questions. The room was *vibrating* with the deafening sound of silence.

Tension, disbelief, shock... sadness. The emotions bubbled up inside of me, swirling like a lethal cocktail, foaming over the glass of my restraint.

I snapped.

I roared, surging to my feet, and hurled my chair across the dining room. The force of my fury had the chair shattering against the wall like twigs in a strong breeze. Breathing heavy, eyes ablaze, rage riding me hard, I screamed again, punching the table. The solid oak *dented* from the force of my strike. I felt bone crunch but couldn't even find enough of my sanity to feel the pain. A few long, tension-filled minutes passed. My vision narrowed, my heart beating a rhythm of disbelief and rage.

Breathe. In. Out.

I had to collect myself. All eyes were on me, some wide with fear, some narrowed in distrust. But one reaction had remained the same among all of Leonid's people.

They all had their fingers on their triggers.

I pushed a hand through my hair. Rubbing the beard I had let grow, I turned back to the table. My breathing was still ragged as I put my hands on my hips, squeezing until I felt the pinch of pain, my eyes downcast to the floor. I took another few moments to wrap my head around everything, shoving back all unnecessary emotion. Trying to clear my mind, my emotion, to see the situation with cold reasoning.

"It doesn't matter." I said, my voice a mere whisper in the otherwise silent room.

"What?! Viktor, of course it matters, Fritz *lied* to us-" Kiernan said. I could tell by his tone he was upset. Hell, he sounded like a kicked puppy.

"It. Doesn't. Matter." I ground out, opening my eyes and raising my head. I looked to Leonid, who had his arms crossed over his chest, his head tilted, simply watching me and waiting.

"We're here for Emilia. I don't give a fuck about anything else." I said, glaring into Leonid's eyes. It was true. No matter what came about from the events of today, I knew only one thing for certain.

I needed Emilia's ass back on her throne.

"*D'yavol* is right. It does not matter." Meiling said, surprising me. She looked me over slowly, then turned to Masamune. "You agree? Or you want to kill Fritz and Korol baby brother?"

Masamune was silent for a moment, his eyes hooded as he stared at Hound across the table. She smiled vacantly back at him, her unfocused eyes and lazy smile revealing nothing. After a long moment, he gave a small sigh.

"When this is all done, I would like some questions answered. But for now, the only thing that matters is getting *Kitsune-san* home." Masamune said quietly, nodding. He turned to Kiernan with an expectant brow raised.

Kiernan chewed his lip, his face distraught. He looked back at Fritz, his eyes sad, betrayed. God, he really did look like a kicked puppy. All droopy ears and sad eyes. Finally, he looked down at his clenched fists on the table and hung his head.

"Aye. I'm with the Jap. We need to bring Emilia home. That's what matters." He said quietly, defeated.

"Why did you do this, scary man?" Meiling inquired softly, her eyes twin lasers latched onto the large Russian Pakhan. "Why did you reveal this now when we already sad about Boss lady?"

"You needed to know. You are all good. Very, very good. I hesitate to say this, but it doesn't make it any less true... you could be the best I've ever seen in the business. It is almost terrifying the sheer amount of raw talent and ruthlessness your group contains." Leonid stopped, fixing us with a fierce stare.

"But it is not enough. Potential only gets you so far if you are held back by your own lies. The secrets you have tried so hard to keep weren't helping you. They were destroying you. I thought to help an old friend," Leonid nodded at me, but I could only gaze back with silent rage. "And, of course, because my Alex asked me to do it."

Leonid's gaze landed on Hound, whose expression was no longer vacant and calm. No, now the emotions showing through the crack of her armor was sadness... and heaping disappointment.

Disappointment? What the fuck did we do?

Even as I thought the question, I knew.

"You were hurting my Foxy." Hound said quietly, her eyes sharpening and landing on me. Rage sparkled for a moment before she caught herself. "You all thought you could just hide behind the fact that you agreed to help her. That you so *graciously* decided to stay with her to bring down Korol. I wasn't buying it from the beginning. Every last one of you was hiding something, and Foxy didn't even care! She just let it happen. Even after I told her every single one of your little *secrets*."

Silence.

My eyes rounded, my shock a palpable force inside of me.

"What did you just say?" I whispered, my insides trembling.

No, she couldn't know. She couldn't. Impossible.

Hound turned to me, eyes clear, face curled into a sneer of hate. Those eyes were twin orbs of not just hate... but accusation.

She knows.

My already-crumbling world was breaking apart, carving out chunks of my soul as it fell.

"Does Emilia know-" I began but Hound was quick to cut me off, every word a disgusted whip of sound.

"Of course she fucking knows. She asked me to find out, so I did. She knew about you- *all* of you- since the first month you escaped Korol together." Hound grew agitated. Her thin body started to tremble, her sneer becoming a full-fledged snarl of rage on her face.

"She knows who you are, where you came from, your entire history. *Everything.* She gave Downswing all of herself, opened herself up to you completely. She has put herself in the line of fire countless times to protect you. To give you everything you never had in your old life. And what did you do to repay her? Lie, omit the truth, hide behind her love for you. You were picking and choosing the parts of yourselves you wanted to give, while she gave you every... last... piece of herself."

Hound was shaking now, her face reddening with her rage.

"She is your fucking *captain*. Your leader. The woman who saved your sorry asses from Korol's prison, and you didn't even trust her enough to be honest with her. She left Korol's prison only to lock herself in a cage of her own team's *lies*. And she let you do it. She let you hold back from her, and do you want to know *why*?" Hound was snarling now, and with the rabid look in her eye and the terrifying snap of her voice, she truly resembled a ravenous dog.

And with her next words, she locked her jaws on our crumbling hearts.

"She let you do it because she said when you truly wanted her to be your captain, you would be honest with her. Share yourselves with her. But just like Korol, you let her down. You *all* let her down."

No.

Denial ran through my mind, but I knew in the deepest parts of my black, shriveled heart that this madwoman was telling the truth. And she was right. All these years, and my Emilia had known about me. My past, the ugly truth of my existence, everything. And not just me. She had known about the members of our team and had told me nothing. I was supposed to be her partner, her trusted other half. She had told me that countless times over the years.

Reminding me repeatedly over the years, giving me every opportunity to be honest with her. And I let her down... every single time.

Just like Korol.

The realization slammed into me hard. So hard, I trembled. I fought to control myself, not wanting to show the sheer *rage*, the bone-deep sorrow, the crushing devastation the truth brought me. All those years of holding back, hiding who I was, shielding her from my past, where I came from... wasted. All those years *wasted*. She had known me. She had accepted me. She had *wanted* me.

She had loved me.

My eyelids fluttered down. God, the *pain*. The fucking agony. My chest hurt from the constriction of my heart. I had denied her love for me, her lust for me, all because of something she had known from the beginning of our relationship. And she hadn't said a word. Not one look of pity, of disgust, of hate. Nothing. She had accepted me wholly and I had paid her in kind by not trusting her. My captain.

My heart.

Opening my eyes, I glanced over to the other members of Downswing in the room. The pain inside my own chest was reflected on all of their faces. Even Fritz looked startled, his blue eyes swimming with regret. Meiling looked fucking destroyed. Tears were streaming down her face and I realized that this was the first time I had ever seen her cry. Kiernan was no better, his big, green eyes swimming with unshed tears, his throat bobbing up and down with the force of his restraint. And Masamune.

What the hell?

Masamune was looking at Hound stoically, but when he glanced at me, he nodded.

"I was honest with *Kitsune-san* from the beginning. She knew everything about my past the first week we acquired our home in Lesbos, before I sent for Mari and Misaki. I was under the impression that the reason we swore our allegiance to Emilia was because she was unlike any boss we had before her. She is a queen not by birth, but by nature. She has done everything in her power to give us the world. To get us the revenge we crave. Why would I hold back any part of myself from someone who would sacrifice her entire life, her very sanity, for the people she calls family? For us?"

"Oh, thank fuck one of you gets it!" Hound screeched loudly, rolling her eyes. "God, I told Emilia *repeatedly* how she should just boot all of your asses to the curb. My sweet Foxy, surrounded by people who refused to trust in her enough to truly lead them. Putting on a brave show for years, my poor baby."

Hound huffed, muttering the next part so quietly I almost didn't catch it.

"No wonder *Maman* abducted my Foxy to see if she has what it takes to bring Korol down. It's all of your faults and I will *never* forgive you."

A pin dropping in the room would have echoed in the sudden screeching silence that statement brought forth. My eyes widened, my jaw dropping. I noticed the same reaction from the other members of Downswing beside me.

"They abducted Emilia..." I trailed off, shock overtaking me.

"You heard me, Ugly." Hound said petulantly, pursing her lips and turning her head away from me. Leonid sighed, giving Hound a look of censure, before bringing his gaze back to us.

"My Alex is correct. I just received confirmation of the truth. Ethyn Dubois had little to do with the kidnapping of Emilia Fox. *Maman* has been gunning for Emilia since the formation of Downswing. He merely... hurried it along a bit."

"What the hell does *Maman* want with our Emilia?" Meiling screeched, wiping her tears away furiously. The small Chinese woman was vibrating with rage, close to losing it. Meiling at the end of her patience was a frightening thing.

Heads would start rolling soon if they didn't spit it out and tell us what they knew.

"Stupid, you really think Alexei is the only person who

wants to see Korol brought down?" Hound huffed, rolling her eyes.

"Korol is a cancer." Leonid said, his eyes flashing danger-ously. "His power and influence keep spreading, destroying everything in his path. There is almost nothing left in the crim-inal underworld without his tainted prints on it. As it stands right now, he is judge, jury, and executioner for us all. Hell, he is so powerful *I* cannot even touch him without losing my orga-nization to him and his allies. Korol is the reigning king of the organized crime world and he is a ruler without mercy. Without scruples. He is a madman. You know this, otherwise you would not have been desperate enough to seek the help of the German boogeyman to bring him down." Leonid nodded his head to Alexei, who remained silent. His silence was answer enough.

We were all well-acquainted with Korol's madness.

No one more so than Alexei and myself.

"The CIA, MI6, Interpol... Korol has his spies stationed in every single one of them now. And the men he has in place aren't just agents. The men he has in place inside the world's strongest Intelligence agencies are the ones calling the shots. He isn't just taking over the organized crime world. He is slowly, quietly taking over the world. And there's not a fucking thing anyone can do about it." Leonid said, his voice grave.

Hound picked up in the same tone of voice, her eyes reflecting the seriousness of the situation.

"He owns Russia. His allies run Europe. His influence is starting to spread across the UK. And the US? Nothing but a plot of land for him to get his drugs and sex-trafficking victims from South America and ship them around the world. He's made dangerous friends, put his allies in places of power, all to protect himself and build his empire. And he did it all without anyone noticing... until it was too late. He is too well-connected. Nobody can hurt a hair on his head for fear of starting World War Three. Not even *Maman* can touch him without repercussion. And *Maman* is *terrifying*." Hound said, her voice quiet, hushed.

"Knowing all of this, how long did you think *Maman*, the assassin group said to have shaped the course of history, the oldest and most lethal of crime organizations, would stand for this kind of madman trying to run the entire criminal under-world?" Leonid asked quietly.

The words resonated throughout the room. I felt like my chest was filled with lead, breathing becoming difficult with each strangled drag of air through my lungs.

I knew Korol. I knew the man behind the legend. His empire began with Korol's father, who had brought all of Russia to heel with his brutal, horrifying reign of terror. Korol had not only followed in his footsteps, he had made sure to ally himself with the most dangerous, most horrifying men in the world to further his own agenda and spread his influence far and wide. I knew this. It was why I hadn't felt one sliver of remorse when I betrayed him for Emilia. I had already planned to challenge him for control of the group before Korol laid eyes on my Emilia.

His reign *had* to end before the world was plunged into madness.

"Why now? Why would *Maman* take her now when she was ready to move against Korol?" Masamune's quiet query had everyone's attention shifting to the Japanese man. His stoic face reflected nothing save mild curiosity.

His eyes were another matter entirely. His sharp gaze was drilling holes into Hound, the silent demand for the truth reflected in his dark gaze. Hound stared right back, her eyes sharp and focused.

"Ethyn." she whispered.

All attention snapped to the bleeding Frenchman. The man's long, tangled blonde hair hung in an unruly mess over his face, hiding his expression. He slowly looked up from his chest, his mismatched eyes revealing nothing as he regarded the room silently. Finally, his lips turned down in a frown, his eyes flashing with sadness.

"I called them." He said simply, looking down at the table.

"Why? What possible reason could you have to interfere in Downswing's business? Other than a death wish." I snarled, my hate for this man burning a hole inside me that was filling with the burning acid of loathing.

Ethyn's eyes slowly trailed from the table to my trembling form. His eyes darkened with a more intense sadness as he looked me over slowly. His pretty face, mottled with bruises, paled further, his distress clear for all to see.

"Because she was falling apart." Ethyn breathed. "I saw her the night you went to the club. She left you, *D'yavol*, alone in that private room... and she went right into the arms of Korol."

The air swooshed from my lungs.

My heart constricted in my chest.

And my mind cracked at the corners, threatening to crumble completely.

"No," I whispered brokenly.

"Yes. And when she emerged, she looked..." Ethyn trailed off, and I leaned forward, needing to hear the rest. My breathing was uneven and loud in the room, my hands gripping the table with such force I swore the wood began to crack.

Ethyn raised his gaze, the mismatched pools swimming in sadness, in pity.

"Trapped. In her mind, Korol still held her in chains. Emilia was never going to be able to bring Korol to his knees if she was still- at least in her mind- held captive by him. So, I needed someone with the power to break those chains inside

J.J. ANATOLIY

her mind. Someone who knows how to break a person down to
the core of their being and build them up again. *Maman* was
already coming for Emilia Fox. I merely asked them to reconsider taking her life. I planted the seed, asking them to break
her completely. So that she can rise on her own feet, bound by
nothing but her own thirst for revenge. Not by the chains of
Korol's madness."

"Why was *Maman* going to kill her? I thought they wanted
her alive to bring down Korol." Kiernan asked, leaning forward,
his green eyes bright.

"Because she wasn't supposed to be the one to bring about
Korol's demise." Alexei said, breaking his silence. He stared at
the table for a long moment, then heaved a sigh, running a trembling hand through his blonde hair.

"She was the only wild card. Nobody saw her coming. I
didn't think she would be the one to form an alliance with all of
you, binding together the team I needed to bring down Korol. I
thought Viktor would be the one to lead you. Not Emilia."
Alexei breathed, realization dawning. His bewildered gaze
locked onto Leonid.

The Pakhan nodded, his arms crossed over his chest, his
face grim.

"Emilia Fox was as you say. The wild card. The perfect
weapon to bring Korol to his knees. And she managed to not
only gain the allegiance of all the members of Downswing, but
of more than half the men, other mafia leaders, who are daring
to stand against Korol. She managed to build a respected,
deadly mercenary group from the ashes of Korol's compound
that you burned to the ground and raise you up to unforeseen
potential." Leonid's eyes sparkled as he warmed to his speech,
his booming voice increasing in volume and intensity.

"The woman who is worth more alive than all of us
combined. If she were to fall, to Korol or to her own demons,

60

the one chance we have to bring Korol to heel and his empire crumbling down falls right along with her. And that makes her the most dangerous woman alive." Leonid said, his voice dropping to raspy whisper that curled itself inside my soul and branded itself there.

"If you were *Maman*, wouldn't you want to make *damn* sure the usurper queen is truly ready to defeat the reigning king?"

FIVE

Viktor

There it was.

The reason my Emilia had been ripped from my side.

The reason Downswing was in a spiral, scrambling to regain our footing in the crumbling path left by the loss of our leader.

Emilia Fox was being tested. And the unspoken words of Leonid's revelation had my brain spinning, circling one thought that echoed throughout the rage-addled depths of my mind.

If Emilia Fox is being tested, then so are we.

And the time had come to show the world just who they were fucking with.

I rose slowly to my feet, my hulking body tensing as I stood to my full height. Masamune, Meiling, Kiernan and Fritz rose along with me, their faces as stoic and lifeless as my own. Without knowing their feelings on all that had been revealed, I knew we were all on the same page as far as our plan of action now that we knew the truth. Even with the lies and half-truths that still lay between us, we were still a unit borne from blood and vengeance. We were hardened killers, professionals, criminals.

And it was time we started acting like it.

"You have given us the information we need, Leonid. For this, I thank you. Downswing thanks you. But that does not excuse the lack of communication for these two long months. It does not excuse you for hiding the one man from us who knew what had happened to our Emilia. You have slighted Emilia and Downswing, even after we forgave you for the incident at your club two months ago that let Korol know we were back in the country."

Leonid's mouth tightened at the corners, but he remained quiet. Hound stared up at us, gaze sharp, limbs held perfectly still. She really did live up to her name as The Hound. I could practically see her ears perking, nose twitching, trying to sniff out the trouble that was brewing just below the surface.

The Hound was on to us.

And so were Leonid and his men.

The assassins in the room all raised their weapons as one, pistols and rifles snapping into place with precise efficiency. Leonid crossed his arms over his chest, his face an impassive mask though his eyes remained trained on me, sharp and focused. Wary. Even Ethyn, shivering and exhausted as he looked, still pulled himself up right, his nose twitching in antici-pation of the upcoming storm.

"I am sorry you feel this way, *D'yavol*. I regret that it has come to this. But I needed to be sure of my information and I couldn't have you killing my man while I unraveled the mystery of Emilia's disappearance. Remember that without me, you wouldn't know jack shit. And without Ethyn, Emilia would more than likely be dead. Ethyn may be a lot of things, but he is still a member of Father of Assassins. A valued member, a good assassin. When Emilia is returned to you and your anger cools, you will see this. Then we will toast with vodka and everything will be forgiven." Leonid said, nodding, as if the matter was already decided.

Yeah, that is not going to work for me.

"That is all well and good, boy-o, but we're going ta be needin' a wee bit more than your sorries." Kiernan drawled; all traces of sadness gone from his face. He clutched Una tightly in his fist, lifting her up to rest on his shoulder.

"Yeah, now we know why Boss lady was taken. We need to know where." Meiling said, pursing her lips and tapping a red claw against her lips.

"And you and your man Ethyn are going to get this information for us." Masamune said, leaning back, a bored look adorning his face.

Quiet descended, all eyes and barrels on us. I watched Leonid stare us down, and for a moment a flash of something like amusement crossed his face before he forced himself to remain stoic.

Yeah, keep laughing, motherfucker. Enjoy it while you can.

"Oh? I have already given you so much as it is. Even with hoarding our little Ethyn here, I have done my part in trying to find Emilia Fox. You expect me to stretch my neck out even more for Downswing? A group who is falling apart at the seams? And what is in it for me, eh? And do not say my Alex's appreciation. That trick will only work so many times." Leonid's voice boomed, the laughter in his voice unmistakable.

"I do not expect you to do it for us. Not for Hound, not for Emilia, not even for Ethyn." I said, my voice a deep rumble in the tense room. I waited stoically, glancing to the grandfather clock against the far wall. I watched the second-hand ticking for six, seven, eight clicks before finally it came to rest on the twelve at the top of the clock.

A crackle came from the clear piece wedged tightly into my ear.

"We're green on the left."

I waited. Three seconds ticked by, then another crackle. A different voice this time.

"Green on the right."

And I waited again. Patiently. Stoically. Staring at Leonid, my head slowly tilted to the side as I listened for the last pieces of the puzzle to fall into place.

The last pieces on the board to align so the game could begin.

"Green from the front."

I waited a solid ten ticking seconds this time. Waited until an annoying Irish voice cackled in my ear. Louder than it should be, like fucking usual.

"Oh, she's looking mighty green from the rear, as well. I imagine she'll look much better after being spanked to a nice, deep red."

For fuck's sake.

Kiernan snorted in amusement, his cheeks puffing out from holding in his laughter. I glared over at him, right along with Meiling and Masamune.

"Are you serious," Meiling hissed, eyes going wide with exasperation.

"We could die right now, and you're laughing. I would venture to say now is not the best time for that." Alexei drawled, though he didn't seem overly concerned himself.

Kiernan's mirth didn't falter. No, he simply twirled that bloodstained bat, grinning like the mad loon he was.

"It's never a bad time for an ass joke."

Fritz grinned, while Meiling, Masamune, and I rolled our eyes.

Morons. They're a bunch of fucking morons.

"Read the mood, idiot." Masamune spat, reading my mind. Though I could swear a tiny twitch was pulling at the corners of his lips.

"What the hell are you going on about?" Hound barked, a thunderous frown contorting her brow. Looking back to Leonid, I merely shrugged at the startled, wary look on his face.

"You left me little choice." I said quietly, waiting for the final piece to fall.

The sound of the buzz in my ear made a smile slowly start to sneak across my face. The answering French voice that was so smooth and quiet that I almost missed the single word that fired my blood and sparked the short fuse on my thirst for vengeance.

"*Vert.*"

Green.

God, that was becoming my favorite color.

Well, second favorite. My favorite color was going to be the red of the blood I was about to spill. And if Leonid didn't do as I asked, I was about to paint the walls with that sweet, beautiful red that called to me like sin to the devil.

My smile stretched my lips.

Woe be it to the man who brings forth the fury of the devil...

And all of his demons.

"We do not expect you to help Downswing for anything short of the lives of not only yourself, Hound, and Ethyn... but of all of your men. And your compound."

My words resounded through the room with all the gravity of a judge's gavel. I smiled my same rage-infused smile, my eyes lighting with the adrenaline pumping through my veins.

"*Zelenyy.*" I breathed.

Green.

And with that, the world tilted on its axis and the game began.

My eyes lowered to half-mast as I heard numerous phones start to vibrate inside the large dining room. Leonid's eyebrows lowered, his face contorting into a fierce scowl that could send lesser men to their knees in fear. Hound's face morphed from outrage to cold, unfeeling calculation as she gazed at me with nothing but pure ice.

"What have you done?" She asked, her quiet voice barely rising above the sound of vibrating phones and startled shouts echoing throughout the large house.

"Sir," Gregor, one of Leonid's head of security stepped forward, his face pale, his phone shaking in his palm. "They've done something to the sensors on the security scanners."

"And what, pray tell, did they do to my state-of-the-art security system while they have been inside my house for the past hour?" Leonid purred, the green specks in his brown eyes sparkling dangerously. And that hazel intensity was focused solely on me.

Not laughing now, are you, fucker?

I simply stared back, eyes still hooded, the grin on my face slowly dimming to nothing more than a smirk.

"I-I do not know, Boss. But the sensors are lighting up around the entire property. Including-" Gregor stopped, his eyes going wide. He looked up at me, then slowly over to my team, and audibly gulped.

"Including... where, Gregor?" Hound inquired; her voice deceptively soft.

Gregor had to swallow twice before he forced the words out.

"Including inside the house. Directly above us."

Leonid's gaze sharpened. Hound raised a brow.

And I smiled.

"What did you do to my system, *D'yavol?*" Leonid asked, his voice a mere thread of sound in the deafening roar of vibrating phones and pounding footsteps and yells from outside. Confusion was descending swiftly, exactly as planned.

I gave a shrug, my face assuming a bored, stoic look.

"I did nothing to your- what did you call it? Ah, yes. Your 'state-of-the-art' system. Your security is much too advanced for Downswing's tech crew to disarm and dismantle. Your team should feel proud." I said, never one to deny excellent work when I saw it.

"Aye, that's right. So, we had ta do the next best thing." Kiernan said, his insane smile spreading impossibly wide.

"We had to actually surround you." Meiling finished, nodding happily.

"Not with men, of course. You would be able to see a full assault coming from miles away. No, this had to be something that would have the same effect as an all-out assault but with less bodies. Something that packed the same punch. Something that would go unnoticed from security sweeps. Something so small and unassuming, your men would miss it every time they did their rounds." Alexei said, looking as if he could yawn from boredom at any moment.

"And, as you pointed out earlier, we have one of the world's leading experts on explosives among our ranks. She also happens to be the leading expert at how to hide them in plain sight. Even from heat sensors." Masamune licked his lips, his eyes hooded.

The glimmer of glee in his eye told me he was enjoying this immensely.

"You and your men are so efficient, it is almost embar-rassing to us, who managed to lose our leader for two months. Do you know how difficult it was for two women to sneak onto your grounds every night? Setting foot on your property was problematic enough as it was, but giving them the task to also hide a tiny, miniscule bomb in plain sight at the same time? Nearly impossible. *If* they had planted more than one bomb per night. So, they didn't." Fritz spoke, his voice quiet, contemplative, calm.

"You said before that you were surprised it took me so long to find your compound, secret though the location may be. You're right, that would have been shameful if I had only just now discovered you. But I knew where you were two days after Emilia was abducted. So, nearly every night since Emilia was stolen from us, Misaki and Mari Usami stole onto your property, and planted one bomb per night in a designated location." I said, pulling Alexei's vacated chair over to me. I sat down slowly, lacing my fingers together on the tabletop, my eyes never leaving Leonid's face.

"They so fast. Your security probably thought they were deer running onto the radar for only a moment before disappearing again. What was their best time? Six seconds? We practice for one week before setting them loose on you. They never take longer than twenty seconds. So, so fast." Meiling purred, propping a hip against the table, puckering her lips at Hound.

"You see, your security system is working just fine. We just disabled the thermal blockers Jazzy installed on each one of the fifty-five ammonium picrate explosives hidden around your property. And armed them." Masamune said, a ghost of a smile trying to consume his face. He was trying to hold back his glee, but god, his excitement was so contagious I almost found myself laughing aloud.

We were all fucking crazy.

As my Emilia would say, it was what made Downswing... Downswing.

At the thought of Emilia, my smile melted from my face, and rage burned bright and hot, consuming me. My heavy-lidded gaze lit with the force of my fury, my hands clenching on the table in front of me. Leonid's men watched in horror as I leaned forward, my expression so dark and foreboding, I knew I resembled the devil that was my namesake.

"As Emilia would say, the slow bet is often the one that wins the hand. And a good poker face never fails in a high-stakes game. So, we were slow. We waited. We planned. We revealed nothing. And we executed." My words thundered through the room, though my voice was low, thick with rage and dark intention.

"We made our play. What's your next move?"

Leonid stared at me, his hands now gripping the back of Ethyn's chair so tightly the wood creaked. His face was thunderous, hard with rage and a glimmer of what almost looked like panic.

"How did you get one of the explosives inside the house?" Hound said, tilting her head, blinking at me curiously. Her blasé attitude was grating, but that was Hound for you.

Irritating as hell, crazy as fuck.

Crunch.

Every head in the room whipped to the doorway.

There, leaning against the doorjambs of the dining room entrance stood Cin Raymes, calmly chewing on the apple he had just bit into, and Silas Deveroux, the Frenchman of Down-swing who had once belonged to *Maman*. I watched Ethyn closely, and when the man noticed Silas, he blanched, physically slouching in his seat. His face flashed with an emotion so piercing, the sight of that telling reaction had all my murderous intent tingling with pleasure.

Terror.

UPSWING

"Bonjour." Silas said blithely, the corner of his mouth curling in a taunting smile.

"Yo." Cin grunted, saluting with the hand that held the apple.

"Hello." Hound answered, waving at our boys. They both grinned at her, Cin even going so far as to throw a wink her way. She giggled.

Crazy. Bitch.

Pistols and rifles snapped to the pair at the door, and I was pleased to note that the hands holding the weapons all trembled. Gregor reached to his ear, presumably to radio to the men outside, but Leonid held up a staying hand. He regarded Cin and Silas with a narrowed gaze, glancing behind their shoulders to the darkened hall.

"And just where are the men that were stationed outside this room?" Leonid asked, his voice that quiet, lethal wisp of sound. If I was in my right mind, it would have terrified me, that foreboding look on Leonid Sokolov's face. He was, after all, the Pakhan of Father of Assassins. No one had dared a move against the underground assassin group in the history of its formation. And even if they had, nobody was crazy enough to try it on their home soil.

I wasn't in my right mind.

I was crazy with worry. With rage. With expectation.

I was out of my mind without my Emilia and playing by the rules was no longer in the cards.

"Oh, them?" Cin hiked a thumb over his shoulder, tsking in disgust. "Dudes were so busy listening at the door that they didn't notice us for a full three minutes. Hell, they probably still won't know what happened when they wake up. Y'all got some major adjustments to make to security inside your house, bro." Cin took another bite of his apple, the crunch loud in the silent terror of the room.

71

"You did not kill them?" Leonid whispered, his green-specked gaze zeroed in not on Cin, but on Silas. The Frenchman gave his signature Gallic shrug, expression bored.

"*Non.* We are not here for that. Not yet, anyway." Silas said, his ice-blue gaze sliding to Ethyn, who moved down even further in his chair.

"Aren't you going to blow us all up? Why did you arm the explosives if you're not going to use them?" Hound said, tilting her head again in that curious, crazy way of hers.

"Insurance." Cin said, shrugging.

"*Oui.* You told us why Emilia was taken, for which we are very grateful. But it was something that I had already suspected, knowing *Maman.* Now, we need one last favor. And we could not get you to respond to us, so we used a little... persuasion to help you along." Silas said, his silken voice wrapping around the room and gripping it tightly.

"Yeah, man, not cool, by the way. Thought we were friends." Cin said, his head shaking in mock sadness.

Tension was thick in the room, clouding the fresh air like a tangible beast. Leonid's gaze slid to all of Downswing's members, one by one, until finally he rested back on me. His men were silent behind him, trying not to look shocked and uneasy. Hound just sat, tapping her finger against her lips, eyes vacant and far-away. Ethyn kept one eye on Silas and another on his leader, Leonid. Finally, the Pakhan heaved a small sigh.

"If I give Ethyn to you to save the rest of my men and my compound, I will look weak. Incompetent. I would rather die than sacrifice the pride of Father of Assassins. I would rather go down in flames than revoke my word as Pakhan." Leonid finally said, looking down at Hound. He reached over and squeezed her shoulder, his eyes speaking all the words he wouldn't say aloud. Her eyes flicked up to him for but a moment before she just shrugged, smiling at us.

"I do not want Ethyn Dubois. Not after what you told us. If what you said is true, and I do believe you were telling the truth about his role in Emilia's abduction, then he saved himself by contacting *Maman* first to plead Emilia's case. If he truly did say that they should take her alive, he is exonerated in the eyes of Downswing." I said quietly, raising a brow. Leonid looked surprised for a moment, before confusion furrowed his brow.

"What is it that you want, Ugly?" Hound asked quietly, her body still relaxed, though her eyes sharpened on me once more. My eyes slid to Ethyn.

"I need him to whisper once again into the ears of *Maman*."

Leonid frowned thoughtfully, looking down at Ethyn.

"None of Silas' former contacts associated with *Maman* will answer his summons. They have vanished right along with Emilia. We could not find a single person who knows how to contact *Maman*, at least nobody we trust to do what needs to be done." I said, slowly rising to my feet once again. Staring down my nose at Ethyn, I focused all my attention on the bound Frenchman.

"I need the one person we know who has access, or at least one contact inside the organization, to plant a seed for us. A thread of discord that will help us find our Emilia. A small idea that cannot lead back to us for our plan to work. Just a small suggestion whispered in the ears of those who will listen to it, let it fester, and let it twist them to do something stupid. A suggestion that would never lead back to Downswing since it is the exact opposite of what we want."

This time, both Hound and Leonid looked surprised. Ethyn stared hard at me, then Silas, then back to me. Dawning realization lit his expression, and for a moment, he looked almost impressed. His expression also said quite plainly that he believed us to be insane.

We were.

Because if the plan didn't work, no one, *no one*, would be safe from the wrath of Downswing. So I breathed the one sentence that I never thought would pass my lips.

"We want you to tell them... to kill Emilia Fox."

Hound's answering scream of pure, bottomless fury could be heard for miles.

SIX

Two days later

Emilia

The world was awash in blinding light.

I squeezed my eyes tight, willing sleep to come. The scorching light was incessant, piercing even my closed eyelids, and I huffed out an irritated breath. I hadn't slept in two days. I knew even hiding my face from the light wasn't going to bring me the void of sleep I sought.

The bright lights beating their seemingly endless rays of manufactured sunshine wasn't what I feared the most. No, not even the lack of sleep and the delirious exhaustion it provided wasn't what had me scared to the bones of my aching body.

It wasn't even the crushing, lonely darkness that terrified me.

It was what the darkness brought with it.

Insanity.

The hissing, venomous voice inside my head that had

grown over the last few months slithered in my mind, whispering to me.

It will come. And you'll be with me again.

No. I couldn't let it consume me. The insanity I had been fighting all my life, the line between right and wrong that I had been straddling, was becoming blurred the longer I was in *Maman's* clutches. I was falling, the crumbling ledge of the precipice I had been standing over starting to break apart inch by agonizing inch.

And that precipice had a face.

It was my own.

And it was horrifying.

The physical torture I could handle. Frankly, I didn't give a shit anymore what happened to my body. It was tired. *I* was tired. But *Maman* had found something that was tearing me apart from the inside, out. They had found the gaping hole in my armor that I had been denying for so long. It was crawling over my being, taking me over slowly. I muttered to myself in the corner of my cell, pulling my knees up to my chest and laying my head on them as I struggled to stay in the present.

They had left me in darkness repeatedly, keeping me for days by myself in the silent cell, in the crushing darkness. And with the darkness came the hated other half of myself that I had suppressed for so long. The other half of me that was starting to become the main voice of consciousness within.

With the darkness came not only the voice of that slithering beast inside, but the soft melody of a woman I would have done anything to forget. The voice of my instructor, the one who had sent me spiraling. The one who had done everything in her power to twist me up, mold me into the insane killer she wanted me to be. The killer that would bear the family legacy proudly. The woman whose words filled the otherwise silent room to the brink with her whispered words of venom. Her scathing recitation of countless acts of violence. Her loathsome instruction of murder and mayhem.

The room was silent.

Except it was so loud, I could no longer hear my voice of reason.

All I heard was the slithering, whispered words of the insane killer inside myself. And the voice of the woman who had brought it forth, culminated it, ensured it would one day rule my conscious mind.

The voice of a murderer.

The voice of my grandmother, Catherine Smith.

The woman who had taught me to kill.

You will do so well, pet, if you would only let go, my grandmother's voice purred in my mind.

If I wasn't clinging to sanity, I would have sworn she was standing before me, the picture of her was so clear. Her smiling, slightly wrinkled face. The beauty mark on her cheek. The cold, hard orbs of her muddled grey gaze. The short, soft strands of her salt-and-pepper hair. I saw her short, petite frame with the hidden muscles, strong enough to take down a full-grown man. The gnarled, scarred hands that had taken so many lives. I swore she was bending down in front of me, whispering in her gentle, high-pitched, grandmotherly tone.

Is this what I taught you? To cower on the ground like some simpering male? My grandmother's mirage sneered, her voice hardening on the last word.

I smiled slightly, still muttering softly to myself.

My grandmother hated men. All of them. The fact that I even existed was funny to me, because that meant she had to have fucked one man, at least once. That had been my grandfather, victim number five if my memory served. I remembered her telling me about killing him in their basement and watching his blood flow from his body, listening to his screams for several hours before finally silencing him forever.

She had said it was the only time he had ever turned her on.

"You're not very nice, Grandmama." I muttered, biting my lip and giggling weakly.

Nice is for children and fools. The mirage of my grandmother ran a loving hand over my hair, and I swore I could feel her gnarled fingers sifting through the filthy lanks.

"You did always like to say that." I muttered rubbing my nose on my hand.

Yes, little pet, and you never did listen. I suppose I have your spineless father and witless mother to thank for that. But no matter. You are my lucky coin, little pet. And you will always be more than you appear.

I had almost forgotten that she liked to call me that.

Her lucky coin.

My little coin. My grandmother's soft voice whispered over me, permeating every cell in my body, making me tremble. *You think you're so lost, so broken. When really, you're finding exactly what you need to win the bet you laid down years ago.*

"I'm actually listening to you. That alone is proof enough that I'm broken." I whispered raggedly, clutching my knees tighter to my chest.

You're healing yourself. Grandmama's smile filled my mind, and I could almost see the sharp edges. *What have I always told you about healing open wounds, my lucky coin?*

"To heal a wound... you have to clean it first."

Yes, she hissed. *You were an open wound. Festering, infected. But the darkness has helped you cleanse yourself. And now, you can begin to heal.*

"What's going to happen to me when I heal, Grandmama?" I whispered brokenly, hating the weak pang in my chest.

You're going to be the woman you always needed to be. The

two-sided coin that no matter how high you are tossed, no matter how many times you spin around... When you fall back down, you will never land on a losing side.

My breath froze in my lungs and a lone tear fell down my cheek.

And Grandmama's voice purred right into my ear.

The coin with two faces. My lucky little coin.

"How can I live with two faces, Grandmama?" I breathed, clutching my knees so tightly I felt my fingernails digging into skin. The soft purr of laughter echoed in my mind.

My little Emilia. You're merely up in the air right now. As soon as you land on one side, you'll know the answer.

"And what side will I land on?" I closed my eyes, knowing the answer even before I asked.

My Grandmama's voice echoed throughout my entire being, the answer filling me with nothing but fear... and anticipation.

The winning side.

Darkness bathed the room in its crushing embrace as I lifted my head. I felt the voices echoing around me, though I knew not a sound was to be heard in the deafening black of my cell.

With that darkness came the unfurling of that serpentine beast inside me once again. At that moment, I felt something shift at the center of my soul. And unlike before, this didn't feel like two misshapen objects trying to jam themselves together, fighting to fit into a single gaping hole. No, this felt like two bodies of water flowing into each other, finally becoming one whole entity, merging seamlessly into a larger force of nature.

The other part of myself was reflected right there in the darkness. My other half, the other side of my coin. I reached out a hand, feeling the clasp of destiny in my fist.

And my face curled into a slow, terrifying smile as I hissed the words into the darkness.

"*I always play the winning hand.*"

"Well, now, isn't that interesting."

Four watched the security monitor with the same expression he usually did when the leader of *Maman* was around-stoic, blank, and unfeeling. He was trapped in the security room with her now and he didn't dare show a single expression on his face.

His eerie red eyes flicked to the head of *Maman*, a tall, statuesque woman dressed in an impeccable pantsuit. Her white hair was pulled back artfully into a neat bun, her skin nearly perfect except for the jagged scar that ran down the entirety of the left side of her face. Her eyes were the one thing about her that wasn't a picture of calm, cool, and polite.

And the whiskey-colored orbs reflected a glee that made Four's stomach sour.

The woman was known by many names, in many different countries, by many different people.

But Four, along with the rest of *Maman*, called her *Grande Soeur*.

Big Sister.

"She's talking to herself more than usual today." Four reported dispassionately. He watched as Grande Soeur tapped a perfectly manicured nail against her lips. Her face was calculating as she turned to Four, Twenty-Two, and Thirty-Six. She regarded them in silence for a moment, then tilted her head.

"Twenty-Two. What do you think we should do with our guest?" She asked, her eyes going to the assassin who seemed to become more skittish the longer he was around Four. Twenty-

Two's eyes flicked to Four, almost as if to ask for his permission to speak. Four lifted a brow but said nothing. Twenty-Two's eyes shot back to Grande Soeur, and he cleared his throat.

"I leave that decision to you, Grande Soeur." The big assassin said, inclining his head. Grande Soeur smiled faintly, her eyes softening as she gazed at the compliant assassin.

"And that is why you are perfect just as you are, Twenty-Two." She said softly, inclining her head. The assassin nodded, along with everyone else in the room. Twenty-Two had made it clear early on in his career that he was fine with his assigned number. He had no plans of grandeur and status; he was a man of simple pleasures and didn't need any more out of his life than what he was currently getting.

The man was the perfect soldier for *Maman*. Happy with his lot in life and only too eager to jump at any command handed to him by Grande Soeur or his immediate superiors.

He was a council favorite.

At the thought of the council that now presided over *Maman*, Four felt a twinge of distaste. *Maman* was an ancient organization, always headed by the one they called *Grande Soeur* or *Grand Frère* – Big Sister of Big Brother. It was only recently, within the last fifty years, that the organization had found itself having to take on a council of leaders aside from the older siblings. The council consisted of powerful men and women from around the world, all major criminal superpowers that had a stake in the happenings of *Maman*. The council was there to act as a buffer between the criminal underworld, *Maman*, and the controlling governments of the nations of the world. It had been decided that working together for the profit of all was the best path for a superpower such as *Maman*.

Four secretly thought the council had been put into play by mafia superpowers as a way to put a leash on the all-powerful *Maman*. And it had worked. *Maman's* funding was now directly tied to the council, and they had somehow gained the power to decide who and when certain people were targeted by *Maman*. The group was no longer the pure weapon of death that it had been in the past. Now, it was a for-profit organization ran by men and women who secretly wanted to keep the world in the palms of their hands.

Dirty politics. Four had no patience for it.

He was pulled back into the present with a soft query from Grande Soeur.

"And you, Four? What is it you think we should do?" His leader's eyes held his own in a tight grip. Unaffected, he merely lifted a brow at the question.

"I think you should send the boy home." Four said, for what felt like the millionth time.

The boy served no purpose. Grande Soeur wasn't going to kill him. She had a fondness for outspoken, hearty youths and the boy was that and more. Ludo Flores needed to go back to where he belonged.

Before I go insane.

Four pushed the errant thought down with a viciousness he felt at the center of his being. Ludo Flores was trouble. The boy constantly fought him, promised to be the death of him, and consistently proved himself loyal and pure to the bitter end for his Emilia Fox. His loyalty and defiance were endless, and his contempt for Four knew no bounds.

He was *perfection*.

And it was driving Four mad. The boy needed to be out of Four's reach for another two years. Then, of course, all bets were off. He would come for the boy and make him his pet. His secret obsession. His possession. His and his alone for the rest of his life.

He would have Ludo Flores if it was the last thing he did.

Two more years.

"Is that all?" Grande Soeur said, lifting an amused brow. "You really want to get that boy out of here. He must be quite the firecracker to test the patience of the infamously stoic Four." She was amused, and Four was fine with that. He let her think that impatience was all he felt for the teenager.

He wouldn't allow anyone to know until it was too late.

"Yes, that is my only thought on the matter. You know the outcome you desire from the game you're playing. It's your move to make concerning Emilia Fox." Four said simply, shrugging.

"Hmm." Grande Soeur hummed, her faint smile still in place. She then turned to Thirty-Six. The imposing assassin was staring at her stoically, though his impatience and anger were clear to anyone trained to notice them.

Which was everyone in the room.

"And you, Thirty-Six? What's on your mind that you need to say?" Grande Soeur purred, propping her chin on her hand and leaning forward. She didn't attempt to hide her amusement, which served to only inflame the insolent assassin more.

"I spoke with Ethyn Dubois today." Thirty-Six said, crossing his arms over his expansive chest. The scarred assassin had never been one of Four's favorite people. And after spending more time with him and seeing his love for inflicting pain on Emilia had only solidified Four's opinion of the man.

Thirty-Six was nothing more than a glorified thug.

He didn't belong in *Maman*.

"Oh? You spoke with Eighteen? I'm surprised he is still alive. I figured *D'yavol* would have found and killed him by now." Grande Soeur purred, her amusement deepening.

"He is a protected member of both *Maman* and Father of Assassins. No member of Downswing, not even *D'yavol*, can kill him so easily." Thirty-Six was smug, though his impatience was still riding him hard.

"Hmm." Grande Soeur hummed again, not commenting further. Thirty-Six almost sneered but caught himself in time. Four still saw it, and he knew Grande Soeur did, as well.

God, the man was such an *idiot*.

"Dubois agreed with me that it is time for Emilia to be executed. She is not what we believed her to be, she cannot even keep her sanity long enough to prove her worth. She is not the one to bring down Korol. The council would agree with me if they knew it was you who ordered her kidnapped." Thirty-Six was warming to his own speech, his smug, conceited tone grating on Four's nerves.

It was no secret that Thirty-Six believed himself to be above his station. The idiot had been trying to move up in the ranks of *Maman* ever since he had been given his number. The only reason he was assigned a number as high as thirty-six was because of his ties with members of the council. Four couldn't count the times Thirty-Six had asked for a trial to test his abilities so he could move up the ranks of *Maman*. Four knew what the idiot man wanted.

He coveted Four's seat at the table of superiors.

The top nine assassins and Grande Soeur were the governing body of *Maman*, with Grande Soeur sitting on the throne. But not even Grande Soeur could escape the numbering system. It had been law since the formation of the group that the older sibling that headed the organization had to prove their worth along with everyone else.

Grande Soeur was ranked as Three.

"So, you would condemn Emilia Fox, even knowing that Two swore his allegiance to her?" Grande Soeur inquired softly, lifting a brow at Thirty-Six.

Silas Deveroux was a former member of *Maman*, though he still held his title as Two for as long as he stayed alive. That was the law of *Maman*. The only two ways to move up in ranks and be reassigned your number was to either win a higher ranking in a trial... or die.

Miraculously, Grande Soeur had not yet ordered the death of Silas Deveroux. The same Silas Deveroux who was now a member of Downswing and had sworn his undying devotion to Emilia Fox. The man who had walked away from *Maman*. The very same Silas Deveroux who was ranked as Two and was *still* whispered about in hushed tones throughout the ranks of *Maman*. He was said to be Death itself, and even Four felt a sliver of fear at the thought of angering his former group member.

But the idiot Thirty-Six merely laughed at the question, his mocking gaze saying exactly what he thought of Silas Deveroux.

"You mean the same Two who turned his back on you and *Maman* and got himself captured by Korol? The man has not lived up to his number for a long time. His lack of wisdom is even more apparent with his oath of loyalty to that weak woman in the cellar."

Grande Soeur went still, her faint smile sliding from her face.

"Careful of your next words, Thirty-Six." She said quietly, her face going blank.

Thirty-Six was smart enough to swallow back the rest of what he had planned to say and merely gave a jerky nod. Four gave him credit, at least he had enough brains not to anger Grande Soeur. Big Sister had some serious issues with Two, but nobody got to smear his name in her presence.

That was her pleasure alone.

"All I am saying is that Two has made some questionable choices in the past few years. I simply do not hold his opinion in as high of regards as I used to." Thirty-Six said, inclining his head. Grande Soeur tilted her head, narrowing her gaze.

Finally, she gave a shrug, that faint, mocking smile suddenly sliding back into place.

"Everyone has their opinion. Now, you were saying we should kill Emilia Fox and be done with it?" Grande Soeur said, waving on Thirty-Six. The idiot assassin gave a slow, sickening smile and answered back in a soft voice.

"No, Grande Soeur, I think we should kill her in a way that will not only show Downswing exactly where their place in this world is... but also show them the extent of *Maman's* ruthlessness."

The room fell silent. Four glanced to Twenty-Two, who looked distinctly uncomfortable. He then looked to Eight, who sat at the monitors of the surveillance feed and had been silent up until that point. Eight was staring right at Four, an exasperated gleam in his eyes behind his glasses, but he said nothing.

Eight was the tech genius of *Maman*, the man who could topple governments in a matter of minutes with a few flicks of his fingers. He was one of Four's favorite people. He wasn't only tech savvy; the man had an eerie ability to read anyone he met within moments of standing in their presence. He often provided invaluable intel when a mark was particularly difficult to understand or locate.

He was also Emilia Fox's number one fan within the ranks of *Maman*. Within two days of her being a prisoner of their group, Eight had stated to everyone that he was certain that Emilia Fox was the one to bring Korol and his organization to their knees. Thirty-Six had laughed in Eight's face, then. He wasn't going to listen to a single thing the tech-genius said now. So, Eight remained silent, though his lips twisted in a moue of exasperation.

"Is that what we are, then? Ruthless and all-powerful?" Grande Soeur murmured, appearing thoughtful.

"We are the world's deadliest assassin organization. We

have been here since the beginning of empires and will stand long after. We need to show our strength to those who would oppose us. Downswing does not yet know their place. But they will." Thirty-Six boasted, his gloating expression almost comical to Four.

"Your proposal?" Grande Soeur leaned back, crossing her hands on her stomach, patiently waiting for Thirty-Six to finish his ridiculous plan.

"I propose we broadcast Emilia Fox's death. Straight to Downswing." Thirty-Six said, his voice thundering in the quiet room. "We give them twelve hours to find their mistress and when they can't, they will see her death at our hands. And they will know that no matter who it is, no matter what status they have, *Maman* can get to them. *Maman* can kill them."

Silence once again reigned supreme. Grande Soeur leaned back in her chair, regarding Thirty-Six with a flat, calculating look. Her faint smile never left her face as she asked her next question.

"And how do we get the word to them about this chance to save their leader?"

Thirty-Six's smile was nothing but pure, sick glee as he answered.

"We have a live stream of her being tortured. So that they can see for her last twelve hours, as they struggle and flounder trying to find her, that she is in agony. They will see that no matter what they do, they cannot even save the leader of their group. Not from *Maman*."

Grande Soeur was quiet for a long time. She simply stared at Thirty-Six, rocking gently in her chair. Finally, she licked her lips, leaning forward.

"And was this *your* idea... or did Eighteen feed you this plan when you spoke with him?" She asked quietly.

Thirty-Six scoffed, a guilty expression flashing across his face for a mere second.

Ah, that answered that question, then. Four almost rolled his eyes at Thirty-Six's stupidity, but dutifully kept his mouth shut.

This was Grande Soeur's show, not his. And he would let her orchestrate it.

"He gave me a vague idea, but it was I who thought through the specifics." Thirty-Six said defensively. Grande Soeur regarded him stoically, then finally nodded.

"Well, then. It sounds like you know what you're doing. You seem to have *Maman's* best interest at heart. And you have spent a lot of time with Emilia, so it stands to reason that you would have the information needed to make such a decision. One question for you, though, before I hand the reigns over." Grande Soeur stood to her full height, leaning back and crossing her arms over her chest. She lifted an amused brow to Thirty-Six.

"What happens when Downswing finds Emilia?"

Thirty-Six's smug smile was back in place, and his answer reflected his sheer stupidity.

"*If* by some miracle they find Emilia Fox, then the answer is simple. We will kill them all. We are *Maman*. Nobody can defeat us. Especially not some second-rate mercenary group with more bluster than good sense."

Grande Soeur nodded again, that same, faint smile still tangling her lips.

"That stands to reason." She said, sending a quick glance to Four. He heard the unspoken words behind that one glance, and merely nodded his head in understanding. She turned her attention back to Thirty-Six.

"This is not the plan that I would have put into place. But I have not spent any length of time with Emilia Fox, save watching her on computer monitors. It is you who has spent the most time with her, Thirty-Six, so I give the decision to you. Is this what you truly think the best plan of action is?"

The question had so many layers to it, Four was a little impressed.

But Thirty-Six didn't hear anything except the top layer of the question, and his creepy, smug smile stretched the entirety of his face as he beamed at Grande Soeur.

"Yes, and I volunteer as captain for the mission. But I request this to be a trial."

Grande Soeur's faint smile deepened.

"I had no doubt. And who is it that you are challenging by trial?"

Four almost laughed when Thirty-Six turned his beady, greedy gaze to him.

"Four. I want Four's seat at the table." Thirty-Six said, the glee in his tone knowing no bounds.

"That is quite the jump in rank, Thirty-Six. But I leave the decision to Four. Do you offer your number as prize for this trial?" Grande Soeur turned to him, and Four caught the flicker of amusement in her gaze before she scrubbed it clean.

Four didn't even pause.

"*Oui*. If the trial is won, he can have my seat at the table."

Thirty-Six's beam of sick elation darkened his heavily scarred face.

"Then, it is settled. Send out the word, Eight. Anyone willing to participate in the trial with Thirty-Six should report within twenty-four hours. The trial will begin in two days' time. Where do you wish the trial to take place, Thirty-Six? I can have Thirteen make the travel arrangements to smuggle Emilia out of the country within the hour, if you so wish." Grande Soeur said, but Thirty-Six shook his head.

"I think having it right here is perfect."

Grande Soeur's eyebrows rose in surprise.

Four had to hand it to the idiot assassin, he certainly had balls.

No brains, of course, but he did have balls.

"This close? You do not wish to make it a little harder for Downswing to find you?" Grande Soeur asked, not bothering to hide her surprise. Thirty-Six smiled a conceited smile.

"They have not found her for two months and we have been here the entire time."

"And what if they hack into the live stream?" Eight finally spoke up, his voice deceptively soft. It was clear he thought that Thirty-Six- and his asinine plan- were insane.

"I will have the full tech team of *Maman* on my side. Downswing contains no hackers, the only thing they are moderately efficient at is security systems. They will not be able to track the feed." Thirty-Six sounded so sure.

Eight scoffed, his eyes rolling to Grande Soeur. She looked at him, glanced back to Thirty-Six, then nodded her head, seeming to come to a decision.

"The tech team is exonerated from all outcomes of the trial. I will insist that *Le Trio* assist with the trial, solely for the purpose of assuaging my morbid curiosity."

Eight looked down, his brows furrowed, but nodded all the same. *Le Trio* consisted of Eight, Twelve, and Thirteen, all three deadly tech geniuses from around the world. Since modern times had seen a spike in wars fought behind computer screens rather than on the battlefield, *Le Trio* were in the highest demand out of all the assassins in *Maman*. There was no one in the world who could rival their abilities or infiltrate their systems.

No one that they knew of, anyway.

"Any other requests that you have of me for the trial,

Thirty-Six?" Grande Soeur asked, and Four waited for the idiot to dig himself an even deeper hole.

He wasn't disappointed.

"Yes. I think the first thing that Downswing should see in the live feed is the death of their little brat, Ludo Flores."

"No."

Grande Soeur turned to Four, who had voiced the denial before he could even think about it. She raised a surprised brow, her mouth twisting up at the corner. Even Eight looked surprised, but he also sported a small smile.

So what if it was a frozen day in hell when Four said no to killing someone?

They didn't have to be so bloody amused about it.

"Is this a stipulation for offering your number up as prize, Four?" Grande Soeur queried, and Four inwardly cursed. There was no way out of it, he was going to have to admit that he didn't want the boy dead.

"Yes." He answered and noticed the spark of interest in his leader's eyes.

Fuck.

"That is fair. No killing the boy, Thirty-Six. Though if Four had waited even a moment to voice his denial, he would have heard me do the same. The boy is not an adult, not legally, and I won't have his blood on my hands. And he amuses me. Request denied." Grande Soeur smiled at Thirty-Six, whose face turned red with anger. He inclined his head all the same, his gaze one of loathing as it shifted to Four.

Ah, god, I hope they kill him painfully.

Because if Downswing didn't, Four would. Group politics be damned. Nobody was laying a hand on what was his.

And Ludo Flores was *his.*

"Well, that's that. Please send out the message, Eight. Thirty-Six is now in charge and the trial will begin in forty-eight hours. Ah, there is one last thing before the trial begins, Thirty-Six." Grande Soeur smiled at the assassin gently, and Four felt a shiver race along his spine.

When Grande Soeur smiled that gently, it was an impending sign of doom.

"You may not kill Emilia Fox before the twelve hours have expired. If you or anyone involved in the trial ends her life before the trial is complete, you sacrifice your own life. Is that crystal clear, Thirty-Six?" Grande Soeur said softly, her gaze unblinking as it bored into Thirty-Six.

The assassin's jaw tightened, but he finally gave a grudging nod in acknowledgment.

Grande Soeur clapped her hands. "Excellent! Now, I think I would like to observe the trial remotely. Good luck to you, Thirty-Six. Four, Eight, you're with me. Ludo Flores will join us. We will send him back to Downswing as soon as the trial is completed. If there is anything left of Downswing, of course."

Grande Soeur began to walk from the room but stopped, turning to face Four. Though her expression and tone were nonchalant, her eyes sparkled with a knowing light.

"Four, please take Ludo to say goodbye to Emilia Fox. We may be ruthless, as Thirty-Six has pointed out, but I do have a heart. Let him say his farewell to his captain."

Four inclined his head in acquiescence.

"Thirty-Six, may death be on your side." Grande Soeur said softly, then turned on her heel, exiting the small control room. Eight followed behind her, typing away madly on his phone, and Four brought up the rear.

"Grande Soeur, I am sorry, but may I join you? I do not wish to participate in the trial."

Four, along with Eight and Grande Soeur looked back to Twenty-Two, who was the one to have spoken. He was looking down at the floor, steadfastly avoiding Thirty-Six's rage-filled glare.

"Of course, Twenty-Two. Come along with us." Grande Soeur said, her tone amused.

A look of relief flashed across Twenty-Two's face as he scurried along after Grande Soeur. Four had to hand it to the big, dumb assassin.

He was smarter than he looked.

Four stared at Thirty-Six, whose greedy, loathing gaze was centered on him. He inclined his head, allowing a small, mocking smile to pass his lips.

"Yes, Thirty-Six. May death be ever on your side."

And as he walked away to get the boy that was his ever-growing obsession, he had one final thought for the foolish assassin. The sacred words of the organization of *Maman*.

May the light free your soul, Thirty-Six, for the darkness is coming for you.

SEVEN

Ludo Flores pursed his lips as he finished mending his shirt, staring with a narrowed gaze at the small needle he held clutched in his fist. Eight, the tech genius of *Maman* that Ludo had actually taken a liking to, had given Ludo his personal sewing kit to mend his tattered shirt. The shirt was a gift from Emilia and when he had voiced his sadness at having to discard the article of clothing because of how soiled and ripped it was, Eight had sprung into action. He had cleared it with Four, the leading asshole that Ludo hated more than anything, and had been able to leave his small kit with Ludo so that he could mend the shirt.

Fool.

Yes, he liked Eight, but that didn't mean the man wasn't a sentimental idiot. Who the fuck gave the enemy any kind of weapon to use against them, even if it was small and unassuming?

Especially if it was small enough to hide.

Ludo stoically slid the needle into the skin on the palm of his hand. He didn't know how yet, but he was going to get it to

94

Emilia. He could think of numerous ways his *princesa* could utilize the needle. All he had to do was convince the asshole in charge to let him get close enough to her.

As he pondered this, Ludo felt the familiar tingle run down his spine that signaled his least favorite person was now in the room with him.

Without turning towards the door, which hadn't even moaned when the asshole behind him had opened it, Ludo simply stood, folding his shirt carefully. His shoulders must have twitched the slightest bit, because the deep voice of his worst enemy came floating over his shoulder, the amused tones making Ludo see red.

"It took you that long to notice me, *minou?*"

"*Vete a freír espárragos.*" Ludo answered back smartly, turning around to face the annoying albino assassin. In English, the phrase translated loosely to 'Go fry asparagus' but in his native Spanish tongue, it was a phrase that could mean 'Go fuck yourself'. Ludo couldn't remember the origin of it, but he had always loved the saying because it was a clever way of telling someone off without them knowing.

Ludo liked clever things.

"You think I do not know what that means, *minou?* You are not being very nice." Four leaned back against the closed door, his long, muscular body filling out the black clothes he always wore. Ludo thought that the black was a poor fashion choice for the albino bastard since it only accentuated how pale his skin was. Wasn't his job to be stealthy as he killed people? He only stood out more if his pale skin was highlighted by such darkness.

Fucking joker.

"What do you want this time, *bobo?* I am not leaving Emilia, and I am tired of having this conversation with you." Ludo paused, pretending to think. "Well, I am tired of having all conversations with you, so I suppose it doesn't really matter what you have to say."

Ludo had been with the assassin long enough to know when he almost smiled.

This was one of those times.

"You wound me, *minou*. Maybe I won't tell you the plans for your Emilia Fox since you have no interest in what I have to say."

Ludo froze, his eyes narrowing on the weirdly handsome assassin.

Wait, no. Not handsome. He was loathsome. *That's what he meant.*

Damn it, being a hormonal teenager was arduous work.

Especially when you were already confused about your sexuality.

"Fine." Ludo spat, irritated as all hell. "You have my undivided attention. What do you have to say about my *princesa?*"

The assassin cocked his head to the side and simply stared at Ludo with a knowing look. His creepy eyes trailed a path of heat down Ludo's exposed chest to his unbuttoned jeans.

Damn it, the sick fuck was going to make him work for his answer. Ludo wasn't in the mood to play games, not where his *princesa* was concerned, and the bastard knew that. Over the past two months, the assassin had been toying with him, making him humiliate himself in exchange for information. The bastard seemed to get off on making Ludo say despicable things and debase himself.

But he had never touched Ludo when they played this sick game. Not once. He simply watched. Listened.

And made Ludo do everything else.

"You won't give me this answer any other way?" Ludo asked, his jaw aching from how hard he was clenching his teeth.

Four's answer was to flick the lock on the door, sealing them in. He continued to stare expectantly at Ludo for a long, irritating moment. His deep, husky voice came next and sent a shiver of dread down Ludo's spine.

"You know what I want."

Ludo glared at the assassin, a snarl curling his lips back. Finally, he heaved a defeated sigh, nodding his head. He swallowed his rage and humiliation as he sank to his knees. A damning flush stole across his entire face and down his chest, making his humiliation burn even brighter. As he stared at the ground in front of him, Ludo vowed to himself that he would never be this vulnerable again. He would *never* be this weak.

Ever. Again.

And as he gathered himself, Four's deep, husky voice echoed in the small, stone room.

"Go on now, *minou*. Tell me."

Ludo bit back the retort that sprang to his lips. He felt an even deeper blush stain his cheeks, and he cursed inwardly at himself. This meant nothing, *nothing*. He couldn't wait to take the assassin's last breath from him. Send the albino bastard to hell with the kiss of his gun and a wave of his middle finger. He needed the assassin's blood coating his hands-

"*Non, minou.* We are running short on time and I have much to tell you. Are you sure you wish to show me that expression?"

Besa mi culo, pinche idiota-

Ludo forced himself to stop the slew of swear words echoing in his brain. Ludo had to be completely blank if he wanted to do this right. He had to breathe deeply three times to get his shoulders to sag down and his hands to unclench. His expression was always the hardest to control. The urge to kill the bastard was always stamped across his face, so it took some time to smooth his features out and control his murderous glare.

Ludo closed his eyes, took one last deep inhale, then slowly raised his gaze to Four.

"Please." Ludo breathed, his soft voice barely loud enough to fill the room. Ludo's eyes were round and pleading, and his full lips trembled slightly.

The albino bastard's eyes drooped to half-mast, and a slow, achingly sensual grin curled his features. This was the only time he showed emotion.

When Ludo was on his knees and begging for what he wanted.

"You can do better than that, Ludo."

Ludo fought the curl in his belly at the sound of his name on the assassin's lips. He hated himself for the reaction. It was all Four's fault. The bastard was turning Ludo's budding sexuality and inexperience against him. Making him want things. Making him confused.

Making him weak.

Ludo trembled, forcing back the sneer that wanted to come forth and take up the entirety of his face. He bowed his head, licked his lips, and forced himself to widen his eyes even further, his bottom lip coming out in a pout.

"Please. I-I need you." Ludo didn't even have to fake the tremble in his voice. It came out soft and breathy, pleading. What the tremble was really from was Ludo forcing back all the curses and insults he longed to hurl at the albino bastard for *days*.

And the fucker knew it.

Four's eyes flared for a moment, but he remained relaxed against the shut door.

"Again."

Vete a la verga culero -

"I need you. Please."

"Tell me what you will do for me."

98

Hate you, hate you, hate you.

"Anything." Ludo forced out, licking his plump bottom lip as he said it.

"Say it."

"I-I will do anything for you. Please."

Four finally moved. This was the end of the game. The most humiliating moment of all. As Four made his way slowly forward, forcing Ludo's head to go back so he maintained eye contact with the bastard, Four whispered his last command.

"And tell me why you will do anything for me, Ludo. Tell me why you need me."

Ludo swallowed, though his gaze never left the fucker that was begging for death in front of him. He knew what Four wanted. Ludo had no idea what the hell to think about all the insane things Four made him say when they played this sick game, but this last part...

This last part was the fucking worst.

"I-I need you. I will do anything for you because... because I'm..." Ludo couldn't force the words out. They got harder every time Four made him do this. He looked up at the albino fucker, and he knew the assassin saw the struggle, the fight on his face.

Four tilted his head, his eyes still at half-mast as he gazed into Ludo's eyes with the intensity of a wolf eyeing it's next meal.

"Say it, *minou.*"

"Because I belong to you."

Four waited, that half-mast gaze smothering Ludo with its possession.

"Say it right."

PUTA!

Ludo took a deep breath. In and out. Then, he forced out

the words he had come to hate more than anything else in the world.

"Because you... you *own* me."

Ludo was shocked when Four raised a hand to his hair, smoothing those white fingers through the long, dark strands. He didn't want it to feel good, but fuck, it felt amazing.

Fucking... *puta*.

"Do not worry. I will own all of that beautiful defiance soon enough. Two more years, *minou*." Four said softly, fondly, almost lovingly. But he stepped back, wiping all expression from his face and Ludo knew they were done. As Ludo climbed to his feet, shame beat at him from all sides. The burn of his humiliation made him resent this fucker so much more than he already did. Ludo snarled out his response, meaning every fucking word.

"*You'll die first.*"

Four turned back to Ludo, his hands in his pockets, a small smile playing on his lips.

"Ah, *minou*. You know just what to say. Now, come along. You're going down to visit Emilia Fox. I will tell you about the change of plans on the way."

Ludo stood there for a moment, his fists clenching repeatedly at his sides.

He slowly, carefully, slid into his shirt, the one he had just mended. He watched in surprise as Four whipped the door to his prison wide open, without blindfolding him first. Ludo saw sunshine leaking in from the hallway, and faintly, he heard the telling sound of people speaking, children laughing. They had never, not once in two months, let him out during the daylight hours. And this was why. Because now he was able to identify telling sounds, sights, and smells that would give the location away.

And he had a sneaking suspicion he knew *exactly* where they were.

Ludo's eyebrows shot up, and his gaze slowly lifted to Four's. The man's secret, knowing smile played on his lips for a brief moment before he wiped his face clean. He became the unfeeling, stoic, perfect soldier for *Maman* once again. He moved forward, clearly expecting Ludo to follow.

Four's next words confirmed Ludo's suspicions of moments before.

"Come along, *minou*. We are going to church."

Ludo stood there, stunned, for but a moment. Then, he grabbed his shirt, slid into it, and he did something he hadn't done in two months.

He laughed.

EIGHT

Emilia

"You look even worse than the last time I left you, *morue*."

This fucking guy.

I rolled my eyes but hunched my shoulders further, intensi-fying my shivering on purpose. I was sitting with my legs pulled up to my chest, face pressed into the corner of my room that was technically my cell, shivering slightly. From the cold, thank you very much. Not from any fear of these assholes. In fact, I had been having an excellent conversation with Grandmama in my head, working out my plan for escape.

Yeah, I knew I was going a bit mad. There really wasn't anything I could do about that at the moment. They weren't feeding and watering me enough and it was affecting my sanity. On top of that, I had no idea what time it was, my sleep schedule was off due to them torturing me with lack of sleep, and any stretching and exercising I could do came in the dark-ness, when my insanity was spinning out of control. Oh, and to put the cherry on my bitter cake of torture, they hadn't even brought me a mattress to sleep on. No, all I had were two blankets and one pillow on the stone floor.

I could have killed these bitches just for that. But now, with my back throbbing, my tits feeling smashed into my chest cavity, and the king of all cricks in my neck, I wanted to kill their entire families and make them watch. Go medieval on their asses and take out their entire bloodline, erasing them from this earth for eternity.

Yeah, I was not a fan of sleeping on the fucking ground.

As Thirty-Six stepped further into the room, I sensed there were more people with him, so I whimpered, huddling further into myself. I wanted whoever was watching to think that Thirty-Six was the most effective assassin for finishing me off. I needed it to be Thirty-Six that was put in charge of my fate.

Because the assassin was the dumbest piece of shit I had ever met.

He was going to screw up. All I had to do was wait.

"Do you see your precious captain now, brat? I merely speak, and she starts shaking like that. The mighty Emilia Fox, reduced to nothing but a simpering coward."

I pursed my lips, tiling my head and sneaking a peek at the open door of my cell. There stood Thirty-Six, the big assassin's haggard face lit with elation. Behind him stood Four, the albino assassin who was the biggest threat to my escape and beside him-

My Ludo. My sweet angel.

He stood, jaw clenched, his face flat and cold. He seemed to be furious but trying to keep it together. Behind that look, I saw something that I recognized from years of training and living together. A hint that had me almost smiling.

Ludo was up to something.

Ah, baby, what do you have for me?

"I wish to say goodbye." He said, his voice small and sad.

"Yes, Emilia Fox. Your young soldier wants to bid you farewell. And do you want to know why?" Thirty-Six's face showed his every emotion, and the biggest one was triumph.

Oh, Jesus Christ. Get on with it, you sorry excuse for a cartoon villain.

"In sixty hours, you, Emilia Fox... will die by my hand."

Oh, really now? I mused to myself, almost smiling at the thought. *Sorry, pal, but that's the best news I've heard since you abducted my dumb ass.*

To cover up my excitement, I gave a sob, clutching my head. Thirty-Six laughed in delight.

"Yes, Emilia Fox. And before you die, your beloved Downswing will see you. See you writhing in agony, begging me for mercy. And they will know that there is nothing they can do, no way they can save you."

I almost whipped around. Swear, it was only my prior experience with acting in front of Korol that saved me from letting this idiot know how 'scared' of him I really was. I got the gist of what he was saying, but his next words, spoken right behind me, confirmed that I had been wrong before.

"In forty-eight hours, I'm going to string you up. And I will bring you pain such as you've never known. I will make you cry for me, beg. You will pray for death before I'm finished with you. And your Downswing will be watching the entire time. For twelve hours, they will have the chance to find you. But the entire time, there will be a live stream going directly to them... so they can watch all the things I'm going to do to you."

Yep, definitely wrong before. This was the best fucking news I'd ever heard.

To hide my excitement, I let out a cry, holding my head between my knees and rocking myself back and forth. Thirty-Six laughed behind me, the sound grating on my nerves.

I'd make sure he was the last one to leave this world when I was freed.

Just so he could see the full fury of Downswing in all its glory.

"Say your good-byes, brat. I want you to remember this moment when you're watching the live stream." Thirty-Six laughed and stepped away. I felt rather than heard Ludo come up behind me. Sneaking a peek back, I realized nobody had come with him to my side.

Four and Thirty-Six stood back, and Four had said something to Thirty-Six that had snagged his attention. Nobody was paying attention to us.

For a brief moment, I had Ludo all to myself.

Dumb. Assholes.

As Ludo's skinny arms came around me from behind, he leaned his cheek right against my head, his lips brushing my ear.

"Good-bye, *princesa. Te amo siempre.*" Ludo said, loud enough for the assassins to hear. I raised my head the slightest inch and barely breathed the next word.

"*Where?*"

Ludo pressed his lips to my ear and mouthed the name against the side of my head.

"*Drezna.*"

And now, I knew exactly where we were.

I let out a loud wail to cover my excitement. As I did, I felt Ludo slide his hand to my bare neck. A sharp pinch, and then something being shoved into my skin. Taking a moment to process the feeling, I realized I knew what this was.

A very small, sharp needle. Inserted right into the skin at my neck.

Ludo stood, wiping his crocodile tears from his beautiful face. He looked absolutely wrecked. His beautiful, wide brown eyes shone with tears, his nose was red, and his full lips were trembling. He gave me one last, long look, heaved a sob, then turned from me, walking to the door, almost stumbling in his apparent grief.

The little shit belongs on Broadway.

As Thirty-Six laughed his way out of the room, I was paying close attention to Four's reaction to the entire scene. I thought I saw a brief flash of what looked like morbid amusement cross his face, but the emotion was gone too fast for me to be sure. When they left, darkness flooded the room once again, and I was left alone with my thoughts.

And the voices in my head.

My Grandmama's voice purred right into my ear.

I told you, my lucky little coin. Eventually, you must land. And when you do... it's always on the winning side.

I smiled against my hands, hunched further into myself, and my shoulders began to shake. Not from crying. Oh no, no, no. I was silently laughing, my hidden face screwed up into a wide, insane smile.

And wherever I land... the Devil will come to collect.

NINE

Just short of two days later

Viktor

"Ah, shite, this wig itches like a bitch."

"Quit complainin', ye wee babe. We're all huddled together like sardines, but ye don't hear me bitchin' and moanin', now do ye?"

"I still don't see why I had ta be the one left behind-"

"We've been over this ye stupid sod. Yer built like a tank, exactly like *D'yavol*, so yer the perfect decoy-"

"But I wanted to go kill these fuckers too-"

"Oh my god, would you both shut up, already. Fuck, Cin, thought you said your new crew was smart and shit. These dumb, leprechaun motherfuckers-"

Smack!

"Ow! Fuck, man."

"You just focus on what you're doing, Coop. You fail, and this scary man here is going to make sure you never touch a keyboard again. And that's only after Silas takes your balls as a trophy." Cin growled, jerking his chin to me.

I glowered but didn't bother to correct Cin. Because he was right. If this kid didn't succeed and we lost our window to save my Emilia, I wouldn't just make sure he never touched a keyboard again.

I'd make sure he lived long enough to see every single appendage removed from his body.

The boy- well, man, but damn he looked so young- gave an audible gulp. His wide, light hazel eyes took me in standing tall behind him, my muscles bulging, my signature black stare focused solely on him, and he gave a long shudder.

Cooper Reed, supposedly a distant cousin of Cin's, turned back swiftly to the plethora of computer monitors that littered the table in front of him. He had two monitors floating on the wall and three more that sat on the table. All were blank, with a buffering sign flashing on the screens. The only thing that had life to it was the laptop that he had brought with him from his shitty apartment in Chicago.

Roy, the former CIA agent that was now a part of Downswing, had gone to retrieve the man from his home in Chicago four days ago, when we had formulated the risky plan we were now putting into play. Cin had given the greenlight to have the kid abducted, and from what Roy had said about the boy's living conditions, we'd done him a fucking favor.

He probably didn't see that yet, but he would when I didn't have a gun pressed to his skull.

If he lived through the next twelve hours.

"Do you have everything you need for this to work?" I asked quietly, and everyone in the room shivered at the soft cadence of my tone.

Yeah, when I went quiet, it didn't bode well for anyone.

When the devil spoke in a whisper instead of a scream, it meant the fiery mouth of hell was close.

"For the one-hundred and eighty-seventh time- yeah, man, I'm good. All this hardware is just icing on the cake. I could've probably hacked these jokers with nothing more than my laptop." Cooper said, typing furiously and chuckling darkly.

"Watch it, Coop. You need to bring your A-game. 'Cuz if you don't and Emilia dies, I'm not even going to try and save your skinny ass. I'm going to help Silas tear it apart." Cin warned, his long, lean body casually propped against the table that contained the computer systems.

Cooper snorted, his multi-colored dreads shaking as he clearly tried to hold in a laugh. His mocha skin gleamed from the lights of the monitors, and his wide, plush lips twitched as he fought a smile. As he pushed his thick-rimmed, black glasses back up his nose, he turned his computer chair slightly to Cin, pursing his lips. His small, too-thin body shook with repressed laughter and his hazel eyes danced with mirth as he looked at his cousin.

"I mean, I know you play for my team now, cuz, but I ain't into that incest shit. Might have to stick to tearing up blondie's ass."

If the situation hadn't been so dire, I may have smiled at that.

But as it stood, my nerves were shot, and I was more than ready to spill a bit of blood.

Humor wasn't in the cards for me.

"Bitch," Cin snarled, looking like he was going to rush his cousin, but Silas stepped deftly between them. He raised a blonde eyebrow to Cooper, his ice-blue eyes stabbing the younger man with a look so cold, the kid shivered.

"I do not think you understand, Cooper." Silas drawled, his tall, lithe body moving sensuously forward. Cooper rolled the chair back as Silas advanced, that look of fear once again flashing across his face. Silas crossed his arms, speaking quietly to the man we had abducted to help get Emilia back.

"*Le Trio* are the best at what they do. They are arguably the most dangerous of all *Maman's* assassins. They are the ones who can build or destroy empires with a few clicks of their keyboards. They are master coders, master hackers. I have not ever seen their equal before or since joining *Maman*. Their leader, Eight, is one of the most frightening men I have ever met. The man can dismantle entire governments in a matter of moments. The only reason you are here is because Cin put his life on the line by saying that *you* can do better. You can beat them. If that is not true..." Silas paused, tilting his head to the right slightly. Finally, a slow, eerie smile split his face, and even I gave a slight shudder at the look.

"Well, let us just say that it is not in your best interest to fail."

Cooper swallowed audibly. He glanced around the room at everyone, his eyes falling on each member of Downswing. Masamune was there, quietly speaking in Japanese to the Usami sisters. Misaki and Mari Usami were the small, tightly compacted Japanese sisters whose legend was spreading across the world. They were the craziest, most ruthless killers I had ever had the pleasure of working with. And they answered only to Masamune Onodera.

And Emilia Fox.

Next to the Japanese trio were Meiling and Jazz, both strapping numerous guns and knives to their bodies. Jazz looked up with a sneer and a middle finger to Cooper, while Meiling merely smiled at him, her eyes promising pain.

Kiernan and three of his four Irishmen that he had brought to Downswing were loading the industrial van that was parked with doors open on the outside of the safehouse we were tucked into. He was grinning like a fool, bloodlust stamped across his face for all to see.

Una the blood-stained bat was tucked safely into the loop of his jeans.

Roy and Kamili were both loading numerous rifles, talking quietly to each other. Well, Roy was instructing Kamili quietly. The little firecracker African girl was nodding along, her jaw set in a hard line, eyes blazing with fury. She had been hit the hardest with the disappearance of Ludo, her best friend and partner-in-crime. She was ready to take back what was stolen from us.

We all were.

Alexei and Fritz stood back a bit from everyone, though it was clear on Alexei's face he would rather be close to anyone else than the hulking German. Fritz sat in one of the few uncomfortable looking chairs, reading a book, a pair of reading glasses perched on the bridge of his nose. Alexei stood by his chair, obviously pissed, but trying to appear nonchalant. The sight of Fritz reading comforted me.

If the German mercenary, the boogeyman, was reading before a raid, it meant he already assumed we were going to win.

"What Frenchie said. If you don't help bring my Foxy home, I'll beat you to death myself."

The voice had me snarling.

"D'yavol. I am sorry we are late to the party. But better late than never, eh?"

I turned to the two voices, my eyes going flat and lifeless. Hound, Leonid Sokolov, and Ethyn Dubois strode into the industrial shed, looking so pleasant they could have been making a social call. Hound was the only one whose eyes were sparkling dangerously, her face reflecting her desire to hurt someone.

"Sokolov." I said stiffly. I still had not forgiven the fucker for all he had done to delay the news of my Emilia, but his generosity in providing the safehouse we were currently stashed in- on top of all the computer equipment Cooper was working with- was going a small way in mending the bad blood between us. I turned back to the computer screens, my eyes snagging on the image on his laptop.

"Is that a live stream from our safehouse in Moscow?" I asked, looking down at the images of a man who looked surprisingly like me yelling orders at other members of Downswing running around the grounds. It looked like a frantic shit show, but that was exactly how we had planned it.

"Yeah, this is live feed from your security system at your place in the city. Gotta' say, for the security system coming from MI6 and you putting in your own private security on top of that... it's no wonder your leader got abducted. Hacking into the feed was laughably easy. Can't even imagine the other security you had in place. Oh, right, yeah I can because I already hacked into that too." Cooper said smugly, pushing his glasses up his nose again, typing away. His keystrokes weren't frantic as I had imagined they would be. They were surprisingly tame, but I could tell every number and letter typed were deliberate.

"So, what are the other monitors for?" Ethyn asked as he drew close, giving me a long side-eye that I ignored. He looked cautiously optimistic that I wouldn't slit his throat on principle.

Oh, the man was still on my shit list, no doubt about that.

If he so much as breathed wrong in my direction, I'd snap his fucking neck.

"These bad boys?" Cooper waved his hand around the impressive display of monitors. "These are for the psycho plan that these assholes came up with all on their own. Just sayin' if I was this Emilia chick, I'd be pissed y'all were gambling with my life like this. But hey, what do I know? I'm just a nineteen-year-old college kid from the wrong side of Chicago." Cooper muttered, checking his wires and still typing in a few codes here and there onto his raggedy laptop.

"When you meet my Foxy, you'll understand." Hound said, shrugging. She turned to me, her face reflecting determination and fire.

"We're coming with-"

"No." I said, my tone screaming that this wasn't up for discussion.

Hound didn't seem to hear the same thing everyone else did.

"We'll be good, I promise. We'll follow your orders and everything. Nobody will know we helped you. I swear!" She was whining now, her bottom lip protruding. Leonid snorted behind her, his tattooed arms crossing over his barrel chest.

"Nobody *can* know we helped them, *myshka*. If word got out that I helped Downswing, it would be seen as me taking sides in their war with Korol by the other mafia lords. And I cannot take that chance." Leonid said solemnly, looking to me. I agreed with him, which was why I was confused as to why the hell he wanted to help at all.

"And Ethyn wants to make up for the part he played in this whole mess. Don't you, dummy?" Hound said, glaring at Ethyn from the other side of Leonid. Ethyn Dubois rolled his eyes, but his gaze landed on Silas as he answered.

"I wish to make amends to Downswing, yes. I do believe Emilia Fox is the one who can lead you to victory against Korol. She belongs on her throne."

"And you want to save yourself from my wrath, I would imagine." Silas practically purred, his blonde eyebrow raising once again. Ethyn blanched, shrinking back slightly. He gave a jerky nod.

"There is... also that." Ethyn agreed quietly.

I snorted.

Can't say the man isn't honest.

"Fine. But you follow my orders. You do something that endangers Emilia and I will shoot you. And it won't be a warning shot." I said, my voice promising death. Leonid shot Hound a dubious look when she nodded hurriedly, but he inclined his head in agreement all the same.

"It has been a very long time since I have been on a mission myself. This will be very good bonding time for us, *myshka*. You too, Dubois." Leonid said, his voice booming. He slapped Ethyn on the shoulder, who let out just a huff of breath at the rough handling.

"And Ethyn here knows how Thirty-Six thinks. He worked with him for a time before he came to me. From what he's told me, this Thirty-Six only gained a numbered spot in *Maman*'s elite because he was planted by the council of leaders that fund the group. If not for that, he would never have passed the initiation." Leonid said.

The big Russian walked over and smiled pleasantly down at the wiry Cooper, who gulped as he looked into Leonid's eyes. Leonid leaned over, whispering something into the techie's ear that had the younger man's eyes widening a little. I noticed a small movement of Leonid's arm and watched, frowning, as it looked like Leonid passed something to Cooper. Cooper pursed his lips but gave a tentative nod to the Pakhan, his shoulder bunching as if he was sliding whatever Leonid had given him into his pocket. The Pakhan looked pleased. My frown turned into a full-blown scowl as I prepared to step forward but was distracted when Silas started speaking.

"I remember hearing something about that before I left. Grande Soeur was not happy about the council forcing her hand in giving Thirty-Six a number. I watched some of his initiation. He cried like a baby." Silas said thoughtfully, looking to Cin, who merely shrugged.

"He's clearly an idiot if he listened to your ass, Ethyn. What I don't know is why that bitch who runs *Maman* is letting this go down this way. When Silas and I dealt with her, she was way smarter than this. Something's up." Cin said, glowering.

"Mmm." Silas hummed, pursing his lips. I saw something in his eyes then that made me think that he had a theory about the entire thing. But when he caught me looking, he wiped his face clean. He simply gave me a small nod and I knew when the time was right, he'd tell me.

No more secrets between us. That was the new rule for Downswing. After the visit to Leonid's, we had decided as an entire group that we were no longer in this for just ourselves. We were a group, a family, and we would never forget it again.

It helped that I promised pain such as they had never known if a single one of them lied to Emilia or me ever again.

When you're in upper management, sometimes you have to be strict.

And threaten everyone with unimaginable pain and death if they don't obey you.

"Oh, fuck yeah."

My head whipped around to the softly spoken breath of awe. Cooper was bent over his laptop, typing furiously, his eyes moving over the rapid codes that were rising on the screen. His shoulders were tense, but his body practically thrummed with excitement.

"You were right, man, these fuckers are *good*." Cooper breathed. I was at his back in two strides, staring down at his frantic fingers and ever-changing screen.

"What do you have?" I barked.

"I... almost..." Cooper leaned forward; his face nearly plastered to his laptop. His fingers slowed, stuttered, then came to a grinding halt. Suddenly, all five of the monitors in front of him flashed, and pictures filled the screens. No, not pictures. I peered closer, and my jaw tightened.

This was live video feed.

"Got 'em." Cooper said, swiveling around in the computer chair. He raised both of his arms, looking up at me in triumph.

"Welcome to the game, boys. Y'all now have control of the board."

"You did it?" Silas breathed, his expression one of quiet surprise. Cooper grinned at him, nodding his head.

"Yep." Cooper said, popping the p. "I'll save you the long, boring version but I was taking notes when you gave me the rundown on these bad dudes. I also heard you when you told me that these *Maman* people were the ones hunting your asses when you were back in Chicago. So, I was doing some legwork while y'all were tugging your balls, being useless." Cooper turned back to the wall of screens, grinning like a loon.

"And I realized I've come up against your hacker boys before. A few years back when you were in Chicago and had me hack into Prince's security, I realized someone else had been there before me. And they had their hands on the files you wanted. So, I did what I do best. I hacked those fuckers and erased their codes before they even had time to cry to their mamas. Got you what you wanted and vanished. I never forget a worthy opponent and these boys know what they're doing. They also have a signature. Like me, they're talented enough not to have to worry about erasing it. But sucks to be them 'cuz they ain't as good as me." Cooper sat back, looking very proud of himself.

"Shut the fuck up, Coop, and tell us what we want to hear." Cin snarled, but his eyes were alight with excitement as he stared at the monitors.

"Okay, okay. Could thank me, but whatever." Cooper

pouted for a moment, but when he saw my dark glower, he straightened up, clearing his throat.

"S-so y'all are hacked into their feed. You can see what they see. And we can make them see whatever the fuck we want. I was waiting for them to hack your shitty security at the house in Moscow. I laid that trap the minute you set me up with my shit. They hacked right in and the second they did, we had 'em." Cooper was grinning once again, and he swiveled around to the monitors.

"Looks like they're ready for the show." Cooper said, pointing to the top left screen. It showed a room that was made up of nothing but black stone, with a large hook dangling from the ceiling. I felt my heart constrict at what had to be the setting of the main event.

The torture of my Emilia.

No. Focus.

"That screen is reflecting exactly what is being broadcasted on all your monitors back at the Moscow house. I re-routed the images to come to us. Looks like they hacked into the video on your property and they're shutting down your security as we speak." Cooper said, blinking closely at his laptop, which was streaming with code.

"He's right. They did what we thought and jammed the signal on the grounds. Duncan is two minutes late for his check-in. He's never late." Kiernan said from right behind me. I glanced back and noticed everyone had come forward to huddle behind me, their attention focused solely on the monitors.

"Mark has also been silent for too long. They're on their own." I said, nodding. That was fine by me, I didn't need the extra chatter in my ear. I had given explicit instructions to my second-in-command, Mark, and I watched as he shouted orders to the guards on sight at the Moscow house. That was the bottom right screen, a divided image of all the cameras that were located on the grounds. We could see them clearly, and I felt a swirl of pride at how well our plan was progressing so far. The boys, including the annoying Duncan, were phenomenal actors.

Emilia would probably insist I give them a pay raise.

We'd talk about it when she was back home.

At the thought, my attention focused solely back on the monitors displayed.

"What are those?" I nodded to the three monitors left that looked like thermal imaging. There were twelve images between the three monitors, and giving them a cursory look, I thought that there might be roughly fifty moving images.

"They're not using regular cameras to patrol wherever they stashed your girl. They're using thermal imaging technology. They'll only depict certain temperatures and movement. Looks like they had a contingency plan in case anybody did hack their feed. With thermal imaging, you can't decipher landscape or noticeable landmarks. I can't tell you a single thing about *where* these cameras are. They're virtually untraceable. They're linked into the signal of whoever is pulling the strings of their security, and that signal is bouncing around all over the world. I could try and track it, but the longer it takes me and the more systems they use, the easier it'll be for them to find me." Cooper said, frowning at the screens. He tapped a few times on his laptop, before grunting in disgust.

"Yeah, that's exactly what they're doing. Each camera is set up to bounce off a different IP address and it changes every few seconds. If I try tracking it, they could find me and boot me out. Don't think you want to take that chance just yet." Cooper said solemnly, glancing back to me. I nodded in affirmation. That was a last resort.

We needed to bide our time.

"I will say, if your girl is as good as you say she is, those thermal cameras will actually be a good thing. I can't hack into them, but I *can* do something else. Something still a little risky but it would take them longer to see what I'm doing. And that would be only if they're looking for it. Which they won't be." Cooper said, frowning in concentration and leaning forward over his laptop, typing furiously once again.

"What you got for us, little gay boy?" Meiling asked from behind me.

"Well, *rude Chinese lady*, I've got something that very few people know about. And by very few people, I mean just me. It's just a little code I wrote myself that will basically freeze their feed. No big deal, but it's the worst thing to happen to security systems since jamming devices." Cooper said smugly, still typing in that same frantic rhythm.

"I can't hack into the cameras, but I *can* send back the signals that they're producing. That means once you know where your boss is, you can sneak onto the property virtually undetected. I mean, the guards will know if you fuck it up, but the feed won't track you until I tell it to. I can play their imaging system on a loop so subtly they won't notice until it's too late. That's the problem with thermal imaging systems. It's easy to trick once you know the way it works. Well, to anyone who isn't a moron."

"My god." Roy breathed, coming forward with Kamili at his side. "You're saying that you've found a way to make thermal imaging systems obsolete."

"Pretty cool, huh, asshole?" Cooper preened, sending an amused glance to Roy, who scowled fiercely.

"I don't think he likes you, Roy." Kamili deadpanned.

"Only downside is... if your girl can't help with the location..." Cooper trailed off, glancing up to Silas, who was watching the top left camera with a deadly focus.

"Then we have to resort to having you track the feed." Cin finished, his lips setting into a grim line.

"Yeah, and if that happens and they catch me, I'll have to pull out quick. Otherwise, they could fry everything in an instant. These boys are pretty decent. I may have a ten-minute window to work with before they catch me and I have to pull out. That happens-"

"They'll either move her... or kill her. They won't chance an assault. Not even Thirty-Six is that stupid." Ethyn said quietly from the back. My jaw hurt from the clenching of my teeth.

The plan was risky. So fucking risky. It depended on so many assumptions and we weren't even sure if they were correct. The only thing we had to go on was Silas' hunch, Ethyn's intel, and faith in our captain.

But we had to make our stand. And we had only one shot. If things went south and they ended up killing Emilia, my Emilia...

The world will burn, and I will bathe in the ashes.

TEN

VIKTOR

"Guys, I think the show is about to start." Cooper said, sitting straight up, body tense, fingers poised over the keyboard. And he was right, there was slight movement on the camera that was depicting the black stone room.

Without warning, a large figure took up the entire screen of the monitor that held our rapt attention. I watched, shoulders bunched into boulders of tension, jaw clenched tight as the figure stepped back into view. I took in the man that was presumably to be Emilia's tormentor.

He was a big fucker. Tight ropes of muscle on top of muscle with a scarred face and cruel eyes. He tried to look stoically into the camera, but it was clear from the sick glee in his eyes, the excitement dancing around his thin lips, that he was enjoying this wholeheartedly.

I'm going to rip out his throat and bathe in his blood.

"Downswing." The man rumbled, his voice like sandpaper over jagged rocks. "We have not been formerly introduced. We may know everything about you... but you sadly seem to know nothing of us. Please, let me correct this egregious lack of manners. I am Thirty-Six, one of the top operatives of *Maman*. And we have something that once belonged to you."

I had only one thought as the camera trembled once again, and three figures strode into the camera's view.

Emilia has always been and will forever be mine.

The big fucker stepped back, revealing the trio that had just walked into the frame of the camera lens.

I could hear voices in the background, but I couldn't bring myself to make out a single word that was being said. All I could focus on was the figure huddled between the two newcomer assassins on the screen. Thirty-Six was standing off to the side, prattling on about his evil plan, his ultimatum of twelve hours to find our precious captain. I couldn't even bring myself to listen to his instructions. No, my gaze was focused solely on the filthy woman slumped down at the center of the room, crumpled on the floor beneath the gleaming hook dangling in the ceiling.

My heart stopped beating in my chest. Air froze, crystallizing my lungs. My large body trembled, every muscle screaming with tension. My soul cried out, piercing every corner of my being as my eyes took in the vision before me.

No...

Her usually vibrant mahogany hair hung in dirty lanks around her face. She was dressed in nothing save a frayed pair of bra and panties. Her body was riddled with scrapes and bruises, the same lush body that was now far too thin. The black, blue and yellow of fresh and fading bruises stood out far more against the deathly pale skin that had previously been kissed by the sun. Her face was hidden, her tangled hair obscuring her features from my hungry gaze.

Until that piece of trash Thirty-Six put his filthy, unde-serving hands on her.

"Now, Downswing. Gaze upon your captain. Your prized leader." Thirty-Six said as he strode right up to the slumped woman. He reached down, grasped her hair tight in his fist, and yanked her to her feet so roughly, I felt the pain in my own scalp. And I finally feasted my eyes on the face that haunted my every waking moment and every nightmare-filled moment of rest.

"Behold, Emilia Fox. Former queen of Downswing."

And there she was.

My Emilia.

Her face was bruised, lips chapped, split and bleeding. Her cheeks were hollowed out from malnutrition and what looked like mild dehydration. Her strikingly beautiful face was a shadow of its former self.

But that wasn't what had me almost falling to my knees. That wasn't what had me screaming silently inside my own mind. That wasn't what had the grief, fury, and *pain* riding me so hard my massive body could barely contain it.

It was her eyes.

My Emilia had eyes like an iceberg standing tall and proud against whatever tidal wave dared rage before her. She had eyes that flashed like lightning, promising the wrath of thunder in her wake. Those grey orbs of icy determination, frozen fury, of pure stormy madness were the very thing that had made her the queen of Downswing.

Those were not the eyes staring back at me.

I flinched, feeling a shudder begin at the core of my being and make its way through every single cell in my body. Emilia was staring into the camera with those grey eyes, and as I stared back, gazing into the once-powerful depths, I saw...

Nothing.

Her eyes were empty.

No defiance. No hatred. No promise of retribution. No icy determination.

Nothing.

Lifeless.

Grey ghosts, dead and gone, were now staring back at me.

No.

"F-Foxy?" I heard Hound breathe from somewhere off to my right. My chest trembled, shuddering in breaths, barely able to inhale the oxygen I so desperately needed.

"My god. They did it. They... they broke her." Leonid said, his booming voice nothing but a whisper of shock.

"Jesus, man. I'm-I'm so sorry." Cooper murmured, his fingers covering his mouth, staring at the screen with a look of profound horror.

All I could do was stare at the shell of my love, my captain, my heart. My head didn't even move as I breathed my next words.

"Pray that this is not what it appears, Frenchman. Or you will pray for death."

I heard Ethyn gulp somewhere over to my far right, behind Leonid.

"You have twelve hours from this moment to retrieve your useless captain. Or she will die by my hand. But in the meantime..." Thirty-Six grinned, yanking on Emilia's hair even harder. Her body shuddered, and a whimper of pain trembled from her lips. My heart lurched in my chest at the sound.

"Let me show you what happens to those who think they can compare to *Maman*."

I watched, a quiet, dark rage curling from the tips of my toes up my entire body as Thirty-Six, the corpse who didn't realize how dead he was, jerked Emilia's hands over her head. He pulled a pair of handcuffs from his back pocket, clicking

124

them snugly around each of Emilia's wrists. She didn't even struggle as he secured them far too tightly, trails of blood running down her arms at the metal piercing her skin. Thirty-Six tilted Emilia's face up, looked into her eyes for a long, tense moment. A slow, evil smile split his face and I knew in that moment, this fucker would never see the light of day again. I felt my eyes widen as the dead man suddenly jerked his arm back and brought it down full force across the side of Emilia's face.

She crumpled to the ground, her head banging against the black stone. She let out a pained whimper, blood bursting from her lips. She looked up at Thirty-Six with something more in her eyes now.

Pain.

And I *shattered.*

I watched, helpless, silently raging, as Thirty-Six grabbed her by the hair once again, hauling her to her feet, forcing her to the imposing hook hanging from the ceiling. He roughly hooked her cuffed wrists into the hook, which forced her feet to leave the ground slightly and her body to sway in the air. She trembled as her chin dropped, blood dripping from her lips onto the cold stone floor once again.

Silence reigned in the small warehouse. Not one person breathed a word as we watched Thirty-Six punch Emilia in the stomach, forcing spit and more blood to spill from her lips. He wrenched her head up, and I could feel my eyelids wanting to close at the look of pain and resignation on my Emilia's face.

"The proud Emilia Fox. How far you have fallen."

As Thirty-Six's hands trailed along Emilia's stomach, his fingers stroking her exposed skin, I felt my stomach lurch. My hands slowly closed into fists at my sides, my breath trapped in my lungs as I watched those fingers find the tender pressure points I knew were right on her abdomen. I heard Silas suck in a breath at my side before Thirty-Six pressed those cruel fingers into the skin of my Emilia Fox.

Her body drew taut, her mouth open, eyes squeezing closed, as she silently screamed in agony. The two men that had escorted Emilia into the room laughed as Emilia's body flailed weakly.

And madness consumed me.

Thirty-Six released Emilia after a long, pained moment. She drooped down, her breaths scissoring in and out like razor blades sliding over stone. She whimpered pitifully as Thirty-Six grasped her chin in his fist, forcing her head up once again so her agonized gaze was meeting his. He smiled a smile so sick, so full of glee, that I felt every atom in my body scream to shed his blood.

"And your entire team is now going to watch as I take you apart. Piece. By. Piece."

As the minutes ticked by into hours with Thirty-Six pushing all the most painful pressure points on Emilia's body, slapping her roughly, punching her every now and again, taunting her with things to come, listing out all of her failings, playing with her mind and torturing her body, nobody in the warehouse said a single word.

We watched. And we raged.

My own mind slid further and further into the murderous rage that was bleeding out from the center of my chest. The rage that was now unchained, unrestrained, free to rampage. And one thought kept chanting over and over in my head. It echoed throughout my being as my eyes stayed glued to the screen, forced to watch the dismantling of my captain, my heart, my Emilia.

The world will burn *for this.*

ELEVEN

Three hours later

Emilia

Oh my god, did this motherfucker ever shut the hell up?

I spat out more of the blood that was swirling in my mouth. I had already swallowed a good portion of it, the metallic taste leaving me grossed out a bit. Still, I gave a mental shrug.

Meh, I could use the iron intake.

Still have your sense of humor, my lucky little coin. That is a good sign.

I mumbled my thanks into my chest as the illusion of Grandmama's words breathed into my ear. She was a constant mirage at my shoulder, talking me through the pain, promising me the wait was going to be more than worth the suffering. I agreed, seeing as how I had noticed that Thirty-Six was a bit frustrated that I hadn't started crying yet.

Not that he was letting that bit on for the camera.

He was also weakening from striking me and pressing into

127

all of my tender pressure points. That kind of torture took a fuck ton of pressure and if one wasn't careful about spacing it out just right, the one inflicting the pain grew tired quickly. Not only that, but what he didn't seem to get was that the more pain he gave me all at once, the more I could zone out and go into a space, a frame of mind, that disconnected me from the pain. Unless he started in with shock therapy or knife play, he was actually taking it easy on me. Yeah, it hurt like a bitch when someone hit you full force, but I had suffered worse with Korol. Thirty-Six had no idea what he was doing as far as torture went, that much was extremely obvious. He was only tiring himself out more than anything.

Yet the stupid fucker just *kept talking* like he knew what he was doing.

Dumb. Piece. Of. Shit.

"I think that is enough for now, Emilia Fox. Never let it be said that *Maman* has no mercy. I will give you a two-hour respite. It will give your highly inefficient team time to *try* and find you." Thirty-Six said, posturing for the camera.

"From what I hear, your compound is deteriorating as we speak. Your men truly have no idea what to do without their queen on her throne. It is laughable that you thought you could ever hope to rival *Maman* with such a bunch of useless, inferior trash working for you." Thirty-Six tried to sound cocky, but he was panting, his arms shaking from exertion. I wanted to laugh out loud but held it back as best I could.

Oh my god, this dumb shit is way *more exhausted than I am.*

Not that I was letting that little secret out, either. I'm sure I looked a hot mess. The fucker had been torturing me off and on for three hours straight. My stomach was in knots, having been hit so many times it had caused me to lose what little food had been in it. The thirst was the fucking worst. My entire being was *screaming* for fluid. And yes, my body was so tired, I had felt my consciousness dimming during the worst parts of the torture.

But my mental fortitude was stronger than ever. I was fully emerged in my madness at this point, and I wrapped it around my insides like a security blanket. It helped dull the physical ache of the torture. It lulled me into its grasp like an old friend, hiding me, protecting me as if it was a tangible wall between me and the fucker trying to take me apart.

I embraced the void inside and the madness that swallowed me whole.

It was giving me life. It was also giving my acting new dimension. I was able to keep up the pretense of being cowed for the camera.

Maybe a little too well.

I'm sure Viktor was pissing himself in rage at the look in my eyes. God, I could see it in my head, that scary glower that I'm sure had everyone else shaking in their boots. I had been practicing that dead look for a while now and from the triumph on Thirty-Six's face, I was a very convincing actress.

And it was all about to pay off.

"Horace, give her water. I don't want her passing out on me too soon." Thirty-Six issued the order with that gloating tone, and I rolled my eyes behind my lids at his stupidity.

It was like he *wanted* me to be strong enough to escape.

God, he was proving to be just as stupid as I thought he'd be.

Lady Luck is finally having mercy on me, eh, Grandmama?

I felt one of the guards lift my head up, and I let him move me around as he pleased. I had gone limp over an hour ago, so I'm sure he assumed I was already half-dead anyway.

As I felt the ambrosia of cool, beautiful water pour down my dry throat, I almost moaned in relief. The guard paused several times to give me time to swallow, but he made sure I drank my fill. At the taste and the soothing sensation in my throat, I felt a shudder tear through me. If he played his cards right, this guard may get to live with how well he was forcing water into me.

Hand to god, this was probably the closest I had ever come to orgasming hands-free.

I let my head loll back onto my neck as he let me go. I heard him chuckle and then he slapped me in the tit, watching it bounce.

I blinked.

Oh, fuck *no you did not.*

It took every single atom of restraint in my genetic make-up to keep myself from lurching forward and tearing his face off with my teeth. I stole a peak from beneath my lashes at this guard that I had *thought* I was going to let live only moments before. I made a mental catalogue of his face, nodding internally. This fucker had just sealed his fate.

He was going to die screaming.

"I will be back soon, Emilia Fox. I leave you with only your helpless Downswing to keep you company. You may wish to say your goodbyes now." Thirty-Six laughed, striding from the room with his two cronies.

It was quiet. Eerily, so. Yeah, it figured they probably had some amazing noise-cancelling technology. But eh, that was all right.

I knew exactly where I was.

A few more minutes ticked by. I simply swayed, strung up on the hook of doom. I went over everything in my head, calculating the timing I would need to adhere to when I put my plan into action. The next few minutes were crucial. If I fucked it up...

I would more than likely be killed.

Lady Luck, I hope you're still on my side.

I heaved out a fake tired sob, my body straining forward the slightest bit. As I shifted around on the hook, I clasped my hands together in the cuffs. As I whimpered and moaned, shaking my head from side to side, I let out another heart-wrenching sob.

"I-I'm sorry. I'm so, so sorry." I sobbed out, hiding my face against my shoulder. Wouldn't help whoever was watching to see my face as I was pretending to sob at the moment. Because there was only one thing I *couldn't* do.

Cry.

I couldn't do it. I just couldn't. I hadn't cried when Korol had me, and I for shit sure wasn't crying now. Couldn't even bring myself to entertain the thought of faking it.

If that was the final nail in my coffin, so be it.

I sobbed out apologies for a full five minutes, my sides heaving. And all the while, my hands were clasped tightly together as if in prayer, shaking, causing the hook to tremble. When my sobs hit their crescendo, echoing off the cold black stone, I lifted my ring finger up the slightest bit.

And I tapped.

I tapped my ring finger against the flesh on the top of my other hand.

In a very specific, measured, sequence of taps.

Completing the sequence four times, I let my hands relax, my body finally calming, slumping against the grip of the hook. I tried not to let the maniacal smile that threatened to curl my lips emerge as I breathed out the last clue that the Devil needed to collect his lucky little coin.

"Forgive me, Father, for I have sinned."

Twelve miles north of Emilia's torture chamber

Grande Soeur, Eight, and Four all shared a long, measured look after the spectacle of Emilia's 'breakdown' on the screen. Grande Soeur glanced over to Ludo Flores, sitting so calm and quiet next to Four. The boy's face gave away nothing, and Grande Soeur was truly impressed with the former cartel royalty.

"He has not contacted you? After *that*?" Grande Soeur asked softly, nodding to Eight. The surprisingly buff hacker gazed at his leader, shaking his head with mock sorrow. There was a smug twinkle in his eye that Grande Soeur noted, smiling.

"Then I suppose he wants us to do exactly what we're doing then, hm? It is, after all, his show to run." The head of *Maman* purred. She turned to Ludo, who was staring at his leader on the screen with that same inscrutable expression.

"What do you think of your leader now, little one?" Grande Soeur asked Ludo softly. The boy finally looked up into her eyes, and she let out a slow breath of appreciation at the sudden change in his expression.

That beautiful face split into a grin so predatory, she thought that the boy must spend a lot of time watching nature shows and taking notes.

"You and I both know that my *princesa* is far from broken." Ludo replied softly, his gorgeous honey eyes sliding back to the image of Emilia Fox on the screen.

"Hm. Why would you admit that to me now when you were doing so good at acting disinterested?" She asked, curious. The boy rolled his eyes, and she was surprised at the droll look she received in response.

"Lady, you're not stupid. If you were stupid, you wouldn't be the leader of *Maman*. You're using us the same way we're about to use you. And I cannot even say that I blame you.

Clearly, you needed to clean house without being *too* obvious."
Ludo drawled, crossing his legs casually. He chuckled.

"Though I think you may have wanted to give Silas a head's
up, at least. He will not be happy when he gets here. *D'yavol*
even less so."

Grande Soeur stared at this boy, this young sniper prodigy
if her intel was to be believed and felt a swell of pride. Weirdly
placed since she was not the one to have brought him, but she
was proud of Emilia for raising this boy the way she had. All
while building a mercenary empire that was the talk of the
criminal underbelly.

And Grande Soeur had the thought, not for the first time,
that if things were different... she would have recruited Emilia
to join *Maman* in a heartbeat.

"Hm." Grande Soeur said, lifting an amused brow to Ludo
before turning back to Eight, who was not doing the best job at
holding in his laughter.

"Keep up your guard, Eight. I promised to give Thirty-Six
the full power of *Le Trio* at his disposal. And I am a woman of
my word." Eight nodded, the laptop he had in front of him
showing multiple screens that the tech genius was working
from.

"Everything is under control. I think they may have tried to
hack into the stream three times, but each time I fried their
systems. You really should tell Emilia to hire a more efficient
tech team. If she lives through the night, of course." Eight said
to Ludo, who just rolled his eyes again in response.

"I will let her know when the devil comes for her." Ludo
grinned, looking to Four with a look of triumph and disdain.
Four merely raised a brow, lounging his long, muscled frame
back in his chair. Grande Soeur studied one of her favorite
operatives from beneath her lashes.

Her sweet albino was hiding something. And it had to do with Ludo Flores.

She would have to dissect that observation later.

Grande Soeur returned her attention to the screen that depicted Emilia Fox slumped over, seemingly passed out. She allowed herself a small smile, feeling respect flow through her at the born leader of Downswing that Grande Soeur had forcibly detained for the last two months. And as she sat back, amused and feeling the excitement of what was to come, she had one thought.

Let the real test begin.

Back in the warehouse on the outskirts of Moscow
At the same exact moment

Masamune Onodera turned to the devil of Downswing, taking in the large man's body thrumming with suppressed rage and violence. *D'yavol* missed nothing. His eyes had taken in every movement that Emilia had made in that stunning display on the video. The violence bled away slowly from the devil's face, replaced with the same emotion that was thrumming through every member in the room.

Blood-thirsty anticipation.

"Do you have it?" Viktor Orlov breathed, turning his head to Silas Deveroux. The Frenchman nodded, a slow smile curling his obscenely lush lips.

"Route the feed to Viktor's phone, my man. He doesn't want to miss a single sound from that livestream, you feel me?" Cin said, slapping Cooper on the shoulder. The small, thin black man with the head full of multi-colored dreads nodded, typing furiously.

"It's there. You're good to go."

"Just like we talked about, man. You watch our backs and I promise we'll have yours." Cin said, nodding down to his cousin once again. Cooper didn't even look up, he simply gave a grunt of affirmation and continued his furious typing.

D'yavol looked down to his phone and gave a nod. He turned from the monitors, striding towards the van, the black sedan, and two motorcycles that would take them to where they were going. The large Russian enforcer breathed the next words into the silence, his voice dark as sin as he said his next words.

"Move out."

"We're coming for you, Foxy..." Hound sang, her face alight with madness as she followed the devil from the room, Leonid and Ethyn on her heels. The rest of Downswing moved out smoothly, save one of Kiernan's men who stayed behind to protect Cooper.

Masamune turned to his angels, the Usami sisters, and gave them a firm nod. Both of their mouths gave an amused twitch before they were spinning on their heels, heading out after their crew.

Masamune smiled. He walked languidly to the awaiting vehicles as he finally sang the first words that had popped into his mind when Emilia had finished giving them their final clue.

"Take me to church."

TWELVE

Two hours later

Thirty-Six grinned at the disheveled woman, swinging limply on the large hook he had installed just for her in the basement of the church. Since killing the priest that had presided there and subsequently giving her location to *Maman*, the small church in Drezna with the hidden rooms had been their base for the past few months.

Emilia Fox truly was a pathetic sight, filthy, stinking of pain and humiliation. This was his favorite part of his job, watching the weak fall into the abyss of madness. He loved tearing down their sanity piece by piece until nothing but an empty husk of a human remained.

It was why he would be the next leader of *Maman*.

That stupid bitch Grande Soeur thought he was gunning for Four. The idea was laughable. Yes, he knew he was far superior to the albino bastard who had held Thirty-Six's fate in his freakishly pale hands for far too long. But that wasn't what he was after.

He wanted it all.

And his connections with the council would ensure his victory.

All he had to do was gain access to *Maman*'s inner circle of freaks, the top nine assassins, and he was in. He already had the loyalty of fifty of *Maman*'s Numberless. There were only forty operatives that were assigned a number in the ranks of *Maman*, and they were the best of the best. The deadliest assassins in the world. But every organization needed foot soldiers. *Maman* could not have conquered the world as they had without having an army at their back. So, forty people received the glory and status of being the assassins of *Maman* and the rest were never assigned a number.

The Numberless.

The Numberless served as the army at the back of forty of the world's most terrifying people. But Thirty-Six had known that there were some among the Numberless that weren't happy with their lot in life. And why would they be?

They were nothing.

So, Thirty-Six had whispered in their ear, convincing them that Grand Soeur saw them as nothing more than pawns, disposable trash. He had tapped into all that simmering jealousy, the thirst for glory, and gained the fifty soldiers who were assisting him in his plan for domination. Thirty-Six didn't want Four's position at the fucking table. He wanted to sit at the head of it and these useless pieces of Numberless garbage were going to help him get there.

Four was simply a pawn in Thirty-Six's plans for making *Maman* his own, just like the idiot Numberless that were working for him.

And the idiot girl that hung before him now was the key to his success.

"Did you have a nice break, *putain?*" Thirty-Six sneered,

yanking on Emilia's arm. The girl gave a start, snorting, blinking open those empty grey eyes. She looked up at him groggily and he frowned at her reaction.

The bitch *yawned*.

Thirty-Six frowned.

Has the bitch been asleep *this entire time?*

He had watched the part of the video feed over the last two hours deemed the most important. That had been the break-down that Emilia had gone through right after he had left her to stew in her own agony. After her breakdown, Eight had asked if Thirty-Six wanted *Le Trio* to do anything more than what they were currently doing, which was maintaining all security feed and making sure nobody hacked the live stream. Thirty-Six had said no, confident that Downswing would never find them, and that Emilia posed no threat.

He was still convinced. Thirty-Six had asked for a report on the ragtag group of mongrels that Emilia had banded together, and Eight had told him that the idiots had scattered, going in the opposite direction of Drezna. Eight said he had made sure to put measures in place that if anyone did hack the live stream- unlikely though it was- it would show that it was coming from an IP address across Russia. Hours and miles away from where they were. Thirty-Six had laughed at that.

God, this was too easy.

Downswing was nothing more than an insect beneath the foot of a giant.

And yes, he was the giant.

"Did I wake you, your highness?" Thirty-Six sneered, back-handing the American girl across the face. She gave a broken whimper, huddling in on herself.

This stupid woman was all that was standing between Thirty-Six and his rightful seat at the table. With just a quick flick of his wrist and a blade to her throat, he could end it all now. But no, he had to be patient. He couldn't kill her before the twelve hours were up, no matter how badly he craved the feeling of her blood on his hands. There was no need to be angry, not really.

She wouldn't be making it out of this room alive.

And he had so much more fun planned for the queen of Downswing.

Thirty-Six started to smile as he realized there was a torture that Grand Soeur had not forbidden. She had given him his orders, such as they were, and this was his show to run. Grande Soeur had said that he couldn't kill the girl, she hadn't said anything about hurting her more than he ever had. The pain in the ass woman who hung like a limp doll before him made his dick hard. She had been a fighter at the beginning, and he had loved breaking her down.

He wanted his prize for breaking the spitfire. He already had her spirit, but he was a greedy bastard.

He wanted *everything*.

"Do you know what I bet your Downswing would like, *putain?*" Thirty-Six purred, sliding a slow hand along Emilia's stomach. Her eyes were still flat and lifeless, but Thirty-Six could swear he saw the corners of her eyes narrow slightly.

Maybe there was some fight left in the girl after all.

Thirty-Six smiled.

Good.

"I bet they would love to see you writhing on my cock." He said, a cruel smile pulling his mouth up. Emilia Fox seemed to stop breathing, and her eyes suddenly sparked.

Thirty-Six kept smiling, trailing his hand down between her legs. He grabbed her roughly, and he watched as her eyes slowly widened. That dead look was starting to lift, and Thirty-Six almost cackled with glee.

Oh, taking her was going to be so much fun.

"Hey, what the fuck-" Eight's voice whispered in his ear, sounding furious. Thirty-Six smiled, grabbing the woman in front of him harder between her legs.

"I believe this is my show to run. Emilia is a full-grown woman and she wants my cock. Don't you, sweetheart? Want me to take the pain away for a while, have you gag on my dick before you die? I know you want it, *putain*." Thirty-Six snarled up into Emilia's face.

Silence met his questions, though he wasn't surprised Emilia wasn't answering him. He waited for Eight to respond, seeing if they would really interfere with how he wanted to deal with Emilia Fox. Finally, he got a short response.

"Fine." Eight said, and Thirty-Six heard the com click off. He rolled his eyes to himself. That soft fucker got way too much credit. He was nothing more than a loser hiding behind a computer screen. He wouldn't do what needed to be done.

But Thirty-Six would. And he was going to have fun doing it.

He trailed his hands slowly up Emilia's sides, grabbing both of her breasts roughly in his grip. The woman before him didn't even flinch, she simply watched him with an unblinking stare. Thirty-Six almost frowned but forced his features to remain carefully neutral.

This wasn't the same woman that had been whimpering while he tortured her mercilessly. Those dead eyes that spoke of a spirit long crushed simply stared at him, not one emotion flickering in the depths. Still, the tension in the room climbed higher, and it was almost as if a sudden change in the wind had begun. A shift in power at the center of the room where the leader of Downswing hung, suspended in the air.

Thirty-Six watched in confusion as Emilia Fox slowly tilted her head to the side. Those creepy, cold grey eyes narrowed on him and Thirty-Six couldn't help the sudden gasp that arose.

The woman in front of him... No, it was impossible. But even as he thought it, the evidence in front of him called him a liar.

Emilia Fox was not as broken as she appeared.

Those cold, grey eyes crinkled at the corners and a slow, evil grin stole over her face.

"You stupid, stupid fucker." She breathed.

Thirty-Six reared back to slap her, rage ripping through him.

BOOM!

The church shook, the stones themselves seeming to groan in protest. Thirty-Six reared back, looking around the room frantically. The two men with him did the same, sputtering in shock.

"What the fuck was that?" He hissed, hearing the click of the com in his ear come on again. "Eight, what-"

"I heard it. The cameras didn't pick up a blast. The thermal feed is picking up nothing but your men. I don't- wait. What the fuck-" Eight began, but the com in his ear suddenly clicked off.

"Eight. Eight! What the *fuck*." Thirty-Six snarled but came up short at the sound of a deep, rusty chuckle from behind him.

Thirty-Six whipped back to the still swaying Emilia. That eerily gleeful smile lit up her pale face. She was swinging back and forth on the hook, giggling softly to herself. Her unblinking stare was still focused on him, and he took an involuntary step back at the look that was now in those eyes.

No longer were they empty, devoid of emotion. No longer were they brimming with pain, dim with acceptance. Those dead, grey orbs had risen from the dead. They had gone beyond death, reached into the furthest realms of hell and pulled the fire and brimstone back to the realm of the living. Resurrected from the grave of torture and pain that Thirty-Six had sent her to these two long months.

Emilia Fox's signature stare was back, and the grey orbs of death were now focused on him.

And they were *freezing*.

Sparkling with an icy rage so acute, Thirty-Six felt the air in his lungs chill with the force of that gaze. His eyes widened as another blast shook the room, this one shaking the stones once again. The room was sound-proofed, so he couldn't hear what was going on outside, but he knew that he needed to handle the situation. And there was a situation, he knew it from the knot that had formed in the pit of his stomach. He knew the impossible had happened.

Downswing had come for their queen.

And the queen laughed softly again, finally blinking those cursed eyes.

"*If you're going to play the game...*" She sang softly, the sound like glass scraping the inside of his brain. He staggered forward in a blind rage, only to pull up short as she hissed the rest of the lyrics to that fucking song that sent terror through every atom in his body.

"*You have to learn to play it right.*"

The lights flashed, flickered for a moment, then everything went black.

A moment passed. Thirty-Six's breaths scissored in and out of his lungs. Then, a sound came that had his blood freezing in his veins.

The telltale whisper of metal clinking to the floor.

Thirty-Six stumbled in the dark room, ducking low to the ground, barreling right into the door. He fumbled with the door handle, listening to the shouts of surprise behind him that quickly turned into pained screams. As he heard flesh beat against flesh, he thrust his entire weight against the door. Over and over he pushed, his body quaking. He finally burst forward, a yell of panic on the tip of his tongue. Right before he slammed the door shut and locked it behind him, he felt a shiver of terror race along his spine at the final sounds that came from the yawning darkness of the cursed room.

Spurting liquid.

Gurgling death rattles.

And a low, rusty chuckle.

Thirty-Six slammed the door shut, locking it with the key around his neck. His breaths came in pants and his whole body *shook*. He knew, without a doubt, if he had lingered even a moment longer in that room... Emilia Fox would have killed him. She had somehow freed herself from her shackles and Thirty-Six realized something that made his entire world tilt.

The crazy bitch had never been resigned to her fate. All that time, all that torture he had administered, it hadn't broken her. *He* hadn't broken her.

She had only been biding her time.

And he had done nothing... except underestimate her.

Thirty-Six turned, swallowing roughly and straightened his spine. Fuck it. What was done was done. Yes, he had underestimated his opponent and lost the upper hand for the moment. But it wouldn't last. He would bring her beloved Downswing to their knees and kill Emilia with his bare hands when this was all over. As the thought passed through his dazed mind, he stumbled in the darkness up the stairs from the pitch-black basement of the church.

Thirty-Six then heard the sounds that had been hidden by the soundproof technology of Emilia's torture chamber.

Weapons firing.

Yells of panic, of pain.

And finally, the screams of dying men outside.

Screams that were *begging* for their lives.

He shook, but still powered through. He had fifty men at his disposal, and he was going to sacrifice them all to make sure every member of Downswing lay dead at his feet. He smiled, adrenaline pumping hard through his veins as a high-ranking Numberless he recognized came running toward him, shouting over the noise of battle outside. He grit his teeth and accepted the weapons that the man thrust into his hands.

This was it.

He was going to bring Downswing down. And Emilia right along with them. He was going to win this challenge, rise in the ranks of *Maman*, and take over the organization. Finally, the infamous assassin group would be *his*.

And his first plan of action was to find the devil of Downswing...

And make him his first kill.

"Call in the reinforcements." Thirty-Six snarled to the man that was still stammering through his accounts of the assault Downswing had brought to their door. Thirty-Six smiled maniacally, his grin splitting his face in two.

"No survivors. That is their order. Tell them to move *now*." Thirty-Six said, stomping up into the light of the main room of the church. Moonlight streamed in through the stained-glass windows, and Thirty-Six finally got a good look out into the vast property the church sat on.

And he stopped dead.

His face drained of color.

And the mad thump of his heart came to a grinding halt.

"That is what I've been trying to tell you, sir!" The man screamed, shaking Thirty-Six's shoulders roughly. The man had blood soaking through his sleeve, terror in his eyes, and panic in his expression. The man swallowed thickly, trembling in fear.

"We have no reinforcements. They've killed them all. We

have twenty men left, but we're surrounded. They're coming at us from all sides and we can't even get a read on where they are. *He* is tearing through our men and we-we can't stop him. They have somehow infiltrated the security system; nothing is showing up on the thermal cameras. They've jammed the signals on our communication devices a-and we can't get through to anyone. What-what are your orders, sir?"

Thirty-Six stared out the window and listened to the death screams, the firing of weapons, the panicked yells and curses surrounding the church like a bubble borne from nightmares. He barely noticed three more men scrambling towards them, his own men, terror on their faces, breaths coming in stuttered, panicked pants.

And Thirty-Six felt something that he hadn't felt in all his years on this earth.

Fear for his life.

So, he said the only thing his terror-addled brain could come up with.

"Get me the *fuck* out of here."

Thirty-Six stilled as a voice came from the darkness that was smooth as silk and rich as blood.

With a familiar French accent.

"Ah, but *monsieur*, why leave now? The fun has just *begun*."

VIKTOR
One hour and thirty-two minutes earlier

"You drive like a fucking maniac, you Chinese witch! I could have been seriously hurt! You-"

"Yeah, but did you *die*?"

145

"Silas, hold my gun. I'm going to *beat* this Chinese witch-"

"So dramatic, *chat*. Meiling is right, you did not die."

"*Thank you*, French gay boy."

"... Though there was that one moment I did see my life flash before my eyes-"

"Silas, you mispronounced *twenty* when you said *one*. I can see where you would be confused being a dumbass-"

Smack!

"Ow! God*damn* it, Si."

"Oh my god, do you guys *ever* shut the fuck up? Jesus, maybe this Emilia chick *asked* these fuckers to kidnap her so she could get away from you arguing like a bunch of blood-thirsty toddlers."

Cooper's voice in our ear thankfully put a stop to the argument going on between Meiling, Silas, and Cin. I was calmly watching the screen on my phone, my eyes fixed on the sleeping form of my Emilia, still strung up like a puppet on a string. She looked so cold in that dimly lit, black stone room. The longer I watched her fair skin darken with fresh bruises, blood periodically dripping onto the floor from her cuts, I felt more pieces of my humanity fall away, exposing the demon inside.

"*D'yavol.*"

I looked up from where I was sitting in the open door of the van, my phone clutched in my hands between my knees. Masamune stood before me, the Usami sisters right behind him. They looked only mildly winded, and Mari had twigs stuck in random parts of her hair.

"What are we looking at?" I asked quietly, my eyes flat and cold as I regarded the efficient Japanese man. Masamune lifted a brow but merely snapped his fingers, which seemed to be code for Misaki Usami, the saner of the two sisters, to start speaking.

"The church sits on one kilometer of land. The woods surrounding the property are occupied by ten men on each side. Ten are in the back of the church where there is a shed big enough to house a vehicle, though we could not confirm if there is a means of escape inside. We have located all the infrared cameras except two. Mari sent on the locations of the cameras to *Megane-kun-*"

"My name is Cooper. *Cooper.* Why do y'all forget names all the damn time?" Cooper's voice grumbled in our ears. Jazzy snorted from where she stood gathering unassuming objects from the van that were undeniably bombs.

"We counted five snipers surrounding the property. They are too spread out to exterminate in one move. Well, it is possible, but it will be difficult." Mari continued, ignoring Cooper's outburst. "Ten more men are guarding the front church yard, but they are clearly meant to draw us out. The real threat are the snipers and the men in the trees. There are also five men inside the church that we saw, with the addition of the three that have been torturing *Onee-sama.*" Mari's eyes went flat at that and her small hand gripped the sword at her waist even harder. My eyes flicked to Misaki and watched the same reaction from her.

The sisters truly loved Emilia. It was a comfort knowing that the pair of psycho sisters would do whatever it took to get her back. I nodded, my eyes flicking to Fritz. The big German was looking out over the city to where the church was located. The church was thankfully far enough away from the town that we wouldn't need to worry about civilian interference immediately. Fritz turned back to me, lifting an amused brow.

"Part of me wants to think that this is an elaborate trap to get us to let our guard down but..." The German shrugged. He looked down at Alexei, who was also studying the far-off the church. Alexei cocked his head as he stroked his jaw, looking

147

lost in thought. Finally, he shook his head, turning back to face me.

"I hate to agree with this mountain of Eurotrash, but he is right. I have spent enough time with you to trust the Usami's tracking. I think *Maman* truly thought that fifty men would be sufficient."

I nodded, having come to the same conclusion. There was something off about this entire situation, I was certain of that now. I looked over to Silas, who was leaning against the van, looking up at the night sky. He sensed my look and answered my unspoken question softly.

"We are not dealing with the full force of *Maman's* assassins. If my hunch is correct, the only numbered assassin that is on the church grounds is Thirty-Six. The rest are all Numberless. Talented, still, but not enough to stop us. Grande Souer would know this. There is something else going on, something we are not seeing." Silas said, his face turning toward Cin who was leaning against the van next to him. The black man gave a shrug, tying his dreads back into a tight bun.

"Don't care much about that. Let's do what we came here to do. What you think, big man, you want to go with Flush or Full House? I think anything higher than Full House would just be overkill." Cin said, looking to me.

"Full House!" Jazz insisted, waving her hands in the air like a maniac. Meiling strode forward, strapping knives to the holsters at her thighs. Which of course prompted Kiernan and his two idiot Irishmen to give an appreciative whistle from where they were loading up with their own weapons. Meiling flipped them off but turned to meet my gaze.

"I don't know, *D'yavol*. We may want to go Straight Flush on this." She said seriously. Masamune and the Usami sisters all gave a grin, nodding in unison.

God, sometimes the Japanese trio was just fucking creepy.

"Woah, there, missy. Ye really tink Straight Flush is the way to go? That's an awful lot of manpower for something we could take care of with just Full House." Kiernan said, frowning.

"Meiling is right. They stole Emmy and Ludo from us. They need to know who they are fucking with!" Kamili insisted, stomping forward and thrusting her hands on her hips. She glared down at me, and I heard a long-suffering sigh come from Roy, who was hoisting his sniper rifle onto his shoulder.

"As much as it pains me to admit it- especially with that language, missy- Kamili is right. The time to hide our strength has passed." Roy said, and I nodded thoughtfully at the middle-aged black man. The former CIA agent was an invaluable member of Downswing. Without his sniper skills and government knowledge- not to mention his patience with mentoring Ludo and Kamili- Downswing would not have made it as far as we had in the mercenary underworld.

Yet another pay raise I saw coming in the not-so-distant future.

"Where *is* Ludo, *D'yavol?*" Kamili asked softly, clutching her rifle to her chest. She looked at me with large, pleading eyes, urging me to say something encouraging. I wished I could give that to her, but we hadn't seen any evidence the boy was even alive.

"I have a theory on that, *mon petit chou.*" Silas answered quietly, stepping forward to put a comforting hand on Kamili's shoulder. "He is alive. I have a feeling that Ludo will make it out of *Maman's* clutches without a scratch on him as soon as we have Emilia. Trust me, *chou.*"

Kamili sniffled but nodded. She straightened her shoulders, her eyes narrowing to determined slits.

"He better be as beat-up as Emmy or I'm going to kick his ass."

A soft click came through the com in our ears and Cooper's incredulous voice spoke again.

"Y'all have some *serious* issues. You're perfect for each other."

Everyone smiled at that. A moment of camaraderie passed between us, and I felt the yawning roar of the beast inside dim for a brief moment. We really were a fucked-up crew, but damn it if I didn't feel the slightest bit of pride at how far we had come. We were one of the most feared mercenary groups in the criminal underworld. And the only reason we weren't the best in the business wasn't because we lacked in skill. It was strategic planning.

Emilia had done that for us. She had brought us together, built us up from nothing, given us a purpose. Her acceptance, her own special brand of crazy, her bottomless font of love... had done that for us.

She deserved nothing less than the best rescue we could give her.

"Leonid." I said softly into the night. "Are you in position?"

The click of the com in my ear came again.

"Hound, Ethyn and I are in position with the package. Hound is a bit upset with you, *D'yavol*. When you said you would let us help, she did not think it would be quite this... boring."

I heard a screech in the background and rolled my eyes.

"Just make sure the jamming device is ready. On my signal, I want communication blackout." I said firmly, not about to argue with Leonid and that crazy bitch Hound again. I had almost had to shove her out of the moving van to get her to stand back from the action. In the end, Leonid had reminded her of her promise to do whatever I told her, and the argument was put to rest.

With those three out of the way and ready to activate the

device that would jam all enemy signals to radios and cell-phones within a fourteen-kilometer perimeter of Drezna, Downswing was about to do something we had been waiting to do until the time was right.

Show everyone *exactly* what happened when you fucked with our queen.

I looked back up to the group, my eyes half-lidded, my lips twitching with blood-thirsty anticipation. I knew the look in my eyes reflected the simmering rage brewing just below the surface. The moment had arrived for me to release my pent-up wrath.

Fuck, I was the devil of Downswing.

It was time to really earn my reputation.

I stood slowly; my phone still clutched tightly in my fist. Glancing down at the time, I did some quick math in my head. The timing for the plan we were about to execute had to be impeccable. Finally giving a nod, my brooding gaze rose back to my team, who seemed to be holding their breaths waiting for my decision.

"Straight Flush, it is."

Meiling gave a whoop, Jazz stomped her feet in excitement, and Kiernan and his two idiot Irishmen gave a deep, belly laugh. Everyone else simply smiled, excitement lighting their features.

"Kamili, Roy, you need to be fully set up and holding position in thirty-one minutes. Everyone else needs to be in position and holding in thirty-eight minutes. Report your coordinates immediately. Cooper, you stay in our ear the entire time and keep feeding me that video stream." I looked down at my phone to make sure Emilia hadn't moved while I gave my orders.

"You got it, big man. The camera feed is already on loop. You guys can move around as much as you need to, they're not seeing anything but what we want them to see. Well, until shit gets real. Then I can probably buy you ten minutes. Everyone remember to keep their coms on this channel. If shit gets switched around and you lose me, you won't be able to get a clear line until the jammer is down. Whatever this plan is that has that lame-ass name, just make sure it's quiet until the last second. You fuck that up, you're going to have a real fight on your hands." Cooper said.

Every member of Downswing smiled.

Alexei blinked, looking at us as if we were insane.

Yeah, baby brother, we're not here because we're sane. We're here to fuck shit up.

The thought crossed my mind, and my blood-thirsty smile spread across my face.

"*Kapitan* is coming home."

Leonid Sokolov listened with quiet intensity to the chatter in his ear. He looked up to Ethyn and caught the assassin's eye. Ethyn gave a quiet, questioning stare back, his hand gripping the wireless camera in his fist. Leonid pursed his lips, thinking the situation over calmly.

His beautiful Alex had whispered a plan in his ear and the idea was starting to take root and grow. He had even managed a quiet moment with the new tech person that Downswing had 'recruited' and been pleased that the man was open to Leonid's little plan. He looked over to his Alex, her strawberry curls blowing in the wind, her tall, willowy body outlined perfectly in her flowing jumpsuit. She gave him a nod, her vacant eyes abnormally sharp.

"Lo-lo." She breathed, her intense green gaze burning a brand into his soul. He loved that about his Alex, that with one look she could send a man such as he to his knees. He also loved the ruthless side to her. That same side that had insisted on going through with this plan that they hadn't bothered to tell *D'yavol* or any other member of Downswing about. The plan that had been brought to him and his Alex right before the torture of Emilia Fox had begun.

The plan that was about to thrust Emilia Fox and Downswing directly into the spotlight of the criminal underworld.

Whether they liked it or not.

It was that ruthlessness and soul-searing gaze that had spared Alex's life all those years ago when she had come to him asking for his help. He had trusted her, believed in her, and it was the best decision he had ever made for himself and for his group.

He wasn't going to question her now after all this time.

Leonid nodded to Ethyn.

"They will make their stand at the front for all to see. Get as close as you can without being detected. Go. Now."

And Ethyn was off like a shadow in the night.

Leonid turned to his beloved and stretched his hand out. Alex's eyes softened, giving him that beautiful look she reserved only for Emilia Fox and himself. He switched the com on his earpiece to the separate channel where only one other person could hear him.

"We are going ahead with the plan. Are you prepared to do what I asked?" Leonid asked softly.

The crackle in his ear sounded before he heard the quiet voice of Downswing's newest tech man.

"Yeah, man, I got you. You positive you gave me the right IP addresses?"

"Oh, yes, I am not mistaken. They were given to me by the owners of said systems." Leonid's voice was amused, and his lips curled into a half-grin.

"All right. And you swear that what you said in this note is true? Because if you fuck with my cousin, man..." The young man's voice trailed off for a moment before he heaved a heavy sigh.

"Let's just say your people will have a *really* tough time finding all of your body parts if you're thinking about betraying Cin and his lady boss."

Leonid chuckled. "Oh, do not worry. I think your cousin will be the first to say that this was a good plan. Maybe not at first, but eventually. Maybe."

"Okay, dude. Your funeral if you're lying. But yeah, I'm ready to go and the feed will go live as soon as you hit the button."

"Perfect. That is all I need. Thank you once again for your assistance. You will be rewarded for your participation in my request." Leonid said, looking up at Hound from his seated position, watching her beautiful face break out into a cheeky grin.

As the com clicked off, Leonid heaved a sigh, his smile slipping.

"Now for the difficult part."

He reached into his pocket and pulled out his cellphone. Scrolling through his contacts, he found the one that he had only recently acquired. Taking a deep breath inwards for courage, he hit send and held the phone to his ear, waiting for that silken voice to answer.

The French accented voice of his greatest competition did not disappoint.

"Are we all set, Mr. Sokolov?"

"Yes. Everything has been arranged according to your specifications."

The silken French-accented voice purred her response.

"Good. Your cooperation has been duly noted. I thank you

and I will be sure not to forget your assistance, Mr. Sokolov. I look forward to doing further business with you."

"We shall see what the future holds." Leonid answered, voice confident, though his gaze stayed glued to Alex. He needed to stay grounded. The bitch on the other end of the line knew he was in awe of her but he needed to be calm, confident and not show his uneasiness.

He wasn't used to this feeling. Though he knew exactly what he was feeling, he found it difficult to process that he was feeling it.

Fear.

But it was true. He was scared. This woman playing them all like puppets on half-broken strings terrified the ever-living fuck out of him.

"A very political answer, Mr. Sokolov. I do so enjoy a smart man with good manners. Until we speak again."

The line went dead.

Leonid Sokolov closed his phone slowly, his gaze never straying from his beautiful goddess. He hit the end button, stood up, and wrapped Alex in his arms.

"Do you think Emilia will truly give the show that crazy bitch is expecting her to give?" Leonid asked softly into the soon-to-be-not-so-quiet night.

His answer was a soft chuckle against his throat.

"Lo-lo... When it comes to my Foxy, you haven't seen *anything* yet."

THIRTEEN

Jazzy Prifti was having a blast.

She laughed uproariously at the thought, having to lean back against a tree to catch her breath as another of her beautiful bomb babies exploded. They were causing so much destruction and they were so *little*. Teeny, tiny harbingers of destruction.

God, her bombs were so cute.

She smiled maniacally as she pressed the next ignition button, lighting the last of her little gifts. Another scream pierced the air and she howled with laughter.

"Ooh, that one sounded painful." Jazzy said in a sing-song voice. She turned excitedly to her two companions who both looked almost bored.

"Come *on* you two! Have some fun! All work and no play make you fucking losers."

Alexei and Fritz both gave her a droll look.

"I am ninety-nine percent certain that is not how that saying goes." Alexei drawled in his high-handed, sarcastic tone. He seemed almost amused, but Jazzy couldn't be sure with this guy. He kept his emotions on lockdown, tighter than... than... Fuck, she couldn't remember the saying. It didn't matter. She didn't care how tight he was.

He was a dick. That was all she knew.

Alexei's lazy expression suddenly sharpened, and his head canted sharply to the left. He closed his eyes for a moment, breathing deep. Jazzy's face screwed up in a confused grimace.

"What the fuck is he-"

"Quiet, *knuddel*." Fritz instructed quietly.

Jazzy frowned but buttoned her lips all the same. She blinked, and that was all it took.

A foot planted into her stomach and with an enraged yell, she went tumbling to the ground. The tree that had been directly behind her head exploded, bark and leaves flying in all directions. She stared at the large hole that could have been her face with a slack jaw and wide eyes.

"Did-did those ass-towels just try to *kill* me?" Jazzy snarled, her face turning a dangerous molten red. She blinked again and almost missed the flash of golden hair and eyes that went hurdling past her into the foliage beyond. Her mouth opened and closed a few times, and she looked up at Fritz in confusion once again.

"Where the *hell* does he think he's go-"

A scream of agony from close by rent the air, cutting off Jazzy's indignant question.

She merely gaped in silence as Fritz, standing so tall and imposing above her, smiled the most sensuous, eager smile she had ever seen on his face. The big German seemed almost proud and...

Turned-on?

What in the actual fuck is up with these two?

"I think you may be right, Miss Prifti."

Jazzy whipped around to see Alexei melting from the darkness. His hands and the front of his shirt were stained with blood, and his amber eyes looked to be shimmering, they were dancing with such revelry.

"I am always right. But what about this time?" Jazzy asked, standing and dusting off her pants.

Alexei's face split into a wide grin, and Jazzy swore the smile lit up the entire clearing they were in. The smile shed years from the Russian's face, and he looked as happy as a kid in an electronics' store.

"All work and no play *does* make me a dull boy."

Fritz's sensuous smile widened.

And Jazzy threw her head back and laughed.

"That is not what I said but you will learn, dull boy. You will learn."

Jazzy had a thought as she led the men further into the dense woods, rushing to their position so they could commence with their battle plan.

Alexei may just fit in with Downswing, after all.

All three of them came to an abrupt halt as a scream so full of terror, so full of pain, split the air that it sent a shiver racing along Jazzy's spine. That hadn't even sounded *human*. And seconds later, another scream followed, so similar to the first that it made Jazzy's heart stutter in her chest.

"What the hell was that?" She breathed, turning wide eyes to Fritz. The big German looked to be on full alert, his eyes scanning the woods around them. Jazzy frowned, jerking her head around as she heard a low, evil chuckle from beside her. Both Fritz and Jazzy stared at Alexei, whose chuckling deepened as they heard the scream again, this time mixed in with some loud begging.

Alexei turned with that same wide grin to Jazzy and Fritz.

"That, little girl, is the sound of the *devil* collecting his souls."

A crackle in their ears sounded, and Kamili spoke right into their ears with a hushed, awed tone.

"Guys... *D'yavol*... holy *shit*."

Another hiss sounded from the com in their ears.

"Abandon Straight Flush. I repeat; abandon Straight Flush." That was Roy, and his tone was brisk, though he couldn't quite hide the awe and fear beneath his words. "New plan commencing. Cover Viktor. I repeat; cover Viktor."

"What? I'm in the back and everyone is running. Where are they going? I wasn't done playing wit da bastards!" Kiernan's voice came next, sounding irritated.

"Guess you better come around front, Irish. Come and see the river of blood *D'yavol* has just provided the church. How thoughtful of him." That was Masamune, and he sounded bored as all hell.

"They're all abandoning their posts to go and take down Viktor? The hell is he do-" Kiernan's voice stopped abruptly in their ears. Jazzy frowned up at Alexei and Fritz. Fritz was listening, his head tilted to the side. And Alexei was... smiling.

Kiernan's voice came again, only this time it was nothing more than a whisper.

"Holy... fuck. What the hell did they do to him?"

"Well, the last I saw on *D'yavol's* phone, that dumb guy, the one who thought he could touch Emilia? Yeah, he, um." Meiling's voice came, and she sounded blasé, but stuttered a bit at the last part.

"What did he do to cause *this* reaction?" Kiernan demanded again.

"He, uh, he grab Boss lady. By her pussy. Then *D'yavol* go crazy and now he like this."

Deafening silence met her pronouncement.

But Jazzy couldn't help it.

She let out a startled, disbelieving laugh.

159

"My god," Jazzy said conversationally, moving forward with Alexei and Fritz on either side of her. They made their way to the front of the trees and came to the clearing that had turned into hell on earth. There were limbs, torrents of blood, and dead bodies scattered around the entire front of the church. And the man making his way through the majority of them was doing it all with a machete...

And his bare hands.

"He *grabbed* her by the *pussy?*" Jazzy asked again, tsking softly. "And you guys think this is bad?"

"Oh no. I'm waiting for the main show. This is just the opening act." Masamune breathed into the com, a smile clear in his voice.

Alexei finally stopped smiling at that and turned to Jazzy, frowning in confusion.

"What?" The Russian asked stupidly. Jazzy laughed.

"Yeah, you think this is a massacre? Just wait until Emilia comes out to play." She said, tossing her hair. Fritz finally reacted, chuckling, turning with a twinkle in his eye to Alexei.

"You have seen nothing yet, *bärchen*."

Viktor

He put his filthy fucking hands on her.

"Please, please, please don't do this!"

He was going to rape her in front of me.

"Oh god, I beg you. I-I-I'll give you anything, just *please!* Oh *god!*"

He grabbed her pussy. Her breasts. Said she liked it.

"Somebody! Anybody! HELP ME!"

He put those... filthy... dirty... fucking hands... on what's... mine.

Awareness was slowly coming back to me. The litany in my mind started to wind down and finally, my red-hazed vision began to clear. I looked down slowly to the man that was trying to crawl away from me. The world was going up in flames all around me, most of that being the work of Jazzy's bombs, I was sure. But as I stood there, staring down at the begging man, feeling the blood on my hands, face and neck from the men that I knew I had just left slaughtered behind me, I finally blinked back to the present.

Glancing around, I saw that I had wound up in the large clearing right in front of the doors to the church. I didn't remember much after watching that *Maman* operative grope and taunt my Emilia. It had all happened so fast. It was like after months of not seeing my love, my *Kapitan,* and then seeing her groped, degraded and objectified like that had finally broken my mind.

And I had went into a berserker rage.

A crackle in my ear came.

"Um. Hey Viktor? You back with us, man? Your machete stopped swinging, so I thought maybe you were... sane. Now." The hesitant voice was that of Roy.

I gave a single grunt.

"Oh, he's back!" Meiling's voice came from the trees to my left. I glanced over as she broke away from the darkness of the woods, holstering her pistols into the straps on her thighs. She smiled a seemingly innocent smile at me as she strode forward.

A rustle in the trees to her right sounded and a blur disengaged from the darkness. A man came running at full speed towards the church, screaming for back-up. Meiling, her smile never wavering from her face, grabbed the pistol she had just holstered with swift accuracy, swinging it up to point at the frantically running man. With barely a glance in his direction, she fired off a perfectly aimed shot that tore through the man's head.

And with a spurt of blood and a final grunt, the man's life ended.

A whistle sounded from behind Meiling.

"Woo-wee, lass. Yer aim sure is improvin'."

I turned to see Kiernan and his two Irish idiots emerging from the trees, grins on their faces and blood on their clothes. Kiernan was swinging Una through the air, blood splattering as he spun, whistling a very uplifting tune as he walked forward.

"I always shoot better than you. Always will. Never forget." Meiling said, holstering her pistol once again with that same friendly grin.

"Och. So feisty. Are there any more boys to play with, Kamili?" Kiernan asked, and I heard the com click in my ear.

"Uh, *no*. Like I didn't shoot them all through their stupid faces the minute they started running from the trees." Kamili's voice was exasperated, but I heard the hint of pride she tried to bury.

"You did very well, Kamili." Roy's calming voice sounded, and I could practically hear the pleased grin Kamili must have been wearing at the praise. Roy had been the one to train both Kamili and Ludo in the art of shooting, and I knew Kamili secretly loved when Roy praised her.

A twig crunched to our right and Meiling's pistols were up and pointed within a matter of seconds, along with that of Kiernan's two bodyguards. I turned my head, rolling my eyes at the sight of Jazzy, Fritz, and Alexei melting from the darkness.

"Woah. You went pig shit crazy, *D'yavol*! Cool." Jazzy said, laughing heartily.

Alexei gave a long-suffering sigh. "Again, that is not the saying-"

"Shut up, dull boy." Jazzy interrupted, still laughing. I turned to Fritz, who just raised an amused eyebrow at me.

"Well, never let it be said that the devil hasn't earned his nickname."

We all turned back to see Masamune striding from the trees behind us with Mari and Misaki at his side. The two women had their katanas out but were wiping them down with identical black cloths. Blood dripped from them as they wiped, and I noticed the excited gleam in their eyes as they stepped closer.

Masamune yawned.

"Well. This was supposed to be a group effort, not a one-man show. When do I get to play?" Masamune drawled, though I could see a slight twitch to his eye.

Ah, he's annoyed with me.

"I did not mean to steal your fun, Onodera." I finally spoke, my accent thicker, my voice quiet and raspy. This was the first time I had gone into a blind rage in a very long time. It wasn't surprising I was reverting to old habits.

"Where are Cin and Silas?" I asked, but before the question was out of my mouth, I heard a terrified scream sound. The scream was so terrible, it sounded as though the one making it had seen hell itself yawning up before him.

"Ah. There they are." Masamune said flatly.

The doors of the church creaked, and everyone raised their weapons, calmly waiting for whoever was inside the dark church to show themselves. I watched as a long figure tore from the darkness, stumbling down the stairs. My eyes widened in rage as I recognized the figure that had just literally fallen at my feet.

My rage dulled and sputtered out as I lifted my head and saw the figure disentangling itself from the webs of darkness from the silent church.

Everything around me dimmed. The sounds of the night, the twinkling of the stars above us, the wetness of the blood-soaked grass beneath my feet. Everything melted away and I was left with nothing but the sensation of my spirit lifting from the frozen hell that it had been encased in for two long months.

My heart gave one loud thump, and it was as if I was brought back from the dead.

Air finally filled my lungs, and life breathed back into me.

And I called out to the only thing that could ever bring me back from hell itself.

"Emilia."

FOURTEEN

Thirty-two minutes earlier

Emilia

What a fucking pussy.

I wrenched the sharp end of the cuffs that I had just escaped from out of the neck of the prick that had dared to slap my tit earlier. He was lucky that I had remembered how nicely he had given me water.

Otherwise, his death would have lasted much, much longer.

When did I become such a bleeding heart?

As the door slammed behind that pussy Thirty-Six, I let my rusty chuckle die out slowly. Pursing my lips, I dropped the dying body of...

Holt? Horace? Bob?

Eh, I couldn't fucking remember.

The tit-slap guy.

His blood spilled at my feet and I tilted my head, watching

it spread like a thick jelly. I could see it almost as well as if the room was flooded in light. By rights, I knew I shouldn't be able to see as clearly as I could in the suffocating darkness. But the endless hours I had spent in pitch-black during my two-month stay with *Maman* had sharpened my senses considerably.

Ah, that reminds me.

I turned to the camera that was still propped up on a high stool. The light was still faintly blinking, which I assumed meant it was still recording. Tilting my head to the side, I let my eyes slide to half-mast, and my face split into an insane, maniacal grin.

"Well, hello."

I gave a little chuckle, biting my lip seductively.

"I didn't see you there."

My footsteps made quiet sucking noises as the pooling blood soaked the ground, making the floor slippery beneath my feet.

"I hope you're enjoying the show."

Licking my lips, I breathed out so harshly, it sounded like a small moan.

"I don't know what your ultimate goal is for this little stunt."

I leaned down.

"And frankly, I don't really give a shit."

My lips curled into a sweet smile, my eyes crinkling at the corners.

"What I do know... is this."

The smile melted from my face like hot wax atop the flames of hell. The cold fury rushing through my veins made my eyes widen and my vision narrow. My head slowly tilted to the side, and I breathed the next words so quietly, so darkly, I didn't even recognize my own voice.

"If you don't bring back my Ludo within the next hour, I

will *hunt* you. I will take your life apart... piece... by... piece. I will carve out all the things you love and leave you with nothing more than a gaping, bleeding hole where your life used to be. You will never be rid of me. And I will *never* allow you to die. I will make sure that for the rest of your very, very long life... you think of nothing but me. You *breathe* nothing but me. You *live* for nothing but me. I will *consume* you. And if there is a single bruise on his body when you return him-"

A huge, toothy smile spread across my face.

"I will feed you your own insides."

I grabbed the camera, leaning close and placing a kiss right on the lens. Leaning back, I fluttered my lashes, giggling.

"You have fifty-nine minutes. *Vous feriez mieux de vous dépêcher.*"

And with that, I slammed the camera onto the ground and gave a long, loud, furious scream.

Twelve miles north, at the exact same moment

Grande Soeur could only sit and stare.

The scene that had just played out before her eyes replayed itself over and over in her mind. She sat, still as stone, face an impassive mask, while inside she felt...

Ah god, so damn amused.

"Eight. Did they just manage to infiltrate our security and wipe out the entire team without us knowing?" She queried softly; eyes still transfixed on the monitors. She saw Eight's jaw clench from the corner of her eye, and her usually positive assassin looked downright murderous.

"They- they did." Eight's voice trembled from the fury that was clearly riding him. "I am sorry, Grande Soeur. I underestimated their hacking abilities. There was *no* possible way they should have been able to reroute and replay the thermal images back to me. I-"

"Figure it out. Make sure it doesn't happen again. Put it in the report." Grande Soeur interrupted, her voice a quiet drawl. She saw Eight's jaw harden once again and he gave a cursory nod.

A quiet chuckle sounded from behind her.

Turning slowly, Grande Soeur tore her gaze away from the monitors to her young charge, Ludo Flores. The Mexican cartel brat sat back in his chair, an eat-shit grin on his face, eyes sparkling with excited amusement.

"So, shall we be on our way? It wouldn't be good to keep *mi princesa* waiting. I am not so sure your insides are delicious enough that you fancy eating them." Ludo was almost humming with suppressed amusement. Grande Soeur pursed her lips, eyes narrowing on the cheeky brat. She held his gaze for a long, agonizing moment.

Finally, Grande Soeur let the smile she had been suppressing curl her lips.

"You are exactly right, *Monsieur* Ludo. Four. Take Ludo back to his family."

She turned around, waving her hand dismissively and laughing softly to herself.

"I do not think we have seen the last of each other, *Monsieur* Ludo."

Grande Soeur felt the young cartel's eyes on her, and she heard the grim determination in his voice as he answered her back.

"Oh, we will meet again, lady. *You can bet on it.*"

She heard Four swat Ludo on the back of his head and the cartel brat's loud expletives as the duo left the cabin. Oh yes, there was something going on there. She would have to be sure to question Four extensively. It was no secret that Grande Soeur had *strong* feelings on the treatment of minors in her care. If she found out that Four had touched Ludo in any way aside from the cursory touches between captive and prisoner...

She would make sure Four never touched anyone. Ever again.

"Grande Soeur," Eight spoke, voice quiet. She turned back to her second favorite operative in the entire organization and raised a brow in question. The man looked positively livid still, but there was a twinkle in his eye that bespoke of a man who was about to try and piss her off.

"I hesitate to mention this," Eight said, though his tone was in direct contrast to the words coming out of his mouth. "But I do have to remind you... that you owe me twenty dollars."

Grande Soeur narrowed her eyes on her insubordinate tech master.

"Hm. Is that so?"

"Why, yes. I bet you that Emilia would put on a show and if that wasn't a show... I don't know what is." Eight tried to blink innocently at her, but she rolled her eyes, not believing it for a moment.

"Is the other camera still recording?" She asked softly. Eight's eyes lost their twinkle and he glanced to the bottom of his screen where a little box was barely visible. He looked back up to her, nodding.

Grande Soeur's lips curled into another conniving, smug grin.

She handed over a twenty from inside her pocket to Eight.

"Just so we're clear, you didn't win because of the show Emilia just put on."

Eight frowned in confusion.

And Grande Soeur's eyes lit with bloodthirsty excitement.

"It is for the show that is about to begin."

Emilia

Damn it, I want out *of here.*

I stared at the locked door, blowing out an exasperated breath.

Well, goddamn it. Even through the soundproof technology that had been built into the room, I could still hear the agonized screams of the men that had taken me hostage. It sounded like Viktor had finally gone a bit crazy and was making his way through the men outside. I mean, that was awesome and everything but... but...

I want a piece of the action too, assholes!

Blowing out another breath, I shifted my ass on the stool and gave another long, loud groan of pleasure. Oh, holy shit, it was so nice to sit on something that wasn't concrete. Orgasmic didn't even begin to describe how good it felt, even though it was wood. Hell, anything was softer than concrete.

My vision started to blur, and I had to pinch myself again to force myself back to attention. I had to keep it together and stay sharp, at least until I got to wrap my hands around Thirty-Six's throat and watch the life drain from his eyes. I didn't want to acknowledge it, but my body was starting to shut down, and my fractured mind was playing tricks on me. I mean, yeah, some of it was the fact that I was half-starved and needed enough water in me to fill a lake. But a big part of it was the torture my body had gone through. My mind breaking had been the best thing for me, sure, but now it was hard to even convince myself anything was real.

No. Must stay focused. Viktor is here. Viktor came for me.

That had to be reality.

It had to be.

Strangely, Grandmama's voice wasn't purring into my ear any longer, and I didn't see her form standing with me inside the room. That was just like her. Only come when she wasn't wanted, fuck shit up, then skedaddle. Well, whatever. She had served her purpose, delusion or not. As soon as I was done with this stupid charade that *Maman* had forced on me, I was regrouping with Downswing and it was time for us to get back to business.

It was time for me to be the leader Downswing deserved.

And with my new outlook on sanity, it was going to be so much *fun*.

I smiled, humming into the darkness. After a moment, my brows raised as I heard a thud, a scream straight out of my nightmares, followed by the sound of deafening silence. I gave a long, low whistle. Well, whoever that was had been in so much agony that I had heard what I was certain was their dying breath through the soundproof walls.

Geesh. Which one of my psychos has that kind of anger management issues?

I answered my own question before I heard the annoyed voice on the other side of the door.

"Mother*fucker*. Fox. You better be behind this damn door or I'm really going to start getting pissed off."

"Sounds like you're doing such an excellent job of that already, Cin." I called out loudly, grinning when I heard a muffled grunt of amusement.

"Well, if it isn't little Katie Kidnapped."

I scowled. "Fuck off. It's not my fault."

"Uh-huh. Anything you say, Katie Kidnapped."

"You're an asshole."

"And you missed me."

I paused for a long moment, the pure relief and elation coursing through me making me second-guess my grip on reality. This seemed too good to be true. I knew my team was good but...

"Cin..." I paused, biting my lip, my body shaking. I needed this to be real so badly, I felt tears prick at the corners of my eyes.

"What now, Fox-trot?" I heard Cin knocking on the door, more than likely testing the strength and locking mechanisms. I closed my eyes and breathed in a deep, calming breath, trying to force my mind to focus on the reality before me.

"You-you're real, right?" I said it just loud enough that if it had been anyone else, I was sure they wouldn't have heard me. But this was Cin, and he was my little mutant when it came to his five senses.

"Yeah, Emilia. I'm real. We're real. And we're here for you. I'm-uh. I'm fucking sorry it took so long." Cin's voice was quiet but I still heard the soft sincerity that was so rare coming from him.

I smiled, curling my feet up onto the stool, hugging my knees to my chest. Closing my eyes, I forced my tears back, knowing that I was running on borrowed time when it came to suppressing the flood of tears that had been building for years. Hell, ever since Korol had kidnapped me, I had been pushing my emotions back, forcing my tears back down into the darkest parts of myself. Now that my mind and heart were where they needed to be, and I was centered, I knew all my repressed emotion was going to come flooding to the surface. And when it did?

It's going to be a fucking blood bath.

"All right, I think I got it." Cin's voice came through stronger, and the soft knocking and kicks against the unbelievably heavy wood stopped.

"Got wh-"

"You standing back, Fox-trot?"

I blinked, cocking my head to the side. "Yeah... but that door is like a million pounds, what are you going to d-"

Yeah, I should have known better. That was my bad.

A heavy thud sounded. Then another. One more, and a crack began at the top left corner of the door. I heard Cin's heavy grunt, rough expletive, and then a louder, harder thud sounded. The crack expanded, and the wood groaned in protest. I heard a loud grunt before the final thud sounded, and the door finally gave way to the force of nature that was Cin.

The door cracked from it's hinges and fell inward.

My mouth hung open in shock as I looked at the huge mass of the door, hanging down by the lock that was still in place. A tall, slim body stepped forward and delivered a swift, hard kick to the lock and finally, the door was down.

My eyes trailed up, mouth still hanging open, to see the vision of milk chocolatey goodness that stood proudly before me. Cin Raymes strode in, calm and cool as could be, blood dripping from his clenched fist. The maniac smiled at me in triumph, raising a cocky brow.

"You think a damn door was going to keep me from getting to you? Yeah, like Silas would ever let me live that one down."

I couldn't believe how hot my team members were.

Jesus, how did I keep a handle on my libido for so damn long with these people around?

"And let's not even talk about how *D'yavol* would react. Well, maybe we should, cuz those screams coming from outside are unreal. I think the big guy has gone off his rocker completely." Cin pursed his lips, striding right up to me. He glanced down and did a double take at the lifeless bodies on the floor next to the fallen door.

Cin gave a low whistle. "Damn, Fox-trot. Guess *D'yavol* isn't the only one who's gone a little nuts, huh?"

"They were mean to me." I shrugged. Cin only nodded, as

if it was completely normal that I had ripped out the throats of two full-grown men with the sharp end of the handcuffs they had put me in. He strode up to me, in nothing but a pair of black, elastic pants and a skin-tight black shirt. I looked him over slowly, drinking in the sight of my team finally coming for me, and gave him a wicked smile.

"I can see the outline of your dick."

"And you're fuckin' welcome for that."

I pressed my lips together, trying not to laugh.

"I'm going to tell Silas I'm sorry that I ever made fun of his walk the day after sleeping with you. The man is a hero."

"Don't tell him shit, he'll think he's cool or somethin'." Cin's signature scowl was in place, but I saw the gentleness behind his stern frown. He nudged the stool I was perched on with his foot. His scowl melted from his face and his warm, penny-colored eyes held my own in a gentle embrace.

"You're running on fumes, aren't you, boss?" Cin's voice was gentle, the deep, soothing timbre of his voice sinking into my extremely tortured muscles. I swallowed roughly, my vision swimming.

"Is it that obvious?" I whispered, letting myself shiver. Yeah, I had been holding back how exhausted I was. God, every single muscle in my body hurt. It felt like Thirty-Six and his cronies had dunked me into a pool of acid. I felt like the air itself was eating away at my flesh. Fuck, I hurt. I was one-hundred percent sure this was how meat felt after it had been minced.

Yeah, I had been downplaying my agony just a smidge.

"Nah, girl. I just know you better than most." Cin said, his eyes still firmly on me. "How much time we got before you pass out?"

I swallowed, taking a mental inventory of my plethora of wounds and gave myself the benefit of the doubt. Hell, I had held on this long, maybe I could force my body to go on just a bit longer. Scratch that, I *had* to force myself to go on.

The queen of Downswing had a fucking point to make.

"Twenty minutes." I answered back, my voice low. Cin gave a nod, pursing his lips again. His eyes lost focus for a moment, and I knew the master strategist was going over several different plans of attack in his mind.

Cin Raymes had many, many secret talents. Among them was being far more intelligent than he let on.

"Okay, this will work. Fox-trot, how crazy do you think you can get?"

I stared at Cin for a few moments. Slowly, my head tilted to the side and I let my mind slide back into the laughing darkness inside.

There, I saw Grandmama's grin taking form in the shadows, teeth as sharp as a predator's. I saw the rivers of blood and agony that I was set to bring down upon Korol's world. And most terrifying of all, I saw my own reflection staring back at me. The reflection seemed to be frozen, curled into a ball of icy terror. Inside my mind, I heard the familiar low hiss, the raspy chuckle... and there it was.

The slithering form of my insanity.

The serpentine specter wound its way around that frozen form in my mind, and I watched as the cold fire inside the serpent's eyes locked onto me. Staring right into my soul, that serpent's jaw unlocked, dropping down to show the dripping fangs of madness inside. And with nothing more than a quiet hiss, another rusty chuckle, those fangs snapped down on my frozen reflection.

And shattered it.

Laughter echoed in my mind.

And Grandmama's voice whispered to me.

My lucky, little coin. My little... Lady Luck.

"Jesus Christ, what the fuck did they *do* to you?"

I pulled myself back to the present. The dark stone room came back into focus, and I realized with a start that my face was split into a huge, eerie grin. Cin had stumbled back, his eyes wide, jaw hanging open in shock. He closed his mouth, gulping audibly. Even the whimpers and pleas echoing down the stairs did nothing to break Cin's focus on me.

He straightened, clearing his throat.

"Well, uh. I guess this plan will work just fine, then. Yeah. Can you- uh. Can you- fuck, why'd you have to freak me out? You threw me off my damn game." Cin's scowl was back full force, and he stomped over to me, glaring down.

I shrugged.

"Don't hate the player. Hate the ga-"

"Nope. Stop it right there. God, you're so fuckin' white." Cin shook his head in mock sadness at me, and I felt my face finally break out into a genuinely happy smile.

That is, until I heard another one of those incredibly terrifying screams that was silenced abruptly with a horrible gurgling noise. My brows shot up, and I looked up at Cin in question. The handsome black man sighed almost dreamily.

"Do *not* tell him I said this but damn, I love when that boy works. He is one insane mothafucka'."

It appeared that being an insane 'mothafucka' was not on Cin's list of turn-offs.

Cin shook his head, looking like he needed to clear his mind off the dirty thoughts about Silas.

No! Tell me about them first, damn it!

"Right. Fox-trot, you want to send a message, yeah?" Cin asked, and I nodded. A slow, eerie smile curled Cin's lips.

And he thought *I* was insane.

"Here's what you're going to do. And you better do this right. Because if Silas is right, and the situation is what we think it is... your ass is still on stage. And we can't have the queen of the fucking show looking like a little pussy bitch, right?"

I curled my legs from beneath me. Every single atom in my body groaned in protest. I had to clamp my jaw tight and tuck my lips together to keep from screaming out in pure agony. Lowering my legs to the ground, I centered myself, allowing my vision to swim again for only a moment before I pushed myself to stand. My body unfurled from itself, and I felt my aches, pains, bruises, scrapes, tortured flesh... melt away. I allowed that crazed other side of myself, that serpentine madness to take over. This time, I didn't allow it to control me. Oh no, I had learned a very valuable lesson from my detainment by *Maman*.

This madness inside? It *was* me. And I was no longer trying to force it down and cage it.

I was setting it free.

And using it to set the criminal underworld aflame.

"If I couldn't put on a good show and show these assholes exactly who they fucked with..."

I stepped forward, breathing my next words against Cin's throat.

"What kind of mercenary queen would I be?"

FIFTEEN

Silas Deveroux couldn't believe this.

He sighed dramatically as he snapped the neck of the fucker that had insisted on sounding off those god-awful screams. Really, though. He had taken only two fingers from the Numberless operative before the man had broken down to nothing more than screams and terror before him. What fun was it to listen to high-pitched, terrified screams?

Well, after a few minutes, at least. The first few screams were...

Silas smiled.

Divine.

Turning back to the hulking, scarred Thirty-Six, Silas lifted a brow at the assassin.

"Well, it did not take very long to put you in your place, did it?" Silas drawled, striding up to the ashen assassin. Thirty-Six blanched, but still had those hate-filled eyes focused on Silas. Silas rolled his eyes at the show of bravado.

"That look would be far more effective if you weren't crying like a child." Silas drawled, wiping his blood-soaked hands on the shirt of the idiot assassin in front of him. Silas stared at this man, this complete idiot, and spoke his musings aloud.

"What on earth was Grande Soeur thinking? This plan of yours was idiotic at best. Did you honestly think Ethyn was on your side? He told you exactly what I wanted him to tell you. He would never dare to go against me. I may not be active in *Maman* any longer, but I am still Two- the second greatest assassin in the entire organization. Did you truly think that the whispers about me were exaggerations?" Silas shook his head in mock sadness and leaned close to Thirty-Six.

"The whispers you hear do not even hold a candle to what I am *truly* capable of."

Silas stood, hearing the welcome sound of footsteps on the stairs leading to the main room.

"You deserve everything you have coming to you, *sot*."

"Damn, Si, I leave you alone for like fifteen minutes and you have all this fun without me. That's cold, man. Thought we were friends."

"If you think we are friends, you are even more stupid than I thought. And I already thought you were *very* stupid." Silas said sweetly, turning back to his not-so-secret lover, the sinfully annoying Cin. Silas watched his lover emerge from the darkness, clad in all black, looking like a deliciously wrapped candy and couldn't help it. He licked his lips. Catching Cin's eye, Silas bit his bottom lip, letting his eyelids droop to half-mast. Cin ran his hot gaze along Silas's entire body, and Silas couldn't suppress a shiver of need.

God, he could not wait to get his idiot home and just *ruin* him.

With a final devastating wink that made Silas's heart throb- not that he would ever tell Cin that- Cin stepped aside and Silas felt his eyes snap wide.

"*Cocotte.*" Silas breathed, the endearment tasting so good on his tongue.

"*Bounjour, mon choupinet. Tu m'as manqué.*"

Emilia Fox stepped around Cin, confident and cool as could be. She gave Silas a happy smile as she told him she missed him in his language. She looked like hell, to be sure, but that was what two months of imprisonment would do to someone. She had to be in agony, Silas was certain, but she was moving steadily forward. The light from the stained-glass windows hit her form, and Silas took in a sharp breath at the sight.

The blue, grey, and purple hues played over Emilia's bruised and torn skin, creating an image of ravaged devastation. She strode forward, steel-grey eyes locked on Thirty-Six's prone form at Silas's feet. Still clad in nothing save her bra and panties, she may as well have been wearing a full gown and studded crown with the air of royalty that she walked with. Her malnourished form didn't seem to be inhibiting her in the least. Silas felt a shiver of apprehension race along his spine, followed by nothing but elation.

God, it felt so good to fear his *princesse* once again.

Emilia came to a stop in front of him, looking down at Thirty-Six with her signature freezing stare.

"Well, this is new and different, isn't it, Thirty-Six? Me, standing tall and proud... and you, groveling at my feet. A very welcome change of pace, if you ask me. But I may be a bit biased." Emilia said, leaning against the pew that had been nearly annihilated by the two men that had tried to escape Silas's wrath. There were five bodies strewn about the church, but there were multiple limbs from said bodies strewn across the floor.

Silas wasn't one to take slights against him lightly.

"You know, this exact pew was where I slit the throat of

Yulian Semenov. The sicko that put his disgusting, filthy hands on Silas years ago. Little did I know your organization was waiting for me to make my move against any one of the men that hurt him. Honestly, I did not think that you would figure out where I was just from that. Have to hand it your leader, her manipulation techniques are beyond-this-world amazing."

Emilia gave a small laugh, tilting her head and lifting an amused brow to Thirty-Six.

"Don't have to tell *you* that, do I? After all, she is the reason you're here now."

With that revelation, the hate brimming forth from Thirty-Six's gaze dulled. Confusion filled his scarred face for a long moment. Emilia waited patiently for the idiot to figure out exactly what she was saying. After a too-long moment, in Silas's opinion, it became obvious that Thirty-Six caught on to what Emilia was suggesting.

The assassin's face drained of all color, and his jaw slackened. His eyes, filled with such hatred before, now reflected disbelief, shock....

And panic.

"You're lying. Grande Soeur would never endanger one of her assassins knowing-" Thirty-Six snarled, his face going from white as a sheet to beet-red. He snarled, his big body lurching forward. Silas kicked out a swift foot, placing it square on the idiot's chest. With a loud *oomph*, Thirty-Six was back on the ground with Silas's foot planted in his solar plexus.

"Move like that again and I take your ear. *Comprenez-vous?*" Silas purred. Thirty-Six coughed, but still managed a tight nod.

"*Bien.*"

Silas looked up to Emilia, nodding.

Thirty-Six wasn't going anywhere. He knew that death had come for him. Now, it was just a matter of *how* he would die. If he was a very good boy, Emilia would kill him. She was ruth-less, to be sure, but she made sure that when she killed, she usually did it as quickly as she could. Now, if Thirty-Six was going to be a bad boy...

Silas would let *D'yavol* have him.

He smiled.

The thought made him horny.

Fuck, they needed to wrap this shit up and get home.

Silas turned to Cin; whose gaze was on him. Mmm. *Dieu*, he loved having his lover's full attention. And from the hot look in Cin's penny-colored eyes, Silas knew that they were on the same page.

"Go now, *chat*."

"Tell me what to do one more time, bitch." Cin snarled, but Silas saw his eyes sparkle with that mischievous light that he had come to crave.

"Did I stutter? Go. Now. *Chat*." Silas purred, pressing his foot down harder into Thirty-Six's solar plexus just to hear the gurgle of protest. Cin licked his lips, prompting Silas's grin to take on a predatory gleam.

An annoyed sigh sounded, and both Cin and Silas gave a guilty start.

"Boys, you know I love a good eye-fuck as much as the next girl but... we're kind of on a time limit, yeah?" Emilia asked, giving Silas a droll stare. Silas rolled his eyes, shrug-ging his shoulders. Surprisingly, Cin gave a snort of amusement.

Silas was impressed. Usually, Cin would try his best to deny their relationship.

Hmm. Was their relationship finally progressing or was it just because it was Emilia that Cin didn't muster a protest? Silas wanted to know.

Even more reason to wrap this up and go home.

With a final mock salute, Cin melted into the darkness and left without a sound.

The man really was as silent and deadly as a panther.

I want him this fucking minute.

"You stupid bitch. You think that just because you're escaping you've won?"

Silas turned back in surprise to Thirty-Six. The man had some balls speaking out of turn like that. A little too much nerve for Silas's tastes. Without a second thought, Silas had his knife in his hand and Thirty-Six's tongue in his fist in less than five seconds. Just as he was about to slice it off, Emilia stopped him.

"Silas."

Her tone brooked no argument. Silas *tsked*, but complied all the same. Raising his foot from the insolent filth, Silas stepped back to Emilia's side. He glanced over at her and was surprised to find her gaze only mildly curious as she took in Thirty-Six's scarred face and his hate-filled eyes.

Silas flicked his eyes down to where Emilia had one hip leaned against the pew, and one of her hands clutching the ever-living shit out of the wood. With her regal stance and detached mannerisms, it was easy to be fooled into thinking Emilia Fox was none the worse for wear. But Silas knew her, he knew her better than he knew himself most days, and she was...

Weakening.

Thirty-Six started to laugh, his ugly face contorting in a desperate, maniacal twist.

"You don't know who it is you've challenged, do you? We did you a favor kidnapping you when we did. You're even more of a stupid bitch than what I thought if you think you can win against Korol. You think *Maman* is terrifying? We have nothing on Korol. He is *everywhere*. He sits on the fucking council of benefactors for *Maman*. They may have betrayed me, but they will *never* fully betray him. No one will. He is in every major government, every underworld crime ring, he is the king of the criminal underworld. He has thousands of soldiers at his command. And what do you have? *Nothing*. You and your band of freaks are *nothing*. You will never win. So, go ahead. Kill me. But that doesn't change the fact that you will go back to being exactly what you were before. Korol's *whore*."

The screams from outside died down. The church was silent save a few dripping sounds coming from the numerous bodies lying about. Silas swore the temperature in the chapel plummeted. Hell, even the wind seemed to stop completely. Silas held his breath, his head slowly turning to his *princesse*. Thirty-Six had said the one thing sure to get a reaction out of the queen of Downswing.

They were not disappointed.

The shift began in Emilia's eyes. Eyes that had been cold but distant suddenly sharpened, narrowing in freezing intensity. Inch by inch, she shifted away from the pew, standing on her own two feet. Her chin went up, her lip curling to the side in a silent snarl. She walked forward slowly, her blood-soaked feet making a *splat* sound on the stone floor as she stalked Thirty-Six like a snake about to strike.

"I have *nothing*, you say?" Emilia asked, husky voice soft. She didn't blink, her eyes widening slowly as she spoke. "You had me at your mercy for two long, agonizing months... and you still say I possess nothing to defeat Korol?"

Emilia continued her steady walk forward. Thirty-Six scrambled back, his eyes wide as he took in the full vision of the enraged queen of Downswing. She pushed forward, her lip curling back even further, a full snarl now transforming her beautiful face into that of a crazed villain.

Silas was so smitten with his captain.

"Who is it that took you down, along with fifty of your

men? Who is it that answered the challenge that *Maman*, the most feared assassin organization in the world, forced upon us? *Who* is it that has managed to rise to notoriety in the criminal underworld in the span of a few short years? And *who is it* that came for me, the *whore of Korol*?"

Emilia's voice was a whip of death now, her face a mask of divine rage. Silas watched as Thirty-Six stood, stumbling to the door of the church. His face was reminiscent of a cornered rat. He shoved the door open with trembling hands, falling down the steps of the church into the night. And Emilia followed slowly, stalking him with that same predatory gate.

The snake was about to strike.

Silas Deveroux grinned, following his *princesse*, his captain, and whispered the mantra that he had uttered countless times before, when he had been an assassin for *Maman*.

"*May the light free your soul, Thirty-Six, for the darkness has come for you.*"

SIXTEEN

Emilia

Well, the fucker was going to die painfully now.

If I could stay conscious long enough to make it happen.

I followed Thirty-Six out onto the steps of the church, the snarl on my face not moving an inch. Damn, the guy had gotten under my skin. Not my best moment, to be sure. But I was tired, in agonizing pain, and all I wanted was a three-week nap and enough water to fill an ocean.

And that was when I heard it.

The sweetest fucking sound in the entire universe.

"Emilia."

I blinked, tearing my gaze away from the frozen form of Thirty-Six. The assassin was looking up in complete, utter terror into the huge form above him. My eyes trailed up slowly, the familiar muscles and breathtaking good looks making my heart thump loudly. My gaze finally came up and collided with burning obsidian, and I almost melted into the stone.

It was the devil himself.

And he was *beautiful.*

"Viktor." I breathed. My throat closed, tears prickling at the back of my eyes. My legs wobbled, and the urge to fall into my head of security's arms was so strong, I almost whimpered. No, I couldn't fall apart now. I had to finish this.

Then I could pass right the fuck out and not wake up for a very, very long time.

There were more yells from around the yard, and my heart warmed at the sight of Downswing- my Downswing- standing before me. They had blood spatter on their clothes, weapons in their hands, and huge, insane grins on their faces. Behind them lay a path of death and agony, with blood, limbs, and lifeless eyes staring back at me.

My gaze lowered to Thirty-Six, who had gone white as a sheet.

"The answer to my questions, Thirty-Six, happen to be surrounding you." I took the steps one-by-one, the snarl from moments before replaced with a calm, cool smile. I stood above the cowering Thirty-Six, and simply stared for a long moment.

"You seem to have gotten the wrong idea about us. Let me correct you." Without warning, I brought my foot down with shattering force on Thirty-Six's right kneecap. He gave a long, terrible scream, his face completely ashen now, his body curling into itself.

"Downswing has more than Korol will *ever* have."

Another crushing kick came to his left kneecap, and with it a broken scream from the assassin at my feet. He tried to crawl away, only to look up into Viktor's stoic face.

"Downswing will come for Korol. We will take his kingdom... piece... by... piece. At the end of this war, we will possess everything. And he will be left with *nothing* but ash and dust."

My foot came again, this time to Thirty-Six's right shoulder. The loud crack of his collarbone was audible in the quiet

night. The scarred assassin vomited onto himself, sobbing pitifully. I stared down at the broken man that had tormented and
tortured me for two long months and felt...

Nothing.

"And do you know why Downswing will win this war
against the king of the criminal underworld?" I asked softly.
Glancing back to Silas, I reached my arm back. Cold metal met
my palm, and I twirled the knife between my fingers, waiting
for Thirty-Six's agonized gaze to focus on the blade. When his
eyes caught the glint of the blade in the moonlight, they
widened in shock. I moved forward swiftly, bringing my arm up
in a graceful arc. With a flick of my wrist, the knife sliced
through his throat in one well-practiced movement.

I stood up to my full height, throwing the knife aside with a
snarl of distaste.

And it was Silas who answered my final question.

"Because we just put our queen back on her fucking
throne."

And with that, my tormentor, the idiot assassin who
thought to bring Downswing to our knees, died in a pool of his
own blood and vomit, betrayed by his own people.

Rest in pieces, Thirty-Six.

You poor, stupid fucker.

Blackness crept into my vision.

Uh-oh.

I stumbled, smiling softly to myself as I heard the concerned
shouts around me. But one voice echoed in my mind above the rest.
I closed my eyes and finally let my exhaustion and agony claim me.

As the darkness surrounded me, I tumbled straight into the
waiting arms of the devil himself and breathed his name on a
broken sigh.

"*Viktor.*"

Ethyn Dubois snapped the video camera closed.

"It... it is done." Ethyn whispered. He heard the com in his ear crackle, and his boss's deep, Russian-accented timbre sounded.

"Well done, Ethyn. Return swiftly."

"*Oui. Comme tu veux.*" Ethyn responded, suppressing the shivers of fear running down his spine from all that he had witnessed.

Fuck, Downswing was much deadlier than anyone had imagined. They had been only using a fraction of their true power and they had *still* managed to bring down more than fifty trained soldiers. Not just any soldiers, *Maman* soldiers, the most sought-after army in the entire world. If the destruction and devastation that had occurred in that churchyard was any indication, Downswing was a group not only to be respected, as Ethyn had thought...

But feared beyond all measure.

Ethyn rose, shaking off the last of his unease. He needed to get back to his boss to deliver the full report. With a graceful twist and turn, Ethyn tensed, ready to run.

And stopped dead in his tracks.

The blood drained from his face, and his tremors came back in full swing.

Fuck, he was going to die here, after all.

"Relax, Frenchie, I ain't here to kill you. Though you may want to work on your stealth skills, you were making enough noise to wake the dead."

Cin Raymes regarded Ethyn from beneath hooded eyes, a lazy grin on his face.

Ah, *fuck.* Ethyn didn't know much about this deadly man,

whose nickname was rumored to have been *the panther* on the streets of Chicago, but he did know one thing.

When Cin Raymes was smiling, the outcome was never good.

Especially for the poor soul he was smiling at.

"We just wanted to be sure Silas was right. Owe that bitch twenty bucks now."

Ethyn stood still as stone, his body tense, ready to battle for his life. Cin unfurled his body from the darkness, striding forward with the grace of the panther he so closely resembled.

"Now, Frenchie. Who did that video go out to? And don't lie to me. I hate liars." Cin said, his voice nothing more than a gentle rumble in the darkness. Ethyn swallowed, trying his best to keep the terror from showing on his face.

"Well, well, Cin Raymes. I would be lying if I said you were not as good as they say. But Silas is always one step ahead of you, *oui?*" Ethyn dared to tease the legendary Cin and earned himself a deep scowl from the nightmare himself.

"Watch it, bitch. If you think I won't kill you just for proving Silas right, you got another thing coming. Now answer my fucking question."

Ethyn swallowed audibly.

"It went out... to exactly who Silas thinks it did. Downswing needed to be seen in action. We simply helped the process along."

Cin folded his arms slowly over his chest, his eyes once again lowering to half-mast as he gazed at Ethyn. A long, tense moment of silence passed before finally, Cin exhaled a loud sigh.

"Yo, Coop. He telling the truth? Did Leonid tell you to send it to that *fucker* on that piece of paper he thought we didn't see?" Cin said, rolling his eyes in exasperation.

Ethyn's jaw fell open with a *pop*.

And Cooper's voice came through on the com in Ethyn's ear.

"Yeah, man. Silas was right. They had me send that video to a few other crime bosses but one of them was definitely that Korol guy y'all hate."

"And you made sure they saw it, yeah?" Cin asked, his gaze still focused and unblinking on Ethyn.

"Yep." Cooper said proudly, popping the 'p'. "They got the message loud and clear, cuz."

"Good job, dude. You're hired. Welcome to Downswing." Cin grinned as sputtering sounded through the com.

"*Fuck* no-"

"Shut up." Cin said, rolling his eyes again. He gave a shrug to Ethyn. "Kids today. Always think they have somethin' smart to say."

Ethyn could only stare, dumbstruck.

"Yeah, huge thanks to you, Leo, and Hound. Our plan wouldn't have turned out so well if your boss and his psycho bitch weren't such meddling assholes. Y'all did us a huge solid, we won't forget that. Almost makes up for the cold shoulder you gave us for two months. Almost." Cin turned away, saluting.

"Well, that's a wrap for us. Oh yeah, *D'yavol* says to find your own way home. Okay, by-eee."

And just like that, Cin melted back into the shadows without a sound.

Ethyn could only stare. After a moment, he found his voice and spoke directly into his com.

"Did Downswing just play us?" Ethyn asked quietly, and he heard an answering bellow of laughter in his ear.

"*Blyad'*. Yes, yes, they did. Alex, did you see that one coming?" Leonid Sokolov's amused voice sounded in Ethyn's ear, and he winced as he heard an outraged shriek that could rival any banshee's.

"This is why we do not give her a radio." Leonid still bellowed with laughter, his amusement finally seeping into the terror in Ethyn's bones. He sagged against a tree, throwing his head back with a loud breath.

"Gregor is coming with the car. Come back to us, Ethyn. I think we all deserve a vacation, *da?*"

Ethyn couldn't fucking agree more.

Pomest'ye Korol
Moscow

The security room was so silent, the guards could hear their own thundering heartbeats.

Zakhar Vasilek- otherwise known as Korol, king of the Russian mafia- stood, staring at the now black screen of the monitors. He was so silent and still, the entire room felt the tension running through like a thin chord about to snap. The video they had all just witnessed had been terrifying enough. But nothing was more frightening than how they thought their boss was going to react to it.

It was the coldest of Korol's personal bodyguards, Anna, who finally broke the silence.

"It seems Downswing has a very accomplished hacker in their ranks we were not aware of. No information was stolen from our systems, but they did manage to use an advanced exploit code to intercept communication inside our own network. A patch code has fixed the issue, and our systems are currently undergoing intense scanning for any other weaknesses." Anna explained, typing furiously on her phone.

Zakhar spoke not a word. Not even a nod came from the supreme mafia leader.

Anna forged on.

"I am sorry, Korol. We were not the only ones to see the stream. The hacker sent it to several of our rivals across Western Europe, the United States, and South America. Our IT department says that the stream was received. Downswing has now been exposed."

Nothing but more terrifying silence from Korol.

It was Lenora Mundez, also one of Korol's personal guards, who spoke next.

"This was carefully calculated. More groups will ally with Downswing now that they have seen what they will do for their leader. And they were very obviously not even at full strength."

Niko, the former protégé of *D'yavol* and another of Korol's personal guards, nodded in agreement.

A beep sounded from Anna's phone that had her looking down to read the text. The famously expressionless woman stared down for a long moment before her eyes slowly trailed up to Korol's still form.

"I... have confirmation, Korol. Of the traitor you said was within our ranks."

Every single guard in the room- aside from Korol's terrifying personal guards- swallowed audibly, shaking in their seats.

Anna's jaw hardened, her eyes narrowing the slightest bit.

"You were correct, my lord. Alexei is the traitor in our ranks. I do not yet know the full extent of his betrayal but-"

Zakhar finally broke his stony silence.

"Of course I was right. I should have put him down, just like I did his whore of a mother. Fucking mongrel." Zakhar's voice was quiet, and everyone promptly stopped breathing, not daring to move a single muscle. He continued his stare at the blank screens, but behind his wire-rimmed glasses, his amber eyes burned bright.

His laughter started out low.

Within a few moments, he was bellowing with the force of his mirth, tears leaking from the corners of his eyes. He let himself laugh, laugh, and continue to laugh.

After a few long minutes, his laughter died down to throaty chuckles. The mafia lord turned around slowly, showing his face to the entire room.

Every single person in the room felt the blood drain from their faces in terror.

Their boss was smiling.

And it was *horrifying*.

"My little Emilia. Even after months of imprisonment and torture, she still shines so bright. *Angel moy*."

Korol, king of the Russian mafia, stood to his full height, that terrifying smile still splitting his face into a mask of pure horror. His next words came out husky and low, full of promise.

"It is time Emilia returns to my side."

Every single one of Korol's personal bodyguards slowly inclined their heads, knowing what the next order from their king would be.

"*Prepare for war*."

Anna slowly smiled, her frostbite grin making everyone in the room shiver.

But it was Zane, the most terrifying of the bodyguards, who spoke. The ridiculously tall, thin man's deep timbre of a voice made the security members in the room shrink into their seats.

"Korol."

Korol turned slowly to Zane, eyes narrowed in question.

Zane stared back, his impassive face showing nothing, not a hint of emotion.

"Choose me as your first strike."

Korol raised an eyebrow in surprise. The eerily quiet man rarely spoke. He only killed, which suited Korol just fine. It made him into the most lethal of bodyguards. And, if he were honest with himself, the bodyguard made Korol... nervous. Which was why when Zane spoke, Korol listened.

And often acquiesced to his suggestions.

"Your plan of attack?" Korol asked, folding his arms over his chest.

Zane uttered the suggestion that Korol knew to be Emilia Fox's worst nightmare.

"Seems to me Emilia Fox has one too many families. I would like to relieve her of the one that we have left alone for far too long."

Korol stared at this man who didn't change expression as he suggested murdering an entire family of innocent people. Not only that, but it was his Emilia's blood that his bodyguard was talking about. Her precious family that she had bargained her compliance and body for, for over a year when she had been at Korol's side.

Korol smiled.

"Anna."

Anna turned.

"After my business trip this week, Zane will be heading to America. He is right, we have been ill-mannered for far too long. We must pay our respects to the Fox family. Make the preparations."

Anna's frostbite smile spread further along her face, and a raspy chuckle fell from her lips.

"As you wish... *my king*."

SEVENTEEN

One week later

Emilia

When did concrete get this soft?

I breathed in the scent of the cotton pillowcase beneath my head, whimpering at the incredible softness cushioning my entire body. The soft cotton felt like butter against my skin, cushioning every part of me perfectly. I was sleeping on fucking clouds. The grin of bliss that had spread across my face died a quick death, confusion clouding my rational thought.

"Ah shit, I died and went to heaven." My throat felt like a thousand needles had pierced through it, and I realized the absurdity of my statement.

A masculine snort came in answer to my quiet revelation. A gentle breeze caressed my skin, bringing with it the barest hints of vanilla and mint. I knew that smell and derisive snort very well.

"You really think heaven is where you are going after death, *mon trésor?*"

My smile returned.

"If you're here, I'm clearly not anywhere near the pearly gates, Silas."

The warmth surrounding me squeezed me gently. I realized I was in a bed, the smell of the sea and sun permeating the air. My eyes cracked open, and a beautiful, familiar room came into focus. Joy filled me at the sight of the large bed with the lavender sheets, and the cream and lavender walls as familiar to me as my own face.

"I'm home." I breathed.

We were back in my room at Downswing's base of operations on the island of Lesbos.

"Yes, Emilia. You are back where you belong."

Ah god, I think I might cry.

I shifted gingerly, twinges of discomfort accompanying the movement. I turned over, seeing the setting sun through the open terrace doors to my balcony. Shifting even further, I looked down to the man who had his body wrapped around my own. The beautiful Frenchman was looking up at me with a face devoid of emotion.

I frowned, a sudden thought popping into my sleep-addled brain.

"Ludo. Where's Ludo?" I made to sit up, but Silas gently touched my shoulder, his touch reassuring.

"He is safe, *princesse.* He was returned to us without a scratch on him."

I heaved a sigh of relief, smiling at Silas, who didn't return the gesture. My smile fled, a frown creeping in.

"Well, what the hell, where's my welcome home excitement? You look like someone died."

That did it.

The stoic Frenchman's face cracked, and it was as if I had obliterated a dam of emotion. Relief, followed swiftly by sorrow, and finally regret twisted the beautiful Silas' face into a hard grimace. He looked to be in such pain that I found myself bringing my hand up and running a finger through the furrow in his brow. Silas looked at me as if his heart was shattering before he clutched me tightly, hiding his face in my breasts. My eyebrows shot up as I heard a sob of pain rip out his throat.

"I... am so sorry, *princesse*. I am so, so sorry." Silas' voice was muffled, but I heard the agony in his words. My eyebrows shot further into my hairline when I felt wet droplets hit my flushed skin.

I could only blink in complete shock.

"Uh-" I said intelligently.

"I should have told you about my past. I should have trusted you more. You are my captain, my *princesse*. Because of me, you were unprepared for *Maman* and the horror they bring. I got you kidnapped by the worst people in the world and still, you let me stay by your side. I do not deserve you as my *princesse*, my captain." Silas' muffled words were said in a rush, and a hiccup followed.

Another blink from me.

"Um-"

"I am garbage. Filth. *Imbécile. Dégénéré. Connasse-*"

"Woah! Dude. That's harsh." I said, flabbergasted.

Silas' head whipped up.

I gasped.

Then immediately snorted with laughter.

"Oh my god. I can't believe it. You're an ugly crier!"

Silas' gorgeous face was red and blotchy, his nose swollen, eyes puffy. He really did look terrible. Horrible. Completely awful. I mean, the guy was still beyond gorgeous, but it was comforting to know he had least cried a little ugly.

"Shut up. I have not cried since I was a boy. It will not stop. On top of everything else, I am nothing but a pussy. A cry-baby, little pussy-"

"Okay, that's enough." I said, shaking my head. I couldn't help but blink in complete astonishment. I had never seen this side of Silas, and we had grown inseparable since our escape from Korol years before. I heaved a sigh, smiling gently into my beautiful Frenchman's face.

"Listen to me, you beautiful idiot." I said gently, wiping a tear from the soft skin of Silas' cheek. He sniffled at me, which I could only chuckle at.

"I *know* you trust me. I know that deep beneath that expressionless face and that superior-to-thou-attitude... that you love me. You all do. Even Cin kind of likes me, and that's a freaking miracle by itself. He doesn't like anyone but you. And if we're being honest, sometimes I don't think he even really likes you all that much."

Silas snorted, rolling his eyes.

Ah, there's my Frenchie.

I looked down at his chest, a sad smile crossing my face for a brief moment.

"You want to know why I never said anything about knowing who you all really were, right?" I looked back into Silas' beautiful eyes and smiled at his shy nod.

Jesus, this dude is adorable when he's sad.

"Because I thought I understood *why* you didn't want to tell me. It's not as if I was wallowing in self-pity, thinking that none of you trusted or respected me enough to be honest with me. Yes, I was sad that nobody except for Masamune and the Usami sisters came clean right away. But do you know why I never pushed the issue?"

I took a deep breath, my eyes closing for a moment in pain.

"I was ashamed." I whispered. Silas frowned in confusion,

tilting his head at me adorably and I almost smacked him for how cute he was. Instead, I sighed, flopping back on the heavenly pillows.

"I was ashamed because you all came from such... esteemed backgrounds. I mean, shit, there isn't a single person in Downswing that isn't criminal royalty. You came from such amazing places to become the talented, terrifying people you are today. And you guys *are* scary. Every last one of you has something amazing about them. After you escaped the mafia's most powerful leader, you decided to align yourself with... me. *Me.* And you didn't just become my allies, you decided you wanted me to *lead* you. Some nothing girl that managed to get herself kidnapped by the biggest mafia lord in the world and didn't even know he was playing her the whole time. So no, I didn't expect the most amazing criminals in the entire world to spill their secrets to some idiot American girl who couldn't hold a candle to your greatness."

Silas looked like he was going to argue, but I put a gentle finger on his lips.

"I said I *was* ashamed. Past tense, boo. Because I realized something over time. You all truly are the most talented, lethal, amazing killers and criminals in the world. But after a while of living together with all of you, I noticed the most peculiar thing."

A slow smile crept its way along my lips.

"Every last one of you... is a fucking train wreck. It is a miracle that any of you managed to survive as long as you had before I came along. Honestly, had I not come along and been such an amazing influence in your lives, I seriously don't think you would have survived much longer. You would have been dead. *Real* dead."

I turned back to Silas, pressing my lips together, eyes dancing in merriment.

"So, really, when you think about it... *I'm* actually the most amazing out of all of you. You. Are. Welcome."

With that, I *booped* his nose.

Stunned silence met my revelation.

One beat. Two.

Then, complete meltdown.

Silas howled with laughter, holding his sides and turning away from me. I put my hands behind my head, smiling smugly.

Yeah, that's right. I was a fucking badass for keeping all these psychos together, mostly sane, and letting them just... be *them*. No strings attached. No threats, no beatings. Just acceptance and respect. I was the glue keeping this fucked-up, jagged puzzle together and I was damn proud of it.

So what if the glue was slightly warped and fractured in certain places? Didn't make it any less adhesive. Yeah. That was it. I was warped glue and I held all of Downswing's crazy together like a goddamn hero.

Bow at my sticky feet, bitches.

Finally, Silas' mirth died down and he sighed contentedly. He turned back to me, his smile brilliant, his face absolutely stunning. It was like he had never cried at all.

This beautiful prick.

"You are right, *princesse*. You are the most amazing. That is why you are not only my *princesse*, but the queen of Downswing." Silas smiled, hugging me tightly.

Well, my Frenchman was certainly lovey-dovey today.

"Thank you." I felt rather than heard him murmur against my throat. I smiled, patting his head and chuckling softly.

"Oh, you are most welcome. Whenever you need a reminder of how much of a badass I am, you just let me know. Okay, peaches?"

Silas nodded, chuckling against my throat.

My heart constricted in joy. I swallowed roughly, pushing back tears.

I had made it.

I had *made* it.

I had really made it back home and I was in bed once again with my lovely Silas. One of the best friends I had ever been lucky enough to have by my side. I wrapped my arms around my perfect Frenchman and held onto him tightly. His familiar scent, his warm skin pressing against my own, his soft words of appreciation against my throat... God, it really was heaven.

There were only a few more things that would make my homecoming even better.

I gave an evil grin over Silas' head.

"Si... where is Viktor?"

Silas leaned back, looking up at me with blue eyes that narrowed to suspicious slits. Yeah, my tone had been a little too innocent to be believed.

Oops.

"What?" I blinked, trying to appear nonchalant. Silas gave a snort, sitting up. He raised a brow down at me but answered all the same.

"This is actually one of the only times of day that the great *D'yavol* forces himself away from your side. You've been in and out of consciousness for the past week and he has been the one to stay with you much of the time. Meiling and Jazz have been the ones to attend to your toilette and bathing needs. I take over when he absolutely cannot stay awake. Even then, he only allows himself a few hours of sleep at the most."

"Jeesh, think he likes me?" I asked, tilting my head and blinking innocently. Silas didn't laugh as expected. Instead, he gave me the most chilling, frightened look that I had seen on him yet.

Woah.

"Emilia, I do not think 'like' is the right term to describe how he feels. That word is far too mundane for the deep, truly terrifying emotions he has for you. I do not know if I envy you... or if I need to find a way to hide you away where he can never find you again." Silas' voice was so serious and his eyes so haunted, I didn't even ask what he had seen in Viktor while I had been gone. It was clearly terrifying and beyond anything that could be considered healthy or safe.

And didn't that just affect me in the most fucked up of ways.

My nipples hardened beneath the soft cotton top I wore. I felt my eyes lower to half-mast, and I unconsciously licked my lips. A low hum escaped me, and I leaned back on my hands, a slow grin curling my lips.

Silas watched my reaction, lifting a brow and finally heaving a long sigh.

"I forgot for a brief moment that you are just as fucked up as I am when it comes to matters of the heart... and of the body."

"Oh *yeah* because I'm the poster child for perfect mental health on a good day." I rolled my eyes as I sat up. Scooting to the end of the bed, I slid to the side and slowly stood on my own two feet. Brief cramping made my legs shake, but after a few minutes of clenching and unclenching the muscles throughout my legs and back, I found myself able to stand. Tossing a triumphant grin at Silas, I strode slowly to the bathroom.

"Now, I have some... maintenance issues to take care of. When is Viktor due back?"

Silas' lips twitched, his eyes starting to spark with mischievous amusement.

Oh, that's not good.

"In another twenty minutes. But if your maintenance

includes ridding yourself of, say, unwanted hair... I believe Meiling took care of that this morning when she and Jazzy washed you. That Chinese witch bet me twenty dollars that when you woke up, you would be ready and, erm, *raring* to be alone with Viktor."

My jaw dropped open.

That bitch, no she did not.

I crouched down swiftly, running my hands along my legs and feeling the suspiciously silky-smooth skin. Shifting my weight from side to side, my eyes went wide. Uncaring because it was Silas, I shoved a hand down the front of my panties. My face burned a fiery red at the smooth skin that met my questing fingers.

"That fucking bitch! She shaved me! She shaved me *everywhere!*" I gasped, feeling weirdly violated.

Silas shrugged.

"She said you would be more comfortable with a bald pu-"

"You shut your mouth when you're talking to me." I snarled, heaving out breaths of indignant air. This caused Silas to roll with laughter and my face to get even more red.

"Are you- are you actually *blushing*? The crazy, fearless leader of Downswing is *blushing* because a woman shaved her pus-"

"Not. Another. Fucking. Word." I huffed, stomping to the bathroom. I came up short as I caught my reflection in the mirror. My eyes slowly widened at the woman staring back at me.

Wow. Captivity had really... I shook my head. Just wow. My body was the thinnest it had ever been, my eyes looking hollowed out with the dark circles surrounding them. The scar that I had gotten during my time with Korol stood out even more at my throat, making it look like an angry purple collar. There were numerous other bruises and scrapes all over my body. At least the hair on my head was untangled and neatly trimmed, and my skin had the smallest bit of color to it. Still, I looked different. More haggard.

More haunted.

Silas came up behind me, wrapping his arms around my waist. I leaned back against his long, lean body, closing my eyes against the contrast of his unmarred beauty against my obvious faults.

"Emilia." Silas murmured, his lips brushing my ear. "You could have a million scars. A million bruises. That would not change what Viktor feels for you. And it certainly would not change the fact that you are the stunning, powerful queen of Downswing. The queen we all adore... and will follow to the ends of the earth."

I opened my eyes, connecting my gaze with his in the mirror. Giving him a warm smile, I heaved a breath and squeezed his fingers.

"You always know just what to say, Si. *Mon coeur*." Silas smiled in delight at my vastly improved French and pressed a kiss to my temple.

"Now, *princesse*. You have sixteen minutes. And he is usually a few seconds early."

I grinned slowly.

"Oh, I'll be ready."

I've been ready for this fucker for years. No more running. No more hiding. We're going to hash this shit out here and now.

Because at the end of the day, who could say when we would die? We weren't in the business of longevity. I wasn't going to live with regrets, with nothing but longing in my heart. Nope. That was not how Emilia Fox was going to handle shit from now on.

Turning in Silas' arms, I leaned up, breathing an evil question right into his ear. His eyes went wide as he stared down at me. After a moment, he reacted the way I knew he would.

He gave his slow, sensual grin, a thousand sins dancing behind his eyes.

"*Oui, princesse.* I have the supplies you need."

I grinned.

Sometimes the only way to take a reluctant devil... is to trap him.

EIGHTEEN

VIKTOR

I'm so exhausted.

As I let the thought slip through, I had to shake myself. It didn't matter how tired I was, how mentally and physically drained I was. Nothing mattered except seeing Emilia wake up.

As I trudged down the hall to Emilia's private rooms, I couldn't hold back a small sigh. God, it had been a week and she still wasn't regaining full consciousness. She had roused herself enough to ingest broth and water and had been only semi-conscious when Meiling and Jazzy had bathed her. I had insisted upon several local doctors- who were paid handsomely to keep their mouths shut- come by and check on her. They had cleared her two days ago. They said she was simply gaining strength and would awaken any day, which was a vast improvement from the state she had arrived home in. She had been dehydrated, malnourished and suffered from severe exhaustion. Not to mention the bruised ribs, numerous cuts and bruises and dislocated shoulder.

All my fault.

I felt my rage, my constant companion, twist its way to the forefront of my thoughts and had to stop for a moment to regain composure. My rampage through the Numberless had only taken the edge off the violent rage inside. Now I had no outlet save sparring with myself in the gym inside the mansion and exhausting myself with swimming in the sea. Nobody would spar with me. They all knew I was in too fragile of a mental state to be able to stop once my anger got the better of me.

They knew I was holding on by a thread.

I reached the door to Emilia's room and inhaled a deep, calming breath. The anxiety and residual fear of losing her drained away, though I had no idea when- or if- it would ever fully leave me. These two months had been torture, pure and simple, and not just for Emilia.

My sanity had suffered so severely, it was a wonder I could even function as a human.

If you call what I'm doing functioning.

My ears perked at the sound of Silas' muffled voice murmuring inside. I could only assume he was reciting poetry to Emilia, as he had since we had brought her home. When I could no longer keep my body from crashing, I would take an hour, maybe two, and rest my eyes and the Frenchman would stay with her. Make no mistake, the French bastard was still on my shit-list for omitting the fact that he was a legendary assassin for *Maman*, but I knew he would never harm Emilia.

Silas was the only one who blamed himself almost as much as I did for Emilia's abduction.

Pushing the door open gently, I stepped into the room, my eyes immediately seeking out Emilia's sleeping form. The anxiousness I felt at leaving her side ebbed completely, leaving me with nothing but relief and elation. God, the sight of her in her own bed, in our home, made my blood sing. She looked so beautiful lying there, still and silent save the deep rasp of her breath.

My beautiful Emilia.

"Any improvement?" I grunted, walking around the bed to Silas, who was sitting in a chair close at Emilia's side, a book of poetry opened in his lap. He didn't even look up, merely shook his head the tiniest bit. My heart stuttered, but I forced myself not to show my despair.

"What is today's poem?" I asked softly, my voice sounding like sandpaper over hardened stone. Silas looked up at me, a half-smile curling his lips.

"*L'Amour* by Marceline Desbordes-Valmore. Beautiful poem. Sentimental drivel. Emilia would love it." Silas said, that same fond smile on his face. I chuckled quietly, making a sound of agreement. Silas stood, closing the book and stepping forward. He clapped a hand on my shoulder, and I raised a brow in surprise. Silas wasn't the touchy type, the one exception seeming to be Emilia. The Frenchman looked into my eyes for a moment as if he was searching for something, and whatever he found there had him smiling slowly. He clapped my shoulder again, stepping around me and chuckling quietly.

"Have a *lovely* evening, *D'yavol.*"

And with that, Silas was out the door, shutting it with a soft click.

I frowned after him, confused by his chipper attitude. I hadn't seen him in that positive of a mood since before Emilia had been taken. And she hadn't even woken up yet.

Whatever.

The Frenchman was fucking weird. That was all there was to it.

Shaking off my musings, I took Silas' empty seat, sliding it close to Emilia's still form. Gazing up at her face, I did as I had so many times in the past week and took her hand in mine, clasping it tightly. I pressed her hand to my cheek, feeling the warmth from her fingers pressing against my scruff, and sighed in contentment.

"Ah, he is a strange one, *Kapitan*. Do you know why he insists upon reading you that stupid fucking poetry day after day? It is so when you dream, you dream of pleasant things. He says it helps to keep the nightmares at bay. Who knew Deveroux had such a soft spot, eh?" I chuckled, pressing Emilia's fingers into my cheek harder. I swallowed, looking at the gorgeous face of my captain. My lips barely moved as I said my next words.

"Please open your eyes, *kotyonok*."

A few heartbeats passed. I waited, holding my breath for a sign that my talking was doing anything to help her wake.

Nothing.

I gave a sad smile, turning my lips to press a soft, lingering kiss to her limp fingers. Putting her hand back down at her side, I stood, pulling the covers closer around her body. I leaned down, resting my forehead against hers, and closed my eyes. I just needed these few moments. I needed to be close to her.

My *kapitan*.

My heart.

My-

"*FUCK!*"

My world tilted and suddenly I was flat on my back on the bed, my arms above my head, with a lap full of vengeful, energetic goddess.

Click. Click.

I blinked stupidly up at my wrists that had just been snapped to the bedposts in handcuffs. My mouth hanging open, astonishment robbing me of all rational thought, I brought my gaze back to the vision before me that had only ever been in my dreams.

Emilia, *my Emilia*, sat back and crossed her arms, a pleased smile curling her lips.

"Hello, Viktor."

Words escaped me. My breath crystalized in my lungs. I could do nothing but stare in open-mouthed amazement. This was a dream. Had to be. My breath left me in a *whoosh*, and my heart started a rapid rhythm, pounding in my chest.

"Am I dreaming?" I asked, my voice coming out as shocked as I felt. Emilia lifted an amused brow, giving that rusty chuckle that haunted my dreams.

"So you *do* dream about me. You learn the most interesting things when you handcuff a man to your bed. I should have done this a long time ago."

Emilia uncrossed her arms, lowering them to my chest and leaning forward. It was at that moment I became fully aware that my *kotyonok* had nothing on save an oversized cotton shirt that slipped off one of her pale shoulders, and some form of panties. That was it. My eyes widened as Emilia leaned forward further, exposing the swells of her generous breasts to my starving gaze.

Oh, holy fuck.

"Emil- *Kapitan*. You are awake. This is wonderful news." I stuttered, blinking rapidly. I tried to force my gaze away from those creamy swells of flesh that entranced me, but I knew that battle was over before it even began.

I did manage to tear my gaze away when Emilia heaved an irritated sigh. My eyes snapped to her face, and I saw that she had her gaze narrowed on me, frustration clear on her face. She pursed her lips, pouting slightly.

Jesus, those lips.

The irritation was still on her face, but a calculated gleam entered those stormy eyes of hers.

"Quick to fall back on that *Kapitan* title, aren't you? What happened to calling me kitten? I like when you say it in Russian. Suits the mood better, don't you think?" She punctuated her question with a slow drag of her hips, rubbing herself over my slowly awakening cock.

I sucked in a startled breath, my eyes flaring with need. Oh fuck, this was too much. My confusion and elation over Emilia being awake, the shock of being trapped in her bed, the pure, animal *need* that gripped me at the movement of those hips, it was all too much. I needed to come to my senses, needed to reign in my desires, needed to-

"Oh, no you don't." Emilia purred. "You don't get to go back to business as usual, *D'yavol*. I have plans for you. And I'm not fucking waiting around for you to come to your senses anymore."

And with that, Emilia pressed her hands down harder on my chest and gave a twist of her hips that had her rubbing along my hardening cock in all the right places. A kiss of pain and a shock of pleasure shot through me, making my instincts kick in and causing me to punch my hips up, a snarl of possession on my face.

"Oh! God, fuck." The irritation was wiped from Emilia's face in an instant, and she threw her head back, exhaling a long moan. My cock twitched in my jeans, now painfully hard.

That's it, kotyonok, *that's what I want.*

Why did she still have clothes on? Why did I? I needed to own her. She had left my sight and now I needed to remind her why she had chosen me, why I was the one at her side. I needed to fucking *brand* her with pleasure. I lurched forward with the full intention of grabbing her and throwing her beneath me.

Snap. My wrists came up short, catching on something. I blinked in confusion, looking up. Oh, shit. Right. I was handcuffed. To the bed. To *Emilia's* bed. She had handcuffed me.

She had planned this ambush. I shook my head violently, shrinking back down to the bed.

"Oh, come on, no." Emilia began, licking her lips and leaning forward again. I shrank back, turning my head.

"*Kapitan*, we must stop. There is too much to discuss. When you left, it created a hole in Downswing that needs to be mended. If you are feeling up to it, we need to get you dressed and hold a meeting, go over security, check in with the rest of the te-"

Emilia had a hold of my jaw in a second. She pressed so hard my lips puckered forward, and she turned my head roughly back to face her. Well, fuck, she had been awake for less than a few hours and I had already managed to piss her off. Rage contorted her pale face, red creeping up her neck, making the scar around her throat that much more prominent. She looked like an avenging Valkyrie, sent to battle the mortal men that would dare challenge her.

And if I wasn't so hard it hurt, that would have done the trick.

"You listen to me, Vik, and you damn well better have both ears open and *really* hear me. I'm not going anywhere. You're not going anywhere. You and me? We've got business to settle. We've been dancing around each other for *four fucking years*. You wanted me when Zakhar had his claws in me, you wanted me after, and you want me now. And I think we both know damn well that I want you."

Emilia's chest was heaving, her eyes glittering with her rage.

So damn beautiful.

"I need you. You fucking asshole, I've wanted you inside me this entire time and I'm *sick* of denying it. I'm sick of this tension between us. I am *sick* to fucking *death* of duty coming before what *I* want. And you are too. I know you are; don't you even try to deny it. We don't have the highest chance of longevity in this business, Vik, that became abundantly clear when I was kidnapped and tortured for *two goddamn months*."

My heart constricted. Fuck, she was so mad. This was not what I expected when Emilia had awoken. I expected her to be soft, hurt, a little broken. That was only natural after the ordeal she had been through. I should have known better. I knew my *Kapitan*, my Emilia. She wouldn't let a small thing like torture and despair get the better of her.

"I went insane, Viktor. Clinically, medically insane. I'm still fighting the effects of my broken mind."

Well, of course she wasn't completely *unscathed.*

Guilt rode me hard, but Emilia must have sensed it because she growled, squeezing my face even harder.

Jesus, that's a strong grip.

"I don't want your guilt. I don't want your apologies. Right here, right now, I want only one thing from you."

She let go of my face, straightening above me. Glaring down at me, she gave me the stare of a queen before a peasant-regal, cold, filled with haughty disdain.

Which only served to make my cock twitch with excitement.

"No more lies. No more secrets. I want you to be honest with me. And I think I have earned that fucking right."

My jaw clenched. She wasn't pulling any punches, that was for fuck sure. God, my heart was twisting in agony at the pain and hurt I had been causing her all these years by omitting the truth about my past from her. But she was right. She deserved nothing less than my complete honesty. So, I stayed silent and merely inclined my head, acknowledging her statement.

Emilia nodded back, then leaned down, putting her face mere inches from mine. Her eyes had me trapped; the constant pull I felt towards her coming forth tenfold. I couldn't help but stare back, hanging on her every word, watching her plump lips form her next words.

"You tell me. You tell me the truth. Right here. Right now. No thought of duty, no thought of repercussions, just you and me."

She leaned forward even further, her lips a breath away from my own. My air felt like it was pummeling my lungs, struggling to get out. My heart was beating so hard I was sure she could feel it against her own chest as she pressed down against me.

Fuck.

I was losing control-

"Do you still want me? If you don't, I will let you go and we will never speak of this again. You will remain as you are, my trusted second-in-command and head of security. Your position here will never be contingent on you sharing my bed. Everything will go back to the way it was. With you at my side in a solely professional manner."

I stared at her, speechless. Ah, god, I needed to say the words. She was giving me no choice, it had finally come to this.

I needed to lie one more time to my Emilia and tell her I didn't want her.

Because I wasn't worth it. She was so far above me, I could never hope to reach her with my stained, tainted grasp. I wanted her to remain out of reach so that I didn't take what light she still had shining inside of her and taint it with my disgusting darkness. If she knew the real me, the darkness lying in wait, the true reason I was called the devil, she would turn away in disgust.

I could never let that happen.

I had to lie.

I need to release her.

A sordid, self-hating part of my brain realized the dark humor in this situation. The fact that Emilia had me restrained, and yet I was the one who had the key to her freedom. Feeling my erection wane swiftly, my heart stuttering, my soul screaming in agony, I prepared to release my beautiful Emilia, my life, my love.

It was time.

"I do n-" My voice stopped, betraying me. I cleared my throat and clenched my jaw. It physically hurt me to say the words, but as I had done so many times before, I forced the words out, guaranteeing my own suffering. The words were hollow, devoid of emotion as they finally struggled past my lips.

"I do... not... want you."

And as the words hung in the air, I felt my heart shatter in my chest.

NINETEEN

Emilia

Oh, what a crock of shit.

I almost rolled my eyes but managed to keep myself under control.

This big, dumb idiot. Really? That was how he wanted to play it? God, I had no idea how he had managed to hide things from me, the guy was the *worst* liar.

He was practically radiating with self-loathing and heart-break. His freaking eyes were swimming with regret and sorrow. And it wasn't the, 'Oh, I'm hurting my boss' feelings' kind of regret. It was the, 'Fuck, I'm going to regret this for the rest of my life because I want her so badly' kind of regret. I knew it. He knew it.

We all knew it.

But there was a problem. The dumb fucker had lied to me.

Again.

When I had *specifically* told him not to.

That shit pissed me off more than him saying he didn't

217

want me, which... had stung a bit. I stared into those obsidian eyes, feeling his erratic heartbeat against my chest, and thought it over slowly.

A memory skittered along the edges of my mind. Silas and I had gotten drunk years ago, right after we had first arrived at our compound on Lesbos and we were still trying to get to know each other. I remember our conversation had been centered around our mutual love for male/male romance novels. At the end of our discussion, I had asked him if his and Cin's romance had been anything close to what we read about in books. The scornful laughter that had followed had nearly blown me over.

"Emilia, mon coeur, you are so sweet. Cin originally said I was nothing more than a deadly piece of ass. I remember, he said that he 'wouldn't mind coming back for seconds. He thought this to be a very high compliment, apparently."

I stared at him, my mouth agape.

"That asshole!" I screeched, hiccupping loudly.

"Oui. He is that. So, the answer to your question is no, ours is not a sweet, loving romance. He still has trouble admitting that he is gay, let alone that we are lovers." Silas' smile was intended to be snarky, but I saw the sadness in his eyes.

"Then, how did you get him to finally take the plunge to becoming a couple?" I asked, curious, hoping the story would cheer him up. And it worked.

A slow, evil smile spread across Silas' face.

"I reminded him that he was not my only option. It may not be nice, it may not be fair, but jealousy and possession are easy tools to use to get what you want. In this case, it was what he wanted, too, even if he would not admit it to himself. So I do not feel so bad, eh?"

Hm. Well. There was that.

Shaking myself back to the present, I sat up, staring down

at the idiot man that I had chosen to give my heart to. I pursed my lips as I tilted my head and watched as his anguished gaze tracked my every movement.

No more Miss Nice Emilia.

It was time to play dirty.

"Okay, Viktor. Fair enough." I said, nodding. "I asked you to be honest, and I assume that you were. Like I said, your place in the household has not changed, and everything will go back to exactly the way it was."

For a man who claimed to want just that, his expression shattered in despair before he schooled his features, hiding his emotions from me. Yeah, no, that wasn't going to work for me. I was about to tear open the fresh wound I had just laid on him. If I didn't, we were never going to heal right.

Grandmama's wisdom echoed inside my head even now.

Makes sense since I'm about to do something a bit evil.

I cleared my throat, sitting up straight.

"Do you know what I kept thinking, sitting alone in my cell, unable to fall asleep for days on end?" I asked softly.

That sure as shit got his attention.

Pain flared in his eyes for a moment before he schooled his features once again.

"I kept thinking... that I might die there. Alone. In that god-awful, cold cell in the middle of nowhere, covered in filth, bruises and blood. And it wasn't death that scared me so much. Nah, death hasn't scared me for a while. But do you want to know what did terrify me about dying there?"

Viktor didn't even blink. Hell, I didn't even think he was breathing.

"It was the thought that I hadn't had anyone except Zakhar inside me for four... fucking... years."

Ah, there he was.

D'yavol.

Jealousy and a burning hatred flashed across his face, contorting those handsome features into a terrifying mask. He couldn't school his features completely this time. Oh, he tried. But the hatred burned bright, searing me with its intensity.

I welcomed the fire.

"It's not even the sex itself that bothered me. No, it was something deeper. It's what it represented. I hadn't allowed myself to open up to someone else for four years. And why? Because I was so consumed with my revenge that I did nothing but study, train, and go on mission after mission. I allowed my job to completely take over with no outlet whatsoever. It made it so easy for *Maman* to crack my mind open like an egg and scramble my sanity."

Sighing, I sat back, toying with the ends of my hair that had grown out over the past two months.

"The weird thing? I'm actually a little grateful that I went a bit mad. It helped me put everything into perspective. I have a new outlook on life. Hell, I even have a new and improved plan to bring Korol to his fucking knees. *Maman* helped me with that. But they also helped me realize that I've been denying myself for far too long. And I'm not going to let it happen again."

I trailed my eyes slowly back up to Viktor's and caught his gaze. I leaned forward once again, putting my face close to his. Running a slow hand up his chest, my lips curled back in a slow, sensual smile. I felt his breath hitch once again and he couldn't hide his hardening cock from me.

"I'm going to release you, Viktor."

His face fell the slightest bit, but he nodded all the same. What a good, little soldier my Viktor was. Ever the fucking martyr.

Wait for it...

"And you're going to summon Masamune for me."

Viktor froze.

And I couldn't help the shiver of excitement that raced along my spine.

Let the game begin.

VIKTOR

What the fuck did she just say?

My body was frozen. My brain couldn't wrap itself around what she had just ordered me to do. I knew what she was saying, but shock made me mute. It couldn't be. She had just handcuffed me to her fucking bed with the intention of solidifying our feelings and fucking it out. There was not a chance in hell she was giving up that easy.

You just said you didn't want her.

Well, that was true, but...

I finally blinked. And then stared. My beautiful Emilia was sitting straight up now, staring down at me, haughty as could be.

"You want me to bring Onodera to you. Right now." I had to make sure I understood what she was asking.

"Yes. That's exactly what I want you to do. And then I want you and everyone else to stay far away from this room until we come down to meet with you."

Okay, no. In a distant part of my brain, I knew what Emilia was doing. She was trying to make me jealous enough where I broke down and accepted my feelings for her. It just couldn't happen. I didn't deserve her, I never would. I was too broken, too filthy, too... dark. My entire existence was darkness personified. She was everything light and good.

I couldn't taint her. I just couldn't.

She didn't understand what having me as her lover would mean. If I got inside of Emilia, if I possessed her body and her heart...

I was never going to let her go.

Never.

She would be tied to the devil for all time.

"*Kapitan.* I-"

"Excuse me, did I ask for your opinion? I gave you an order. That will be all." Emilia said coldly, producing a key from what seemed to be out of thin air. She leaned forward, avoiding my eyes and I felt a heavy panic settle in the pit of my stomach.

No. Be strong. This is for the best. She needs someone better for her.

"But Onodera?" I didn't even realize I had posed the question out loud until Emilia gave a rusty chuckle. The handcuffs opened, and my wrists were freed. Emilia got up, sliding off the bed gracefully. I saw her wince once, but she looked to be handling the residual pain well.

"Mmm. I don't trust anyone from outside the group. And I know Masamune will keep anything that develops between us discreet. Plus..."

Emilia paused, looking back at me as I sat up on her bed and rubbed my wrist. Her eyes were sultry, her lips curled in the most sensual smile. My dick twitched at the sight of my powerful captain in all of her disheveled, carnal glory.

"I'm not easy to handle. Masamune can gave me what I need."

Masamune can give her what she needs.

The words thundered around in my brain for a long, tortured moment. My heart stopped; my breath seized in my lungs. A black, suffocating emotion gripped me. Before I knew what I was doing, I was on my feet, stalking toward my beautiful Emilia.

"How do you know this?" My words were soft, almost a whisper. My feet were silent as I closed in on her. She looked back at me, her eyes widening. She whipped around, backing away slowly. A defiant, cold look came over her face before she gave a bitter laugh.

"Why do you care, Viktor? You just said you didn't want me. It stands to reason I would find a replacement." Her chin went up in defiance, but she was still backing away, a cautious look in her eye.

"How... do you know... he can give you... what you want?" Rational thought had fled. I watched as Emilia swallowed, a nervous tremble to her lips. I didn't miss the flare of need in her eyes. God, she was beautiful like this.

I wanted her in tears for me.

I'm a fucking monster.

I almost stopped my prowl forward at the thought, knowing that indeed I was nothing but a monster, not fit to lick my captain's boots. But then, she stopped, her back pressed against the dresser. She took a trembling breath, her eyes now flooding with carnal need.

"Because he told me what I need before I knew it myself. He was right."

Emilia raised gentle fingers to her lips, her eyes looking far away and drenched in need as she breathed her next words.

"And I knew it the moment he kissed me."

No.

I stopped dead in my tracks. I took in her trembling form, the tongue that flicked out to lick her lips, the heavy-lidded gaze and realized she was remembering it. She was remembering a kiss between her and that bastard and it had her trembling.

The thought of kissing Onodera has her like this.

The memory of him touching her.

She looks so beautiful, so full of need... because of him.

And I lost my mind.

I moved forward so fast; my feet barely touched the ground. Emilia gasped as I stopped right in front of her. Leaning down, my eyes locked on her own startled gaze, I grabbed her by the backs of her legs and lifted her up. She gave what could only be described as a squawk and wrapped her hands around my shoulders for support.

"Viktor? The *fuck* are-"

"Shut up. Shut the fuck up." I snarled, my face inches from my precious Emilia's. Utter shock took over her entire face and she went limp in my arms. Her mouth hung open and she just stared at me, eyes as wide as saucers.

"You've never told me to shut up before." She whispered.

I snarled, gripping her thighs harder and tugging her even closer. Her legs wrapped around me and I rubbed my erection against her in a single aggressive thrust. She gasped, letting out a needy whimper, but her eyes were still round and full of shock.

"What did I just tell you, *kotyonok*? Shut. The fuck. Up." I punctuated each word with a thrust of my hips and that wide-eyed look of hers melted away and was replaced with nothing but heated desire.

"Is this what you wanted? You wanted me jealous? I'm not good enough for you, Emilia, I never will be. I'm assaulting you like a fucking monster. How can you even stand to look at me?" I was breathing hard, but I didn't care. It was as if years of my pent-up desire, wrath, jealousy, possession was spilling forth in a lethal cocktail.

And I was helpless not to let us both drown in it.

Emilia blinked at me, confusion and what looked like *anger* contorting her face.

"Wait, what? Seriously? *That's* why you didn't want to fuck me? Why you thought we couldn't be together? Because you were too much of a monster?" She glared at me and suddenly, she was rearing her head back and snapping it forward, head-butting me.

"*JESUS, FUCK!*" I yelled, dropping her. I clutched my head, feeling the red bump already forming. Christ, for such a small woman, her head felt like a fucking *rock!*

"You stupid, idiot, motherfucking-" Emilia cut off her tirade with a long scream of rage.

It was my turn to stare at her with a gaping mouth and wide eyes.

"Listen up, bitch, because I'm only going to say this once." Emilia thundered, stalking forward now and making me stumble back. She thrust her index finger right into my chest and ground it in.

"*Ow.*"

"You think I don't know a monster when I see one? News flash, asshole. *We are all monsters here.* I'm not some unicorn angel that shits glitter-magic and lactates rainbows, 'kay? Don't you dare put me on that pedestal. I'm a broken, shameless, foul-mouthed dickhead just like the rest of you. And all I want is you. All I have ever wanted since we've met... has been you." Chest heaving, fury stamped across her face, Emilia backed me right back up to the bed.

"You got a problem with that, go cry about it like a scrotum. I'm *no one's* angel. And if you want to keep me out of your reach, that's fine. I'll go and get Masamune and he can take care of it. Now, get out of my sight."

She turned from me, but she had just dropped a bomb on the already overwhelming emotions swirling inside of my chest. The last reserve of restraint I had snapped, and I was done. When Emilia whipped around, heading for her walk-in closet, her body still radiating fury, I swiftly moved to intercept her, tossing her over my shoulder.

Again, that bird-like squawk that was so endearing came out of her.

"Put me *down*, you asshole! I am your fucking captain, listen to me-"

"Jesus, you're mouthy." I muttered, and while she was still prattling on, I reached my hand up and smacked her ass hard enough to get her attention.

Well, that certainly had an interesting effect.

Emilia melted into me, and I swear to god I almost heard a purr come out of her. I almost came on the spot. She was compliant for a moment before she started sputtering again.

"No, *kotyonok*. Let us go back to you being quiet." I smacked her ass again and yes, there it was, a purr deep in her throat and a sensuous roll of her hips. Licking my lips, my cock hard as a rock, I grabbed her supple ass cheek in my hand and gave the warm flesh a rough squeeze.

That resulted in a needy whimper that had a predatory grin contorting my lips.

"You talked. Now you listen." I said, my voice nothing more than gravel and sex. "You are my captain. You will always be more to me than you know. But you are right. We are all monsters here. You know what you want, so who am I to tell you what you need? And you need someone who is going to challenge you. Masamune is not that person, *kotyonok*. I am."

I set her down, gripping her hair in my hand and forcing her head back. She looked up into my eyes with parted lips and a glazed, almost drugged expression. I grinned down at her with a grin so dark, I felt the shiver of fear that raced along her spine.

"If you want to pray to the devil, who am I to stop you?"

We stared at each other for a long moment, tension-filled moment.

And at the same time, we rushed forward, slamming our lips together.

Ah god, fucking finally.

Jesus, the taste of this woman. She tasted like vanilla and sunshine. She tangled her tongue with mine, pressing her generous breasts into my chest and wrapping her arms around my shoulders. I clutched her hair tighter, almost in a brutal grip, and she mewled like the kitten I kept calling her.

I swung us around, lifting her into my arms, and slammed her back against the dresser. Belatedly, I realized that fuck, she was still injured.

Tearing my mouth away, I panted. "*Kapitan*, are you all ri-"

"Mouth. Need it. Please, please, please." Emilia panted, clutching me with desperation. Her pleas were soft and whiny, and I felt an answering twitch in my dick. I looked down and felt all reason leave me at how plump and wrecked her lips looked.

"Yeah, you fucking need it, don't you? Poor *kotyonok*, I made you wait, didn't I?" I ran my tongue over my lips, taunting her. She gave a long, loud whimper, clutching me tighter. Her face reflected pure desperation.

"You want my mouth again?" I asked softly, my voice so rough I barely recognized it myself. I was almost sure this was a dream, something straight out of my fantasies when my Emilia nodded, looking so eager.

"Then you tell me who it is you want. Tell me who can have you." I growled, punching my hips forward sharply again. My cock thrust against her panties, and I must have hit a tender spot because her eyes widened, and she trembled violently in my arms. Words seemed to have escaped her.

Oh, you're going to tell me.

"Tell me who you're panting for. Say it, *kotyonok*, and I will let you have my lips again." I whispered, barely brushing her lips with my own. She lurched forward, but I had her hair in my grip. I jerked her head back and she cried out.

The most beautiful fucking sound in the world.

"V-Viktor. P-please. I want it." She panted. Her throat was exposed so I leaned forward and gave a solid bite to the side of her neck.

Her shout of pleasure echoed in the room.

"Oh, fuck yeah. Do that again. Do it." She snarled, clutching me tighter.

I slapped her ass again, harder this time. She gave another of those beautiful cries, nearly sobbing with need in my arms. Leaning back, I caught her gaze in my own.

"You are not in charge here. Outside these doors, you are my *Kapitan*. My leader. Here, right now, you are my *kotyonok*. You yield to me, do you understand?"

Emilia gave a long, slow lick to her bottom lip.

"Say it. You answer me right and I'll give you what you want. What you need." I stroked a firm hand over her ass and gave a rough squeeze. Panting, she found her words.

She found *a lot* of words.

"Yes, please, please. You're the one I need. You're the one I want. I swear. Please, Viktor." She was desperate now and I grinned down at her.

Ah, my dreams had nothing on my beautiful kitten.

"Good girl." I murmured. My eyebrows shot to my hairline at the long, greedy whimper that came forth from that.

"Ah, my *kotyonok* likes when I praise her? Are you going to be a good girl for me? That's a surprise." I chuckled, running my lips along her exposed collarbone.

"Fuck you- *ahn.*" Her caustic words ended on a moan of need when I bit down on the tender spot between her shoulder and the curve of her neck. She squirmed on me, rubbing herself shamelessly against my hard cock.

"I told you to be good." I rumbled, licking the spot I had just sunk my teeth into. "Who is in charge here, *kotyonok*?"

"Y-you are. I'm sorry." She panted, pressing herself once again against me. Mmm, and wasn't that the sweetest sound, her breathless remorse.

"You should be sorry. Now apologize for kissing Masamune and liking it." I bit that same spot again and Emilia let out a sob.

"I-I'm sorry, Viktor. Please." She was panting, out of her mind, and I couldn't be any fucking harder. The woman drove me to the brink of insanity.

"Good girl, *kotyonok*. You wanted me; you have me. Nobody else gets to touch you. You tell me that and I'll finally give you what you need."

Emilia looked up at me, dazed, but a calculated gleam crept into her eyes. She leaned forward, licking her lips, pressing her breasts tightly to my chests. Her lips brushed my ear and her little tongue came out to flick the lobe.

Ahhhh, fuck.

"No one else. Nobody else gets to touch me but you. I'll give you anything. I'll give you..."

She bit down on my ear, giving it a long, slow lick.

"*Everything.*"

TWENTY

Emilia

Well, that certainly got his attention.

The teasing fucker wrenched my head back and slammed his lips into mine. Ah, yeah, that's what I needed. My brain was fried, but my body knew exactly what I wanted. The *taste* of this man. Jesus.

If fury and leather had a flavor, that was what Viktor Orlov tasted like.

And I lapped it up like a fucking kitten.

Yeah, so what, I liked when someone took charge in the bedroom. Just because I had, had one giant asshole prick loser inside of me that I hadn't given my consent to did not mean I couldn't enjoy whatever the fuck kind of sex I wanted.

And what I wanted, no, *needed* was Viktor's sex.

It wasn't nice. It wasn't flowery, pretty, or magical.

But neither was I. Neither was he.

All I wanted, all I needed, was the all-encompassing, burning desire that I felt in every inch of my body. I saw that same need, that same possession, that same *obsession* reflected back at me when I looked at him.

We were not the perfect picture of mental health.

But we were owning it.

Just like he's about to own me. Bam.

"I'm not going to go easy on you, *kotyonok*. Are you ready for me?" Viktor growled, those obsidian eyes searing me. I licked his cheek, biting his bottom lip.

"Ruin me."

One growl later and we were tearing each other's clothes off.

"Please, I want to feel you inside me. Jesus, you're thick. You're going to hurt me." I panted, rubbing my hand over the intimidating bulge in Viktor's pants.

A flash of uncertainty crossed Viktor's face.

"We don't-"

"Did I say I didn't want it? Get inside me already. Fuck, how many more times do I have to say it?" I growled, gripping his dick tightly. Viktor sucked in a sharp breath, then gripped my hair tighter, yanking my head back.

Oh yeah, that's it. Pull my hair.

He bit me in that spot that made me shudder, a rush of hot need flooding through me.

"Watch your tone, *kotyonok*." I felt another firm slap to my ass and almost came on the spot.

Oh god, yes, sir, just get inside me!

We were ripping, tearing, shoving and licking our way through his clothes. Viktor's mouth didn't leave mine and I let out a loud, long whimper of need. He gripped my shirt in his hands, ready to rip it in half.

God, fuck yes!

Finally, finally, we were going to fu-

Bang, bang, bang!

We both froze.

No, it can't be.

"Emilia. I am so sorry; you know if it was not important I would not interrupt. We need you downstairs." Silas' voice floated through the door, full of regret and what sounded strangely like urgency.

Viktor and I just looked at each other, neither of us comprehending.

"Viktor, we need you too, buddy. Sorry."

And there was Cin's voice, equally as urgent but with the absence of regret.

You. Have. Got. To. Be. Kidding. Me.

I couldn't help it, I really couldn't.

I gave a long, loud, horrible scream of rage.

"*God DAMN it!* I finally got you to stop being a pussy and *this* is what fucking happens?" I screeched. I really couldn't hold it back.

Viktor just raised that sarcastic brow at me and I almost punched him in the throat.

"Come along, *Kapitan*. Apparently, we are needed." Viktor said, smoothing his clothes back into place with ease. I stumbled away from the dresser on wobbly legs, muttering under my breath the entire time.

"Yeah, I fucking need. I need you inside me but *ohh* no. Emilia doesn't get what she wants. Emilia gets to suffer some more. Awesome. Cool. Neat. *Great.*"

I yanked on suitable clothes, my movements jerky and swift. Viktor stood at attention, completely put back together and looking cool as a cucumber.

Oh my god, what an asshole.

"Are you ready, *Kapitan*?" He asked, lifting that sarcastic brow at me.

Someone was aching to be throat-punched.

"Yes, I'm *ready*, Viktor." I hissed. Together, we strode to the door and yanked it open. There stood Cin and Silas, both looking grim.

My irritation fled, concern rising.

"What's wrong?" I asked, frowning. Silas looked at me solemnly and answered in a quiet voice.

"Jane Smith is on the phone. She says she needs to speak with you. She says... the matter is extremely urgent."

Well, that wasn't good. I frowned, following Cin and Silas down the stairs. The MI6 superior, and Downswing's secret benefactor, was not someone who would use the term 'urgent' lightly. A warm hand stroked the small of my back, and I looked back at Viktor, who nodded his encouragement.

We strode down to the large, open foyer and walked on swift feet to the front living room. Cin threw open the doors, announcing our arrival.

"Emmie!"

"Well, there she is!"

"About time you woke up, ye lazy bum."

A slow smile spread across my face as I looked upon the most wonderful sight. Downswing, my Downswing, was gathered in the room. Masamune, Misaki and Mari stood off to the side, all giving me nods of greeting. I felt Viktor growl behind me and I turned slowly to the devil at my back.

He was glaring daggers at Masamune.

The Japanese man raised a brow.

"What did I do?" He asked in surprise. I pressed my lips together, donning an innocent look that earned me an amused snort from the handsome Japanese man.

Kiernan sat with Meiling on the couch, a glass of whiskey clutched in both of their hands. They raised their glasses to me and I gave them a warm smile. Roy stood off to the side with Kamili and my sweet Ludo, who looked healthy and happy. I smiled brightly at them, and they all gave me a huge smile back. Ludo's was cautious, but I didn't let that bother me. He and I would have a talk later. I needed to reassure him that he had played his part perfectly in our capture and I was so happy to see him returned to us without a scratch.

I turned to Jazzy, who was perched in one of the bigger armchairs. Her feet dangled off the ground and she gave me a bright, excited smile. I waved at her and then turned to the hulking German of our group.

And stopped.

"What in the *fuck* is he doing here?" I said incredulously, my eyes widening at the sight of Alexei standing in my living room. The second-in-command for Korol stared back at me, his face devoid of emotion.

"Good question." He answered flatly.

My eyes bugged, and I stepped forward with the full intent to kill the smarmy bastard.

Viktor stopped me.

"There is much we have to bring you up to speed on, *Kapitan*. That is one of those things." Viktor said, his hand lingering on my elbow.

"Yeah, no shit." I huffed, still incredibly baffled.

"I hear Emilia. Emilia, where are you?"

At the sound of Jane's voice, I frowned severely. The leader of a secret sept of MI6 usually had such a chipper voice that it grated my nerves. I had never heard her have such a grave tone before. I pushed forward, marching up to the computer monitor.

And again, came up short at the sight of another strange man.

"And who the hell is this?" I shrieked. What, were they just letting anyone come and hang out with us? In the computer chair, tapping at the keyboard, was a young black man with beautiful multi-colored dreads and thick, black hipster glasses. He was a beauty, with large, light hazel eyes and full lips made for-

Well, I wasn't going to be crude.

Cock. They were made for sucking cock.

I lied. I was crude.

"Yeah, hey. I'm Cooper, a relative of Cin's. I helped get your ass out of that situation you found yourself in. You are very welcome, and you can tell them to take me home now."

Apparently, this Cooper was sassy.

I liked him.

I slowly smiled at him.

"Ah, shit, you want to keep me now, don't you? Damn my charming personality." Cooper scowled darkly, turning back to the monitor.

"Oh, you're fun, aren't you?" I laughed, forgetting for a second that whatever had brought me here was dire.

"*Emilia.*"

I blinked down at the monitor and there was Jane Smith, Ringmaster for the Back Yard. A ridiculous title, but she was apparently some major badass in the most secret part of MI6. The stunning blonde, usually so well put-together, looked haggard and almost panicked. She had dark circles under her eyes and her jaw was clenched so tight, it looked like it was about to snap.

"Jane. What's going on?" I asked, leaning forward. The British woman usually bugged the hell out of me, but I still secretly liked her. Seeing her like this did not leave me with a good feeling.

"Emilia. There is so much I need to tell you. There is so much that everyone needs to tell you, but- but we do not have time. You have to go." Jane was gripping her desk hard, leaning right into the camera of her laptop.

I frowned at her urgency.

"Go? Go where? What-"

"You have to go home."

I snapped up straight, blinking in shock.

"Home, as in..."

"As in the United States. Michigan. Your home. You need to go there, and you need to go now. And you need to be armed and ready."

A heavy feeling crept into the pit of my stomach. My breathing sped up, my heart stuttering in my chest. I had to swallow twice before I managed to get my words out.

"It-it's not what I think it is. Tell me it's not what I think it is." I whispered.

Jane's look shattered, and she heaved a heavy sigh.

"I am so sorry, Emilia. He found them. Korol found your family."

The world tilted. Every single nightmare of this exact situation that had been a constant part of my life for the past four years came flooding back. I gasped for air, my eyes widening painfully.

"N-no. You told me they were safe. You *promised* me!" I screamed, clutching my hair tight in my fists. I felt Viktor come up behind me, putting his hands over my own. I wrenched out of his arms, careening forward and gripping the edge of the desk in my fists.

"How did this fucking happen? HOW?!" I screamed, my heart breaking in my chest.

No, no, no, this can't be happening.

"It was- it was your father. He gave them up to Korol."

Everything stopped. The weather. The voices in the room. Time. The universe. Everything came to a grinding halt, and I felt my heart give one loud, solid *boom* in my chest.

And when it all came crashing down on me, I gave a long, tortured, brutal scream of pure *rage*.

I felt hands on me, but I fought them, punching, hitting, scratching anything within reach. I screamed over and over again until my lungs burned, and my throat felt like someone had strangled me with barbed wire. And still I fought, my rage a beast that was consuming me.

"Jaysus, fuck, hold on to her!"

"I can't! If I hold her, she'll hurt herself more."

"Ouch! Fuck, Emilia, get ahold of yourself."

"*Kotyonok*. Stop it."

I knew it was Viktor, and I knew he was the one taking the brunt of my rage, but I couldn't stop. My body, my soul, my mind were shattered and I had to let it out. I had to fight.

I had to *kill*.

Rough arms suddenly grabbed me, and an arm came around and wrapped itself tightly around my throat. I gasped, sputtering, a strangled scream ripping its way from my already tortured throat.

"Fritz! What the fuck!"

"She is going to hurt herself and us if we do not stop her."

The German's booming voice came from right behind me. I fought for air, but my vision was dimming, my body slacking. Consciousness was fading, and the fight left my body in a *whoosh*. Fritz suddenly released me, and I crumpled to the floor. Gasping, I struggled to bring precious air back into my lungs.

Fury rode me. Rage. Loathing. *Hate.*

And in that moment, I swore I saw Grandmama standing before me, smiling that empty, cruel smile.

You can't kill him if you let your emotions get the best of you. What am I always telling you, pet? Feel nothing. Give nothing away. If you let him take a piece of you, he will hold it forever and you will never win the game.

My vision came back to me, my heart slowing down to a calm, steady rhythm. Viktor was kneeling on the floor beside me, his hand gentle on my shoulder. I felt everyone staring at me, waiting for their captain.

Waiting for their orders.

Because they were the aces in my pocket. My lucky hand.

My Downswing.

I looked up slowly, my gaze cold as ice, my heart as frozen as my father's corpse was going to be when I got my hands on him. My gaze traveled along the room, taking in the deadly underworld royalty from around the world.

My very own army of killers.

I gave a cold smile that promised pain.

And my eyes promised death.

"Prepare a jet. We leave at sunset."

TWENTY-ONE

Women's Erie Valley Correctional Facility
Redford, Michigan

"Sorry, ladies, seems I've won again."

A collective groan rose from the three other women sitting at the table. Betty threw down her cards, looking in disgust at the old woman who never seemed to lose a game.

"I call bullshit. You're cheatin'."

Silence met the pronouncement, the two other women at the table looking up slowly to the newcomer's outburst. They both sucked in a breath, not daring to move. The older woman who had just won and was collecting cigarettes from the other women raised a haughty brow.

"Oh? My dear, I do not cheat. I simply play to win. And Lady Luck seems to be ever on my side." The older woman with the salt and pepper hair and dead grey eyes said, her smile holding a thousand secrets. Betty wasn't a fan of the old bitch. She had heard from others in the prison that this harmless old lady ran things here and that didn't sit right with Betty.

"Yeah? That what got you locked up for life, you cheating bitch?" Betty snarled, rising from her chair. The older woman gave a small sigh, shaking her head in mock sadness.

"You're new here, yes? But you've heard of me. They all hear of me before I meet them." The woman said, looking up with pity at Betty. That pissed her right off. Betty didn't need pity from anybody, especially not from some old bitch with more bark than bite.

"I don't give a shit who you are, bitch, you're a lying, cheating wh-"

Betty never got to finish her sentence.

In the blink of an eye, the old woman was across the table, grasping Betty by the hair and slamming her head into the table over and over again. The newcomer lost consciousness, blood spurting from her nose and mouth, but still the old woman kept slamming her into the table.

The guard in the corner swallowed audibly but stayed exactly where she was.

The other two women at the table sat perfectly still, even as Betty's blood flew onto their jumpsuits. Finally, after she was satisfied, the older woman let Betty go and watched her larger body flop to the ground.

"Trish. Would you be a dear and clean that up for me? I apologize about the mess, but you know how these things can get." The older woman chuckled, blinking innocently at the guard. Trish's bulky frame shook but still she nodded, giving the older woman a smile.

"You got it." Trish said, her words wobbling. Another guard knocked, coming into the room. She looked down without surprise at the prone body of Betty, then back up to the table of convicts.

"Smith. Warden is asking for you."

Catherine Smith smiled at the new guard and stood,

dusting her bloodstained hands on her jumpsuit. Whistling the tune she had loved singing to her granddaughter years ago, she strode from the room. The walk to the warden's office was uneventful, only marked by the guard wiping the blood from Catherine's hands, neck, and face. The guard nodded in satisfaction before knocking on the warden's office door.

"Enter."

Catherine smiled at the guard, thanking her quietly. She slipped into the office, her smile warming a few degrees as she gazed at the serious face of the warden. The warden was some-where in her early fifties, with a tall, statuesque build and striking features. Her name was Elizabeth Martin, one of the only female wardens in the state of Michigan.

"What has you so serious, my love?" Catherine purred, sidling up close to the warden and wrapping her arms around the much-taller woman.

Elizabeth Martin also happened to be Catherine Smith's lover.

"You had a message from that person again. They said it was an urgent matter." Liz said, running her hands through Catherine's soft hair. Catherine purred, rubbing her face on Liz's chest.

Her lover had the bosom of a goddess.

With none of those pesky male parts she detested with all of her being.

"Mmm. Thank you, Lizzy. Do you mind if I read it now?" Catherine asked, already sidling up to the desk. Liz nodded, smiling. She tilted her head, regarding her older lover for what must have been the thousandth time.

"I will never get over how much like Helen Mirren you look. Really, I should have known as soon as I saw you that you were going to be my downfall." Liz said, wrapping her arms around Catherine from behind. The older woman laughed, patting Liz's head.

"You flatter me, Lizzy. Give me a moment and I'll show you just how much I appreciate you. Why don't you get more comfortable while I finish this business?" Catherine's smile was pure carnality and Lizzy shivered in anticipation.

"Of course, darling." Lizzy murmured and began to strip.

Catherine winked in response, turning back to the letter that had been left unopened. Lizzy was such a good girl, Catherine thought to herself as she opened the parchment.

She stopped after a moment, having to read the words multiple times before it sank in. Her gaze narrowed, and a snarl curled her lips into a terrifying mask of hate.

"That *idiot*. I should have drowned him when I had the chance." She snarled quietly to herself. Tearing the letter to shreds, she threw it in the waste bin at her feet. Hearing Lizzy's sympathetic noise from behind her, she turned to her lover.

And found her in nothing save a very sheer white negligee and a smile.

Goodness, Lizzy was *such* a good girl.

"I will be just a moment, my love. But I need to use your phone. Where is it, Lizzy?"

The warden smiled warmly at Catherine, nodding to the desk. Catherine smiled back fondly, walking around the desk and opening the drawer. She pulled the phone out, dialing the familiar number and held it to her face. Turning so her lover couldn't see her expression, her eyes went dead and cold as the incessant ringing blared in her ear.

A click sounded and Catherine was greeted by a very familiar, very snarky, soft voice.

"If you call and check up on me one more time, I swear by every fashion goddess in existence that I will come to that prison and-"

"Tsk, tsk. Is that any way to greet your elder?" Catherine smiled, leaning back against the desk. An overly dramatic scoff was her answer.

"But since you asked," Catherine purred, the smile slipping from her face. She stared ahead, unblinking, her eyes as sharp as blades as she breathed into the phone. "Why do I not have an update on that *trash* we discussed during our last call?"

Silence met her question. The voice that answered her was devoid of all snark and had lowered an octave. She almost smiled at the loss of the mirth and sass.

"I'm working on it."

"Hmm." Catherine hummed, allowing a small, evil grin to curl her lips. "I distinctly remember telling you to take out that trash when we last spoke. I don't like waiting, Elijah, dear. I thought I made that perfectly clear."

A disgusted sigh was her answer. "I *told* you, I can't just go around taking out garbage at a moment's notice. The garbage man might notice if I take it out too early. I want to smell it even less than you do but-"

"I appreciate excuses even less than I appreciate being made to wait." Catherine breathed.

The little shit was starting to get on her nerves.

"And I told you to go fuck your-"

Well, that was enough of that.

"How is Michael doing, sweetheart? Is he enjoying his new apartment across the street?" Catherine's softly spoken, gentle inquiry would have been almost endearing to anyone listening who didn't know her.

But Elijah knew her. Elijah knew her almost as much, if not more, than her sweet Emilia. He didn't just know her; he knew the underlying threat buried beneath the sweet words. Her gentle question was met with a quick inhalation of breath followed by complete and total silence for a solid two minutes. Finally, Elijah spoke, his tone low, furious and rumbling.

"I will take the trash out tomorrow."

"There's a good boy." Catherine said, her smile widening.

"I hate you." Elijah's voice trembled slightly as he said the low, vehement words and Catherine laughed.

"Now, darling, if we weren't so similar, I would take offense to that." Catherine laughed. Elijah sighed on the other end, but his sassy, higher voice was back as he fired back.

"Anything else, oh lord and master?" Elijah quipped, and Catherine could almost hear the eyeroll. She sobered completely as she remembered the reason for her call.

"We have a problem."

The other end went silent for a long moment. Finally, her Elijah was back on the line, his voice quiet and serious.

"Emilia?"

Catherine allowed herself a small smile.

"Rescued last week and doing better than expected."

A sigh of relief was Elijah's response, but Catherine didn't let the matter rest at that.

"It is *you* who seems to now have the problem, dear."

More silence met her statement.

"Ah. So, I'm finally going to have some visitors, huh? About time. I bet Emilia is absolutely *furious*." Elijah purred, to which Catherine gave a chuckle.

"Oh my, yes. Especially since it was *Garridan* who seems to have invited these guests right to your door."

Elijah Fox heaved a long sigh on the other end of the line. A few more moments passed by before the snarky voice was back.

"Hm. Well, seems I'll be seeing sister dearest sooner than I thought."

"The Russian has already dispensed his bodyguard to find

you and your mother. He should be there within the next two days if my calculations are correct. And let's face it, they always are." Catherine smiled, leaning back.

"God, I hope he didn't send that little Igor fucker. Just reading about that little shit gave me the creeps."

"No, dear, it's much worse than that." Catherine purred, a cold smile encompassing her face.

"Oh? Don't keep me in suspense, tell me, tell me." Elijah said, his prissy tone making Catherine chuckle.

"They've sent... Zane."

There was a long silence where Catherine heard nothing but Elijah's soft breath.

Finally, his deep chuckle came over the line.

"Two days, hm? That's more than enough time to get ready. I can't wait." Elijah purred, that sassy tone of his as endearing to Catherine as the thought of her own son's head on a platter.

"Zane is the one we know the least about. You be extra careful, just like we discussed." Catherine said, turning back to her lover, still waiting beautifully still in the corner of the office.

Catherine almost felt the grin on her grandson's face through the phone.

A deep chuckle sounded.

"This is going to be *fun*."

Catherine Smith snapped the phone closed, looking up slowly to the ceiling.

And the bloodthirsty grin she couldn't suppress any longer stretched the entirety of her face.

Welcome home, my lucky little coin.

SNEAK PEEK

*Here is a sneak peek into Bad Beat: Lady Luck Part Three
The prequel to Emilia Fox and Downswing's adventures*

Available now on Amazon!

PLEASE NOTE

Please note; Bad Beat is centered around Silas and Cin.
The story tells how they met, where they came from, and who
Maman *really is.*
Yes, this will be a male/male romance.
But Silas and Cin both agree that using the word 'romance' to
describe their relationship is using a bit of creative license.

Consider this your official warning.

ONE

Disgusting pig.

Silas Deveroux let his lips curl up in distaste at the man that was currently in the throes of passion beneath him. The pervert whose dick Silas was currently riding seemed to be having a very good time. Silas, on the other hand...

I'm so bored I could die.

The prick currently inside him had thought that Silas was much younger than he was, which was why he was being paid so handsomely for the fuck he had agreed to. Silas had just turned nineteen, but he knew his porcelain skin, slight frame, and wide, crystal blue eyes gave him the youthful appearance that attracted filthy perverts to him like flies to hot garbage.

The man gave a long, low groan, and Silas felt warmth fill the condom inside of him. Silas had been the one to insist upon protection. The disgusting pig had told Silas in a haughty-as-shit tone that he would be going home with less money for insisting on the condom.

That suited Silas *just* fine.

The man was an even bigger fucking idiot if he thought

Silas was leaving with anything less than everything he had on him.

Collapsing into a blissed-out heap on the bed, the idiot looked to almost be entering subspace, he seemed so relaxed and satisfied. Silas lifted a brow at the fact he hadn't even needed to force himself to harden for the entire exchange. The man was well aware what Silas thought of him.

Apparently, that had been a part of the appeal.

The man had approached him outside of a sleazy club in La Marais, the gay district in Paris. He had swaggered up to Silas- who had been wearing threadbare jeans and a mesh tank top- posturing like a damned peacock. The first two questions out of the idiot man's mouth were, 'how young are you', and 'how much for the evening'. Silas, being bored and offended by the man's haughty manner, had played along with the john, not correcting the man to his actual occupation and status.

Silas was a man of opportunity, after all.

He didn't look a dead horse in the mouth.

Especially when it was braying at him like an ass.

Silas gracefully extracted himself from the man, rolling his eyes at the way the idiot mewled and tried to hold onto him. He had been hopeful that the man would at least give him a halfway decent fuck, since the idiot was built like a tank and seemed to have the brain of a cockroach. Big and dumb, just the way Silas preferred his men. Silas pressed his lips together in irritation at having been deceived by the man's size and swagger.

The lay had been as lousy as the man's personality.

Fucking waste of my valuable time, Silas thought dispassionately as he pulled out the handcuffs from his jean pockets. He always kept two pairs on him when he went out to La Marais, just in case he needed them for any kind of situation.

Silas turned, smiled at the fucking idiot man, and sauntered back over to the still-panting piece of trash.

"You did not think I was finished with you just yet, did you, daddy?" Silas purred, noticing the man's dick twitched at the endearment. He rolled his eyes at the sight, which only managed to spur the idiot on more.

"Oh, did you have something more for daddy, dear one?" The man's voice rumbled, and he waggled his too-bushy eyebrows at him. Silas stared at him flatly, smiling inside when the man's face turned red from embarrassment. Which only made the idiot's cock twitch more.

Jesus Christ, this is almost too easy.

"Wrap your hands around the bed post." Silas said simply, continuing to stare in the same flat, uninterested way that seemed to do something for the big idiot in front of him. The man squirmed, his cock twitching again, and did just as Silas told him.

And I thought this idiot could scratch my itch? Fucking laughable.

Silas almost sighed at his own miscalculation, but still went ahead with what he had originally brought the man back to the room to do. He handcuffed one hand, waited for the idiot to get used to the idea, then did the other arm much the same way. The bed was sturdy- Silas had used this particular motel room before- so he knew the man wouldn't be escaping any time soon, even if he wanted to.

He looked down at the man, whose breath was coming in excited pants with pupils blown from anticipation, and Silas almost felt sorry for the fucker. But, considering the wholly unsatisfying fuck he had just received and the fact that the man had made it very clear that Silas was to pretend to be younger than his nineteen years, the sympathy that he was trying to pull forth sat disinterested at the bottom of his black soul.

With that done, Silas turned from the man, bending down to reach into the pocket of his jeans that he had shucked onto the floor. The fucker behind him growled at the sight of Silas's pale, rounded ass, and Silas sighed aloud in irritation. He straightened, bringing the phone up to his ear. Behind him, the big idiot seemed to finally realize that what was happening wasn't as sexy as he was probably imagining.

"What are you doing? Who the hell are you calling-" The man thundered, but Silas shushed him.

"Patience, daddy. I'll get back to you in just a moment." Silas said silkily, bending down to retrieve the big idiot's wallet from his jeans. Silas felt the man's eyes on him, and heard a swift, furious intake of breath when he realized that Silas had his wallet clutched in his fist and was just about to go through the contents.

"You fucking *whore*, you are not going to rob me-"

"Yes I am, daddy." Silas said simply, moving the phone that had been ringing over and over to cradle against his shoulder as he used both hands to rifle through the man's wallet. He slowly turned back around and looked up at the idiot handcuffed to the bed. The big man was yanking against the handcuffs, putting up a valiant effort to get free, but only managed to cut into the flesh of his wrists. The man roared at him, flinging loud insults over and over, creating a ruckus.

Not that it mattered. There was no one around to hear him.

No one that didn't know what was happening, anyway.

Silas waited the man out, the incessant ringing still playing in his ears as he blithely went through all of the man's credit cards, identification cards, and cash. Pocketing the cash with a little wink at the big idiot, Silas finally let the remains of the wallet drop to the floor. All the while, the pathetic pig on the bed continued to berate him, scream at him, call him every single name under the sun, but the one that Silas thought the most hilarious was one, single word.

Whore.

He *loved* that word. He especially loved all the men that called him that before ever asking him who he was, where he came from, and what it is that he did. They just assumed he was some streetwalker because he dressed like trash, was usually hanging about some sleazy club, and looked too young and too beautiful to be doing anything else but giving up his ass to whatever john was paying the highest.

Silas *loved* it.

It made his job so easy; it was almost laughable.

If he wasn't so goddamn *bored.*

Finally, the large idiot on the bed in front of him wore himself out and flopped back down to the pillows, blood running down his wrists from his struggles. The man didn't even have the decency to look frightened. He merely looked at Silas the way a spider would look at a particularly annoying fly. Irritated, but smug in the fact that he was going to have Silas for dinner.

Stupid fucker.

"You have no idea who I am, little one." The big idiot rumbled, laughing maniacally. "When I get free from these, I am going to hunt you down, lock you away, and *break* you. And after I'm done, I'll sell your sweet, young ass to the highest bidder. There is nowhere you can hide, no hole you can crawl back into, that I will not find you. You stupid, filthy, little *whore.*"

Silas stared at the big man, naked and panting against the sex-rumpled sheets of the shabby hotel room bed and lifted an eyebrow. He had to fight the smile as the phone finally clicked, and a soft breath whispered against his ear.

"Name the sinner."

Silas let his eyelids drop to half-mast, and a slow, evil smile stretched his lips as he answered back in the same soft whisper.

"Bernard Lefevre."

The big man jerked on the bed, his name leaving Silas's lips clearly startling him.

The soft whisper on the other end of the phone was silent a moment, but Silas could hear the soft clicking indicating that the speaker was typing.

"Personal or business?"

Silas pursed his lips, considering the man through his half-closed eyes, and finding that he didn't really care, either way. Personal or business, it mattered not to him, so long as the end result was the same.

"Business." Silas said flatly.

"Good answer, Two." The voice whispered, the amusement bleeding through. They quickly got back to business.

"Cleaning crew dispatched?"

"Next door."

The voice was silent and more clicking sounded. Silas waited, watching Bernard and raising an eyebrow as the man screamed. Not in terror, but in pure rage. Silas had to give it to him, he truly didn't think Silas was capable of anything more than a simple robbery.

Looking like a doll had its advantages.

"You're clear. Device 19B is now out of service. Report is due at 0200."

The soft click at the end of the line had Silas's half smile expanding. Silas tossed the phone back onto his jeans, but not before glancing at the time. He had a half hour. Perfect.

"Who were you talking to?" Bernard demanded, rattling his wrists against the handcuffs once again. Silas slowly walked over to the poor bastard who had irritated him and crawled onto the bed. Bernard's eyes widened, and he couldn't hide the twitch of his dick as Silas slowly made his way up his body. Exhaling loudly, Silas leaned his head back and closed his eyes, rolling his neck on his shoulders.

"Answer me, you little-"

"Shut up," Silas breathed, his eyes still closed. Silas slid his hand up the man's abdomen and heard the sharp inhale of breath that accompanied the movement. Moving his hands slowly and lovingly over the man's stomach, Silas found the spot he was searching for. His mouth twitched in an amused smile as he ground his thumbs into the pressure points he sought.

And listened to the music of Bernard's agonized screams.

Bernard's body was taut as a bow as pain wracked him in waves. Silas had been on the receiving end of this particular brand of torture.

It was... *excruciating.*

Silas smiled.

Finally, he relented, releasing his thumbs with a soft hum of pleasure. Bernard flopped back to the mattress, this time panting from sheer agony. Silas finally rolled his head forward, opening his eyes almost bashfully and staring down at the man. Bernard's eyes were wide, bloodshot, and his lip was bleeding from where he had tried to stifle his screams and bitten into it with his teeth.

"You know, I love men like you the most." Silas purred, moving back down Bernard's body. The large idiot's eyes tracked him, the only sound in the room his harsh breathing and Silas's hum of pleasure as he laid his long, graceful fingers against the insides of Bernard's thighs. Bernard sucked in a breath right before Silas pressed firmly with his thumbs once again, right into the pressure points that he knew would rob Bernard of speech.

He was right.

Bernard's mouth was wide in a silent scream, his face screwed up in agony.

Beautiful.

After several long minutes, Silas released him once again, and the man fell back on the bed, whimpering and crying. His eyes were more red than white now, and snot and spittle ran down his face. Silas tilted his head, smiling serenely down at him.

"You roll around in your power like a pig, taking what doesn't belong to you, basking in the fact that you're untouchable by the law. You think you're invincible." Silas breathed, sliding back up Bernard's large, muscled body. Bernard flinched back from him, whimpering, begging. Silas shushed him quietly, trailing his long, graceful fingers up Bernard's stomach and to just under his armpits. Tilting his head, Silas puckered his lips in a kiss before pressing into the pressure points his fingers were resting against.

Bernard's silent scream wasn't so silent this time, but he had little to no control over his voice. Pig-like grunts and disgusting gurgling noises erupted from his throat instead, and Silas pressed harder, wanting to take Bernard to that edge of pain where the agony was so intense, your mind started to free itself and your body became nothing more than a husk of pain and surrender. It usually took a lot longer to get there, but Silas knew it wouldn't take that long for Bernard.

He was just like all the others.

Weak.

Silas released the pressure from his fingers as he felt Bernard's body start to relax. Looking into the large man's eyes, Silas noted with satisfaction that they were glazed, lost, and a bit broken.

"But you're the furthest thing from it. It takes nothing more than a slip of a man like me to bring you to your knees. Make you beg. Make you cry. Make you anything I want you to be." Silas continued, his voice a soft purr in the night. He licked his lips and let out a slow breath.

Silas leaned forward, and pressed a soft, lingering kiss to Bernard's sweat-dampened forehead. Reaching slowly upwards, Bernard's unfocused, agonized gaze trying to track his movements and failing terribly, Silas's hands finally came to rest on either side of Bernard's face. With a soft, loving smile, Silas whispered against Bernard's forehead.

"Make you my *whore*."

With a flick of his wrists, Silas snapped Bernard Lefevre's neck, silencing him forever.

He felt Bernard's last breath leave him, and he smiled against the dead man's forehead.

Ah, that sound was so sweet to him. That final breath stolen by his own hands.

There was truly nothing more satisfying than that.

Silas made himself get up, pushing his mop of platinum hair back from his forehead. Quickly dressing himself, Silas went through the list of groceries he was going to need for his apartment. He had forgotten to pull the chicken from the freezer, so he wasn't going to be able to make his favorite dish, chicken marsala. He sighed.

That was disappointing.

He turned his head as a soft knock came from the door. Silas waited a moment and heard three knocks in quick succession follow the first. Nodding, Silas walked to the door, and flung it open, wrapping himself in Bernard's too-big, but very warm coat. He nodded to the four men that swiftly entered and took a moment to look back at Bernard's big, naked body on the bed. He felt like he was forgetting something.

"Ah, *merde*. I almost forgot."

Silas reached into the big coat, pulling out the flower that he had hidden from Bernard before he had let the big idiot fuck him. Silas twirled the white lily in his fingers, watching the four men that had entered gulp at the sight of the delicate flower. Silas chuckled, tossed the flower onto Bernard's dead body, and whispered the ancient words that were the creed of his organization.

"May the light free your soul, Bernard, for the darkness has come for you."

Silas turned without a backward glance, unable to contain the small smile that curled his lips. And as he softly whistled to himself, Silas Deveroux vanished into the black embrace of the night.

ABOUT THE AUTHOR

JJ knew she was going to tell stories about strong characters who had to overcome tremendous odds when she had her Barbies work in tandem with her dinosaurs to bring down broccoli at the dinner table. JJ lives in Detroit, Michigan and couldn't be happier about it. She writes the city into her stories in one way or another because she believes in the hope and love that are alive and well in the Motor city. JJ lives with two gorgeous men who just so happen to love each other's parts instead of hers. She continues to be oblivious when people flirt with her and manages to botch every attempt at adulting. She also may or may not love wine much more than she should.

You can follow JJ on social media:
Twitter
Facebook
Instagram

Become one of JJ's Jaybirds and receive exclusive content, news, and prizes.
All the cool kids are doing it.
JJ's Jaybirds

And please consider leaving a review on Amazon or Goodreads.
It helps independent authors so much. Thank you!

ALSO BY J.J. ANATOLIY

Lady Luck series

Downswing

Upswing

Bad Beat

YOU CAN BET ON IT

Emilia Fox and Downswing will be back soon.
You can bet on it.

www.ingramcontent.com/pod-product-compliance
Lightning Source LLC
Chambersburg PA
CBHW030237200626
46816CB00002BA/397